She knew what she wanted...

She drew her hands to the front of his shirt and unbuttoned the cloth that strained across his chest. He wrapped his long fingers around hers. "Sara?" he murmured. "Are you ready for this?"

Her hand closed into a fist inside his grasp. "It's—it's just your shirt," she stammered. "If you don't want me to..."

"Sara, I care for you. I want you. I want you very much. You know that." Randy sighed, his fingers stroking hers, melting the fist. "But you're special. I don't want to hurt you."

She measured his words, unsure of exactly what he *did* want. He wanted her, but not to hurt her. Did he think that by making love to her he would hurt her? Did he think she was incapable of deciding what she was ready for?

"Should I leave?" she asked.

"No."

ABOUT THE AUTHOR

Judith Arnold says she can't remember ever not being a writer. She wrote her first story at age six and, after getting her master's degree from Brown University, pursued a successful playwriting career. Judith devotes herself to writing full-time, except for a rather large diversion—her one-year-old son. She and her family live in rural Connecticut.

Books by Judith Arnold

HARLEQUIN AMERICAN ROMANCE
104—COME HOME TO LOVE
120—A MODERN MAN

These books may be available at your local bookseller.

A Modern Man

JUDITH ARNOLD

Harlequin Books

TORONTO • NEW YORK • LONDON
AMSTERDAM • PARIS • SYDNEY • HAMBURG
STOCKHOLM • ATHENS • TOKYO • MILAN

Published September 1985

First printing July 1985

ISBN 0-373-16120-4

Printed In Canada

Chapter One

Soon it would be raining again.

Leaning against the closed bottom half of the Dutch door, Sara gazed out at the damp early April afternoon. The recently tilled acreage of the farm to her left and the dirt roads bordering it were sodden from the morning's shower, and swollen, lead-colored clouds hung low over the earth, almost kissing the spired tips of the pines that lined the southern edge of the farm.

The dank air felt refreshing on Sara's alabaster cheeks and throat. Behind her, the kitchen was stuffy with the heat of the fire baking her bread, and her clothing also rendered her warmer than she might have liked. She wore a floor-length dress of beige calico, with a fringed linen shawl covering her shoulders, and a lace-trimmed white bonnet capped the waist-length black hair she had plaited into two braids and coiled about her head. She appreciated the clash of chilly and hot air where they met around her in the half-open doorway.

She spotted two figures in bright yellow slickers ambling along one of the muddy roads abutting the farm: a tall man and a child with short dark hair—the hood of his raincoat was off his head. A boy, she assumed. His feet were protected by unwieldy rubber boots. He raced clumsily ahead of the man to a rut in the road left by a wagon wheel, then waited until the man approached. When the man was within firing distance, the boy leaped into the rut, spraying the brown rainwater that had accumulated there across the lower portion of the man's jeans. Sara heard the deep muffled roar of the man reacting to the attack.

Father and son, she surmised.

The fragrance of her bread baking in the oven impelled her to turn from the door. She passed the rough-hewn wood table, where a plump mound of dough was rising, awaiting its second kneading, and moved to the vast fireplace that nearly consumed an entire wall of the cozy kitchen. She used a metal implement to unlatch the door of the brick oven that was built into the fireplace and peered in at her bread. It wasn't ready yet. After shutting the iron door, she added another log to the fire and returned to her dough.

Sara adored her job at Old Harkum Village. She felt at home in the ancient house, its whitewashed walls and low ceiling suiting her as much as the archaic clothing she wore. Ever since she was a child she believed she had been born in the wrong century, but here, working in the Willoughby House, she could pretend that the universe's clock had been readjusted to fit her soul.

After shifting the whale-oil lamp out of her way, she uncovered the dough and dug the heels of her palms into its warm, pliant mass. There was something sensuous about massaging the dough, something basic and primal about hammering at it in gentle karate chops and then folding it onto itself and digging in again. So much more satisfying than her former career, teaching in a Brooklyn inner-city high school and being coerced into accepting a more modern view of the world.

A light drizzle began, striking the peaked roof and echoing in the attic above her head. She could hear it through the open trapdoor, from which a slanting ladder-stair descended to the kitchen beside the straw pallet bed. The gentle patter mingled with the occasional crack and hiss of the fire in a beautiful song. Sara smiled and added a handful of coarse flour to the wood surface of the table to keep the dough from sticking.

The drumming of the rain increased, abruptly transforming from a drizzle to a downpour. Through the window she noticed the two slicker-clad creatures darting toward the house. Old Harkum Village had few visitors on this raw, rainy Saturday in April, and Sara had enjoyed the relative solitude of her day. She braced herself for the intrusion of the man and the boy.

She heard their footfalls—one heavy and one sprightly and light—on the plank front porch, and then they swung open the lower half of the Dutch door and ducked inside, laughing and spluttering. She looked up from the table and wiped the flour from her palms with a handwoven towel.

Father and son, but they didn't look much alike, she mused as her large gray eyes took them in. The boy was perhaps seven or eight, small and wiry, with close-cropped brown hair, olive skin and sad dark eyes that seemed to bulge out of his drawn face. The man was fairer, his hair a pale chestnut color, light brown blended with blond and red streaks that were visible despite the dampness that naturally darkened them. He had a square, open face, a broad nose, a dimpled smile and absolutely riveting green eyes. Sara swallowed as she acknowledged the undeniable power of his gaze as it met hers.

His stare seemed to devour her petite form. One discerning upward sweep of her five-foot-three-inch body culminated in an interested perusal of her heart-shaped face, her pale skin, her delicately sculpted cheeks, lips and nose, and her finely lashed eyes. His scrutiny seemed to transfix her. The only part of her able to move was her slender fingers, which plunged into the dough before her as if in desperate search of something to cling to.

"This isn't the horses," the boy announced, shattering Sara's trance. She was grateful to the child. *The man's child,* she reminded herself, although she couldn't keep herself from dropping her view to his strong hands. Ringless. As if that meant anything nowadays. Modern men frequently didn't wear wedding rings, she knew. They saw wedding rings as manacles, marking them as prisoners.

"No, it isn't the horses," the man unnecessarily confirmed, his eyes never leaving Sara. "We'll go look at the horses when the rain lets up."

"What smells?" the boy asked.

"Bread baking," Sara replied.

"Where's the oven?"

She gestured toward the fireplace. The boy approached it. "Not too close," she cautioned him, and he obediently backed up a step. His raincoat, and the man's, dribbled small puddles of water onto the bare floor.

"We're getting the house all wet," the man apologized.

"That's all right. It won't shrink," she reassured him.

He smiled. He had white, even teeth and long dimples, Sara noticed. *Why,* she chided herself. Why should she notice such a thing? "You want to tell us about the house?" he cued her.

She snapped into her professional personality. "This

is the Willoughby House," she recited dutifully. "It was built in 1791 in what is now North Hempstead. Josiah Willoughby was a farmer by trade. The Willoughby House is typical of its time."

The boy peered up at the ceiling. "Was he short?" he asked.

A standard question from visitors surprised by the low ceilings. "According to the diary of his wife, Julia Willoughby, a photocopy of which is on display in the main building, Josiah Willoughby stood nearly six feet tall." *About as tall as you,* she almost added to the man, who continued to stare at her with disarming curiosity. "The ceilings were built low to conserve heat."

"Did he have horses?" the boy asked.

"Several. Everyone did in those days," Sara informed him.

The boy appeared mildly restless. He prowled the small room as if in search of horses. Reaching the door that led to the parlor, he lifted its latch and swung it open.

"Not so fast, tiger," the man said, snagging the boy's arm. "First you've got to ask permission from Miss..." He hesitated, his eyes sparkling as they coursed over Sara. His grin expanded and he winked. "The lovely Miss Willoughby."

Sara recoiled slightly. The nerve of him, flirting with her in front of his son! She had no patience for the antics of modern fathers after her own dismal experiences with that particular breed. "That's the parlor," she addressed the boy, "and yes, you may go in there as long as you don't touch anything." The boy quickly vanished into the parlor. The man positioned himself in the open doorway, keeping a close watch on the boy even though his attention was on Sara. "Mrs. Willoughby," she declared frostily, hoping to forestall any more flirting from him. "There was no Miss Willoughby."

"Oh?"

She slipped into her routine recitation, seeing it as a solid defense against the man. "The Willoughbys had four sons, two of whom survived to adulthood. The elder son, also named Josiah, took over his father's farm after marrying. He sired three children, all of whom died in infancy."

The man seemed interested. "And the younger son?"

"The younger son became an itinerant lay preacher. In 1837 he was shot to death by a jealous husband."

"Shame on him," the man said, his tone underlined with soft, husky laughter.

Sara shot him a quick, irritated glance, then crossed to the oven to check on her bread. "His guilt was never proved," she informed him before sliding the loaf out of its baking chamber on a long-handled wooden spatula. The crust was an even gold color, and she tapped the bread with her knuckles to test its hardness. Satisfied that it was fully baked, she set it on the table, then shaped the fresh mound of dough into a loaf on the utensil's wood surface, and slid it into the oven.

"If the jealous husband's wife looked like you, I can understand why he'd shoot anyone who came within two miles of her," the man noted playfully.

Sara cast him another piqued look, then turned to the parlor door, eager to remind him that he was a father and that, as such, his behavior was way out of line. "Would you like a slice of bread?" she called to the boy. He immediately reappeared, his eyes round with delight. Sara sliced a thick slab of warm bread and handed it to him. He presented her with a snaggle-toothed smile.

"What do you say?" the man coached him.

"Thank you," the boy blurted hastily before taking a bite of the bread.

Sara was aware of the man's gaze on her. "You want one, too?"

"You bet I do," he replied. Reluctantly she cut him a slice and extended it to him. When he took it from her, his cool hand stroked her warm, floury fingers. *Accidentally,* she wondered, drawing her hand away as if it had been burned. In fact, it did feel burned; a searing heat shot through her bones to the pulse in her wrist, causing it to accelerate slightly.

Why in the world was she responding to him, she wondered angrily. He was just another father, escorting just another child through the Village. She'd had her fill of fathers and sons, thank you. Modern fathers and sad sons. That this particular father struck her as remarkably attractive was unfortunate, but she wasn't a fool. She scraped the flour to the center of the table with the blade of her knife and tried to ignore the man's intensely virile presence.

"How come there's a bed in the kitchen?" the boy asked, his words garbled by the quantity of bread in his mouth.

"The fireplace in the kitchen is the largest in the house. The Willoughbys slept here for warmth. Their children slept upstairs in the attic."

"What about bundling?" the man asked.

Her eyes flashed their glittering gray at him. "I beg your pardon?"

"Bundling. Isn't that what it's called?" His mischievous gaze remained unwaveringly on her as he nibbled his bread. "I read somewhere that in the olden days people used to climb into bed in pairs and bundle together to stay warm. Body heat is more effective than a fireplace, don't you think?"

Sara decided it wisest not to tell him what she thought, that his lewd remarks were totally unwelcome and not a little unseemly. "Since the Willoughbys managed to have four children, I'm sure they figured out ways to stay warm on a long winter night." She coolly provided her standard answer to the common question, then instantly regretted the suggestive statement. It usually brought laughter from her visitors. This man only smiled—a quiet, oddly pleased smile.

"What do you think, Petey?" he asked the little boy, who was staring at the lumpy bed. "Would you like to sleep in your mother's kitchen?"

Your mother's kitchen, Sara noted. He was divorced, then. A divorced father with weekend custody. No wonder the boy had that sad, soulful darkness in his eyes. She knew from personal experience the special misery that afflicted children of divorce.

"Think of it, Petey," the man continued. "You could raid the refrigerator at midnight and nobody would ever know about it."

"There's no refrigerator here," the boy logically pointed out.

"Spoilable food was kept in a springhouse," Sara instructed him. "A spring ran through the building and kept it at a reasonably cool temperature. You can see a springhouse behind the Boodner House down the road."

The boy obediently moved to the Dutch door and peered out, searching for the springhouse. "You can't see it from here," Sara said, then continued her lecture. "A springhouse was usually kept stocked with some dairy goods and certain unsmokable meats after a slaughter, but much of the family's food was obtained the day it was needed—milk, eggs, vegetables from the garden. Spoilage wasn't an enormous problem."

"Can we go see the horses?" the boy asked, his interest in the Willoughby House having been satisfied.

Good idea, Sara thought, eager for the man to leave. She didn't know why she was so disturbed by his presence, but she knew intuitively that she would feel much more comfortable when he was gone.

His eyes zigzagged between her and the boy. "It's still raining pretty hard," he observed.

"So what?" his son challenged him.

"So..." The man grappled for an excuse. "So if the stable doors were kept open, the inside'll be all mucky and gross."

"So what?"

The man frowned, deep in thought. "So, you know what horses smell like when they're wet?"

"Like horses," the boy sensibly replied. Sara offered him a silent cheer.

The man thought some more, then unzipped his rain slicker and reached into the hip pocket of his mud-spattered jeans, retrieving a souvenir map of Old Harkum Village and unfolding it. "I tell you what, Petey," he compromised. "You're interested in the horses and I'm not. Why don't you go on by yourself, and then we can meet at the stables when the rain lets up. How does that sound?"

The boy appeared mollified, but Sara was enraged on his behalf. His father, who probably only saw him on weekends, was willing to ship him off to the stable on a rain-soaked afternoon, irresponsibly abandoning him for the opportunity to stay with Sara, who certainly didn't want his company. She glowered at the man as he hunched over the map with the boy, pointing out various sites: "See, this is where we are now, the Willoughby House," he narrated as his index finger roamed over the map. "There's the farm, right? There's the church, remember? And the hatmaker's shop. And here—" he traced a path on the map "—here's the stable." He guided his son to the door. "Down this road and to the left. Do you think you can find it?"

The boy nodded energetically and yanked on the Dutch door's lower half.

"All right. If you get lost, just go into one of the houses and ask someone. But you'll find it; don't worry. And you stay there, tiger, until I meet you, okay? I'm going to wait for the rain to lighten up."

"Okay," the boy eagerly promised. "Is it okay if I ride one of the horses?"

"I don't think they'll let you," the man warned. "If they say you can, you come back here and get me first."

"All right!" the boy hooted before racing out the door.

The man closed the door behind him and turned to find Sara glaring stonily at him. He seemed surprised by her disapproving scowl. "You don't think I should let him ride a horse?" he asked.

His face was so open, so frank and friendly, that she lowered her eyes. They came to rest on the beige flannel shirt visible under his slicker. In spite of the shirt's loose fit, she could imagine the firm breadth of his chest beneath it and the slim muscles of his abdomen above the leather belt of his jeans. She felt unreasonable resenting his well-proportioned physique, his long legs and multicolored hair and the humorous glint in his eyes. "I don't think you should let him go running around the Village by himself," she scolded, although she knew she had no right to criticize him.

"Oh, he'll be fine," the man reassured her. "He'll find the stable without any difficulty. He can handle Old Harkum Village. He's navigated through minefields."

Like your divorce, Sara guessed silently. "Doesn't he want to spend the day with you?" she asked as she drifted to the oven to check her bread. The dough was puffy but still white.

"He sees more than enough of me," the man replied, settling himself comfortably into one of the ladder-back pine chairs near the table. "Is it all right if I sit here?"

"The chair won't collapse beneath your weight, if that's what you're asking," Sara answered, shutting the door of the oven but remaining near the fireplace, across the room from him. She suspected that what he was really asking was whether she minded his company, which she did, but she couldn't rudely throw him out of the house. He was a paying visitor to the Village, after all, and part of her job was to be pleasant to visitors.

Still, the steady green light of his eyes unnerved her, and fussing with her utensils as she wiped off the table didn't distract her. "How old is he?" she asked, tilting her head toward the doorway where she had last seen the little boy.

"Eight," the man replied.

"That's awfully young for you to send him running off on his own," she scolded.

"What's going to happen to him? Do people get mugged at Old Harkum Village?"

Not as many as get mugged in the corridors of a public high school in Brooklyn, she answered silently. "It just seems to me," she said in a quiet, reproachful voice, "that you ought to be a bit more concerned about your own son."

"My son?" The man's eyes grew round and he sat straighter in his chair. "He's not my son."

"He's not?"

"No." The man chuckled and relaxed again. "He's just a stray I picked up."

"A stray?" Sara suspected that the man was mocking her, and she determinedly prevented herself from reacting to his teasing. "Do you collect many strays?"

"Nah, one's enough. As it is I've got newspapers spread out all over the floor of the kitchen, but boys will be boys." When Sara refused to join his laughter, he let it die. "He's the son of some friends of mine. I'm just taking him off their hands for the day."

"I see." Sara couldn't hide the compassionate frown that darkened her brow. Isn't that what happened to unlucky children? They were taken off their parents' hands, as if they were a dreadful burden, something to unload whenever they became inconvenient. Hadn't her own parents always farmed her out to boarding schools, summer camps or willing relatives so they could indulge their own selfish interests—disappearing with this or that lover, splitting up, reconciling, divorcing, dating, dating each other.... Oh, her parents were avant-garde, sophisticated, in step with the latest fads. The only thing that slowed them down was their daughter, but she was easily disposed of here and there. She rarely got in their way while they ran around pursuing their modern life.

She wondered why she should be thinking about her own miserable childhood. Then she knew why. She had recognized the loneliness in the little boy's eyes. She had instinctively understood that, whoever his parents were, they had dumped him on this strange man for some reason. Her disapproval of his failure to accompany the child to the stable was tempered by the understanding that he was giving the child more attention than did the child's own parents. In spite of his silly flirting, the man deserved some respect from Sara.

Slightly embarrassed by the emotional memories that had welled up inside her, she stooped to check her bread. "You just checked it a couple of minutes ago," the man pointed out.

She straightened slowly and shut the oven door. "It has to be checked frequently. I haven't got a timer."

"How many braids have you got tucked into that cap of yours?" he asked.

A faint flush stained her cheeks. One of the disadvantages of having such clear, porcelain skin was that it turned uncontrollably rosy at the merest uneasiness. "Two," she answered softly. Even if the man was absolved of being the irresponsible parent of the boy, she wasn't interested in his attention.

"So—" he reached for the knife and sliced himself another piece of bread "—what's your real name, Mrs. Willoughby?"

She bit her lip. She didn't like the way her body felt beneath his gaze, a weird tingle rippling along her nerves. "I think the rain is easing up," she announced.

A distant rumble of thunder belied her claim. The man chewed and smiled. "What's the matter?" he challenged her. "You don't like it when a randy man makes a pass at you?"

"Randy?" She laughed.

He rose and extended his hand. "Good guess," he praised her. "Randy Zale. And you're...?"

She couldn't resist a small chuckle at his having tricked her into speaking his name. Nor could she resist his warm, shimmering smile. "Sara Morrow," she told him.

He gathered her hand in his, and his eyes seemed to gather the glow in hers as well. He was standing much too close to her, she thought vaguely. The subtle spice fragrance of his after-shave seemed to overpower the rich aroma of the baking bread for an instant. "Sara," he murmured. "What a perfect name."

His nearness, and the suddenly hushed timbre of his voice, made her nervous. "Perfect?" she echoed, extracting her hand from his and wiping it on the towel as if she could wipe his warm, oddly potent touch from her.

"A beautiful name for a beautiful woman."

"It seems like Randy is a perfect name for you, too." She hoped her brisk tone would stifle his obvious interest in her.

He laughed, not at all offended. "This bread is incredibly good," he complimented her baking. "Mr. Willoughby must have been one lucky guy. There's nothing like coming home at the end of a hard day and entering a house that smells of baking bread."

"Mr. Willoughby was not a lucky guy," she argued, absently sweeping the edge of the hearth, where some cinders had spattered, with the broom she had woven herself. "Judging from her diary, I'd guess his wife wasn't a very happy woman."

"After losing two children and three grandchildren, I don't suppose she would be," Randy commented. "Life must have been pretty tough back then."

"It had its compensations," Sara noted.

"And what were they?"

"Besides a house that usually smelled of baking bread?" She balanced the broom in a corner and returned to the door to stare out at the deluge. Her gaze softened, growing distant as she reflected. "Things were simpler then. People had enough genuine challenges that they didn't have to go out of their way to manufacture them the way they do now."

He weighed her words thoughtfully. "Do people manufacture challenges today?"

"I think so."

"You busy tonight?"

The non sequitur jarred her, and she turned to face Randy. He stood squarely in the middle of the room, his feet slightly spread and his hands in his pockets. He looked as if he owned the house. "That sounds like a manufactured challenge if ever I heard one," she remarked with a wry smile.

He laughed.

Damn the man for having such a musical laugh, she thought angrily. The last thing she wanted in her life was a man. Stu had cured her of any desire for male companionship. After leaving him, she had relocated to Long Island, taking the job of her dreams in Old Harkum Village, submerging herself in the simpler world she wished she had been born into. She did not want or need any more modern men in her world, this well-built honey-haired intruder included.

He continued to watch her, his green eyes bright with amiable humor. She bowed to check her bread again. "I could bring you a timer," he offered.

"I don't need a timer," she shot back. "I've got eyes."

"I noticed."

She cringed, glad her face was averted from him. She could feel the blush rising in her cheeks again, and she wanted it to subside before he saw it. "We don't like anachronisms in Old Harkum Village," she explained, relieved by the steadiness in her voice. "Mrs. Willoughby didn't have a timer."

"Did Mrs. Willoughby have such a sexy figure?"

She turned sharply, no longer caring about whether he saw her blush. "Honestly! Don't you ever let up?" she charged.

"Historical curiosity," he defended himself. "I was just wondering whether Old Harkum Village lets you wear anachronistic underwear under your prissy little frock."

That Sara was wearing a lacy brassiere and matching pink bikini panties beneath her dress was certainly none of his business. "Randy is perfect," she muttered, her eyes hardening to the color of flint. "Were you a fresh-mouthed infant, too, or did your parents just get lucky when they picked out your name?"

Another spirited laugh emerged from him. "It's a perfectly legitimate question, Sara. All the people who work here dress the part, and do the crafts, and act like early-nineteenth-century citizens. I'm only wondering precisely how accurate you are."

"*Very* accurate," she retorted dryly, then added, "If you want to know the truth, I'm wearing hand-knit long johns and a camisole tied with a double knot."

"Well." He shrugged agreeably. "There's something to be said for prolonging the anticipation."

She fidgeted with a small mound of flour on the table. As handsome as Randy was, she'd had enough of his seductive taunting. "I...I've got more baking to do, Mr. Zale, so maybe I'd better get back to work. And you should probably go find your stray boy."

"Probably," Randy concurred. "But first you've got to answer my question."

"What question?"

"Are you free tonight?"

"Not as far as you're concerned."

His smile expanded, cutting delectable dimples into

his cheeks. "As far as I'm concerned," he drawled, his voice a hypnotic, husky purr, "you're absolutely beautiful. Even in a double-knotted camisole."

She tried unsuccessfully to smother her smile. "Flattery will get you nowhere, Mr. Zale," she warned him.

He eyed her curiously. A rainy gust slammed through the kitchen, causing flames in the fireplace to dance wildly. They cast intriguing shadows across his golden skin. "Give me a hint," he requested. "What can I say that will get me somewhere?"

His unflagging good humor touched Sara. Irked by the realization that she found him formidably attractive, she glanced out the door. "You can say, 'So long, Miss Morrow, I've got to go find that lonely child now.'"

"Lonely?" Sara didn't see him take a step, but somehow he seemed closer to her. "What makes you think he's lonely?"

It takes one to know one, she replied without speaking. "His eyes," she told Randy.

He continued to study her, his gaze softening as the fire gentled in the returning stillness. "He is lonely," he confirmed. "His parents are in the middle of a divorce, and he's taking it badly."

Sara was startled by the accuracy of her guess. It *did* take one to know one, she mused. "And how do you fit into the picture?" she asked, wondering whether Randy was somehow involved in the mess.

"Petey's my friend," Randy explained, crossing to the door and peering out, as if he could see the stables from the Willoughby House. "So are his parents. It's all a big mistake, as far as I can tell, but nobody's asking my opinion. So I keep an eye out for Petey while his parents are preoccupied with their stupidity."

That he shared her harsh judgment of divorce appeased her. "That's very kind of you," she said, wishing someone had taken such an active interest in her while her parents were engaged in their various shenanigans.

He clearly sensed her softening toward him and pressed his advantage. "So, tonight, are you free?"

No, she thought. She wasn't interested in men. She had sworn off men after Stu. But Randy wasn't like Stu, she realized. He cared; he cared about lonely children. Stu hadn't cared at all. "What did you have in mind?" she asked, feeling strangely at sea as she watched all her resolutions about avoiding men dissolve.

His smile lit his eyes, imbuing them with a delightful emerald shine. "Tickets to the Islanders game."

"Hockey?" Her eyebrows dipped in a frown.

"You don't like hockey?"

"I..." She didn't even know enough about hockey to know whether she liked it, but she suspected that she wouldn't. What she did know, from her neighbor Mick Sharkey, was that the Islanders were a superior hockey team, so tickets to their games were forever at a premium. She had no doubt that Mick would treasure Randy's invitation much more than she did. "Surely you didn't go out and buy tickets to an Islanders game hoping to share them with a stranger."

"I... Actually, I had considered taking Petey to the game with me," he admitted.

"Petey probably needs an Islanders game more than I do," Sara pointed out.

"I've got needs, too," Randy reminded her, the corners of his mouth lifting impishly.

Good Lord, the man was forward! Did he expect that even if she did attend some silly hockey game with him she would feel obliged to answer his needs? "Do you dare to be specific?" she goaded him. "You have a fetish about double-knotted camisoles?"

His smile erupted in deep, soul-melting laughter. "Go out with me tonight and I'll tell you all about my fetishes."

"That's just what I'm afraid of," she muttered.

"All right," he conceded. "Go out with me tonight and I won't breathe a word about my fetishes. I rarely talk fetishes on a first date, anyway."

His infectious humor was getting to her, and she struggled not to succumb to it. "Look," she demurred. "I'm not really interested in dating at the moment...."

"Involved with someone?" he asked.

"No, but..."

"You find me obnoxious," he guessed, his tantalizing dimples shaping his cheeks.

"No," she honestly admitted, "but..."

"I'm overbearing, oversexed, and you think I'll attack you."

"You are a bit randy," she admitted with a laugh. Why was she teasing this man? Why was she playing with him? It would only encourage him, she chided herself.

Indeed it did. "So wear a chastity belt. Did they have those things in 1791?" he asked.

Perhaps overbearing and oversexed, she allowed, but certainly unusually forthright. Subtlety clearly wasn't Randy Zale's long suit. She provided a cryptic answer to his question. "Wouldn't you like to know."

"Fine," he said with a congenial shrug. "Put yours on, hide the key, and come to the game with me tonight. I'll be a good boy."

"Is that a promise?" Why was she teetering toward an acceptance of his invitation?

"If you wear a chastity belt, what choice have I

got?" He pulled his map from his jeans pocket again and a pen from the chest pocket of his shirt. "What's your address?"

"I don't even know you," she faltered, staring at the strong, bronze hand that clasped the silver-toned pen.

"You'll get to know me tonight. Address?"

She heard herself recite it, her voice sounding alien to her. She felt as if she were eavesdropping on another woman.

He flashed her another intoxicating smile. "Levittown. I'll look the street up on the county map. Is seven-thirty all right?"

"Seven-thirty?" she echoed numbly.

"I'd ask you out for dinner, too, but I promised Petey I'd take him to this pizza joint that's dedicated to people shorter than five feet. You'd almost qualify," he added thoughtfully as he surveyed her diminutive form.

"What do you mean?"

"I mean the child-adult ratio is abouty twenty-eight to one. It's Petey's favorite place, and I promised I'd take him there. His parents aren't into cooking dinner these days." He glanced at his watch, then out the door again. The rain was still falling in constant silver sheets, and he zipped his slicker shut before unlatching the half door. "So I'll come by for you around seven-thirty. See you then." As if unwilling to give Sara a chance to change her mind, he swung through the door and started in a relaxed lope down the mud-red road in the direction of the stables.

Sara watched his departure through the open upper half of the door, trying to figure out what she had gotten herself into. Since her breakup with Stu a year earlier, she hadn't entertained any interest at all in finding a male companion to complete her life. In fact, her life seemed much more complete, much more stable and serene, without one.

Living with Stu had had its exciting moments, but Sara didn't value excitement very highly. To her, excitement had always meant coming home from school on a vacation and not knowing who might emerge from her parents' bedroom. It had meant not knowing from one day to the next whether her parents were talking to each other or talking to their lawyers. With Stu it had meant brief interludes of joy interspersed among the arguments, an erratic life that was exciting because, for a while at least, she could keep hoping for those sporadic interludes of joy to salvage the tempestuous relationship.

She no longer valued that kind of excitement, if she ever had. Her relationship with Stu, she realized in retrospect, was based on her foolish imitation of her parents' strange marriage. It was the only role model she'd had, and at the age of twenty-four, she had believed her life wouldn't be full without a man in it.

But she knew better now. She knew that she was more fulfilled by peace and solitude than by excitement. She knew that her life derived its meaning from the dependable rhythms of the earth, the spring rains, the renewal of life and its subsequent loss in autumn. She knew that her happiness came not from the pursuit of instant gratification, which seemed to obsess everyone around her, but from patience, from waiting. Bread that was kneaded by hand and baked in the brick oven of a fireplace was far more fulfilling than bread that one found wrapped in cellophane on a supermarket shelf.

The bread! Turning from the door, she raced to the oven and opened its door. The loaf inside was crusty, beautifully shaped, a rich, even brown. A perfect loaf, she decided as she set it on the table to cool. Not exciting, but vastly more fulfilling.

Chapter Two

The first thing she did when she got home was to check her sprouts. The house she rented in Levittown was one of numerous, nearly identical houses on a winding, tree-shaded drive. Although the houses were painted different colors, and although many of them had undergone alterations over the years—a full shed dormer here, an extra garage there, an enclosed porch somewhere else—the houses were essentially the same. William Levitt, the town's founder and builder, had been a pioneer in the science of tract housing, holding down the cost of each house by building them all the same basic shape and size. The concept of clone housing was an anathema to Sara, but the modest rent her landlord charged her was all she could afford, and she was lucky to find a cheap home in a safe neighborhood. Old Harkum Village paid its employees much less than she had been earning when she worked for the New York City school system.

The house Sara rented was small and drab, but it boasted a pretty yard with a garden already carved into one corner. Sara had never plied her gardening skills in a real garden before. Growing up, she was never around her parents' house long enough to plant a garden, and during the three years she lived in Brooklyn, first in her own minuscule studio and later in Stu's larger brownstone apartment, her farming labors were confined to window boxes set on rusty fire escapes. The tomatoes she had cultivated there refused to flourish; soot clogged the soil and dwarfed the plants, rendering them unproductive in spite of Sara's ministrations.

She had moved to Levittown the previous August, too late to start a garden. But this year she was prepared. Her living room and kitchen windowsills were cluttered with seedlings sprouting from seeds she had planted in whatever she could find: egg cartons, cut milk cartons, empty jars. She loved the budding plants; she thought of them as her babies. It would have been simpler to buy seedlings and plant them directly into the garden a month from now, but Sara was a purist. She wanted to grow her food from scratch.

She wanted more than that, she admitted as she carefully watered her numerous plants. She wanted to live in a house like the Willoughby House, where she could split her own wood and cook over a fire, where in the winter she could boil water for her bath and in the summer she could cleanse her body in an adjacent stream—if there were any unpolluted streams left in the universe. Sometimes she fantasized about buying a cabin in the woods, in the mountains, away from civilization, where she could test herself against nature, where she could appreciate survival in the most fundamental way. But the fantasy was farfetched, she acknowledged. She could no more return to the simpler era she pined for than she could stop the planet from spinning.

Once she had doused her plants, she carried her Old Harkum Village costume to her closet and hung it up. The Village considerately provided its employees with dressing rooms where they could change into civilian clothing, so they wouldn't have to drive through the streets of Long Island in antiquated frocks or knee breeches.

After storing the dress, she stripped off her jeans and blouse and headed for the bathroom. She unwound her braids and unraveled them, letting her glistening black hair tumble down her back. Then she adjusted the shower spray to a comfortable temperature and stepped beneath it. She ran the soap over her slender, shapely body. Her breasts, while small, were full in relation to her petite height. Her waist was delicate, her hips on the narrow side. Her skeleton was almost fragile in appearance, though Sara knew that it was strong enough to endure the rigors of pioneer living. After all, that was what she did every day at the Village.

As she lathered shampoo into her hair, she contemplated the man with whom she would be spending her evening. Accepting his invitation had been an awfully impulsive thing to do, and she wanted to believe she wasn't that impulsive anymore. She had been impulsive to fall in love with Stu, and look at the heartache he had caused her.

Of course, she wasn't in love with Randy Zale. How could she be? She didn't even know him. All she knew was that he was stunningly handsome, funny and fresh, and that he cared for a lonely little boy whose parents were too engrossed in their own marital nonsense to attend to him. That alone, she imagined, was why she had agreed to see the hockey game with him.

But hockey? What in the world was she going to do at a hockey game? She rinsed the shampoo from her hair and tried to recall what little she knew about the sport. It was played on ice—she knew that—and with long wooden sticks. She had caught glimpses of hockey games on Stu's television set once or twice while passing through the living room, but she had never seen an actual game. And she didn't own a television set herself.

She wrapped her hair in a plush towel, dried herself off, and returned to her bedroom, where she searched her bureau for appropriate clothing. Assuming that one dressed casually for a hockey game, she selected a colorful boat-neck sweater she had crocheted herself and a pair of clean, slim-fitting black jeans. As she slipped on her lacy underwear she remembered what Randy had said about her wearing a chastity belt. Well, she had something just as effective, she decided—her mouth. She was perfectly capable of saying no.

Once she was dressed, she brushed out her long, lustrous tresses. She wondered whether her hair would dry before he arrived. Although the rain had tapered off, the air was still quite humid, and she didn't own a hair dryer. If her hair stayed wet, it stayed wet, she conceded with a shrug.

Determined to learn something about hockey before Randy arrived, she left her house for the Sharkey house next door. In the eight and one-half months she had been living in Levittown, she had grown surprisingly close to the Sharkey family. Jean Sharkey, at forty years of age, was twelve years Sara's senior, which made her too old for a big sister and too young for a mother, but the relationship had developed into something comfortably in between—that of a special aunt, perhaps. Jean's three children were obstreperous and feisty, but Sara enjoyed being around them. The Sharkeys were a family, a *real* family, like the one Sara had never had.

She knocked on the Sharkeys' back door and Jean opened it. Tall, her thick brown hair sprayed with premature silver strands, Jean burst into a welcoming smile and swung the storm door open for Sara. "Come on in. We're just having dinner. You'll join us, won't you?" she asked.

The youngest boy, whose nickname, Pipsqueak, was justified by the shrill soprano pitch of his voice, was trying to wrestle a bag of potato chips out of his brother Jimmy's hands. Donna, the fourteen-year-old, sat at the kitchen table, trying hard to look supercilious. Jean hastened back to the stove, where a pan of hamburgers was sizzling. "I didn't come for dinner," Sara explained as she closed the door behind herself. "I just wanted to ask Mick something about hockey. Is he home?"

"Did I hear someone say hockey?" Mick Sharkey bounded in from the living room, an open beer can in his hand and an Islanders hockey jersey clinging to his broad barrel chest. "Did you say hockey?" he bellowed at Sara. "Lady, you're singing my song."

Jean gently shoved Sara into a chair and set a hamburger down before her. "Why in the world do you want to know about hockey?" she asked.

Before Sara could reply, the bag of potato chips ruptured, cascading crinkled yellow disks over the floor. "He did it!" Pipsqueak immediately protested.

"Like hell!" Jimmy objected.

"Watch your tongue," Jean calmly ordered Jimmy as she thrust a broom into his hands. He stretched his tongue out and attempted to watch it, his eyes sliding drunkenly toward the bridge of his nose.

"They're such creeps," said Donna, sighing. "I don't want any potato chips, anyway. I decided I have to lose five pounds."

"Where, in your brain?" Jimmy taunted, sweeping the strewn chips into the dustpan Pipsqueak held for him.

Jean efficiently served the rest of the meal and dragged a chair from the dining room to sit on. "So what's this about hockey, Sara?"

Sara gazed at her hamburger. She knew Jean would be furious if she didn't eat it, and reluctantly she applied some catsup to the patty before closing the bun around it. "I'm going to an Islanders game tonight," she said.

"Oh, my Lord." Mick clutched his chest, as if in the throes of a heart attack. "How in the world did you manage that? *Saturday night tickets?* Just before the play-offs? I'm gonna faint."

"Don't faint," Jean placidly ordered him. Sara marveled at the way Jean maintained her calm in such a disorderly family.

"Well, how'd you do it? Did somebody die and will them to you?" Mick questioned her. "And furthermore, will you smuggle me in under your coat?"

Sara accepted his teasing banter with a smile. "No, but I'll ask you what hockey is all about. It's played on ice, right?"

Jimmy groaned. "What a waste!" he complained. Pipsqueak added a derogatory opinion about the relative uselessness of girls. Donna rolled her eyes.

Mick grew solemn. "Hockey," he explained soberly, "is art on ice. It is art, power, grace, strategy...."

"And everyone beats everyone else up," Donna concluded. "Then they go sit in a penalty box with a dunce cap on their heads."

"Really?" Sara's eyes grew wide. Pipsqueak and Jimmy made raucous snorting noises.

"They sit in a penalty box if they commit a penalty," Mick explained, adding with a glare at his daughter, "No dunce caps. I won't lie and say the game doesn't have its violent moments." Sara grimaced. "But that's not the point of it," he quickly added.

"Says you," Donna sniffed.

"Why in the world are you going to a hockey game?" Jean sensibly asked.

"I was invited by someone I met at work," Sara answered.

"A man?" Jean tried to stifle a grin. She had tried several times to set Sara up with available men she knew, but Sara had refused to go along with her attempts at matchmaking. She had told Jean enough about her affair with Stu to rationalize her insistence upon swearing off men. "Someone you work with?"

"No, he was a visitor," Sara revealed.

Pipsqueak immediately broke into a singsong chorus of "Sara's got a boyfriend! Sara's got a boyfriend!" Donna poked her thumbs into her ears and wiggled her fingers at him to shut him up.

"And why did you agree to go out with him?" Jean asked, bristling with curiosity.

"Because he..." Sara set down her half-eaten burger and considered her answer. Because he had the most beautiful eyes she had ever seen? Because deep inside her she had enjoyed his lascivious teasing? Because for an instant his spicy male aroma had swamped her senses? "Because he was taking care of a lonely little boy and I thought that was nice of him," she replied.

"He sounds very tame," Jean declared, somewhat reassured.

Hardly. Sara once again recalled his mischievous remarks about fetishes and chastity belts. She recalled the untamed glitter in his eyes, the untamed warmth of his grip when he took her hand, the untamed reaction of her nervous system to his presence. "Well, I don't know. . . ." she hedged. "I'm a bit apprehensive, but I thought if I knew something about hockey . . ."

"Here's what I say," Mick decisively announced. "Pretend you know nothing about it."

"I don't have to pretend," she interjected with a small chuckle.

"Pretend you know nothing about it and then turn to him during breaks in the game and ask him to tell you what's going on. Bat those big gray eyes of yours and hang on his every word. You'll have him eating out of your hand in no time flat."

"Ugh!" Pipsqueak grunted. "Who wants a guy to eat out of your hand? Ugh!"

"You're an old-fashioned man, Mick," Sara ribbed her neighbor. "Men today don't want ignorant women. They expect women to know something about sports."

"So you want to impress this man?" Jean asked.

No, of course not, Sara almost responded. But then, what was she doing at the Sharkeys' house, grilling Mick about the game, if not to impress Randy? She shook her head slightly and decided that she didn't really want to impress him—just to get through the evening without appearing to be a total ignoramus. She wanted the evening to go pleasantly, that was all.

Yet that alone was a revelation. She cared enough about some strange man with honey-colored hair and magnetic eyes that she wanted her evening with him to go pleasantly. The abrupt understanding disturbed her. It wasn't like her to care anymore about what a man thought of her. She had written men off, hadn't she?

"Coffee? Dessert?" Jean offered as she stood up.

"Dessert!" the two boys hollered in unison. Donna looked tempted, then shook her head.

Sara glanced at the wall clock above the range. After seven. "No coffee for me, thanks," she said, carrying several plates to the sink and filling the dishpan with sudsy water. "He's coming in twenty minutes."

"Be forewarned," Jean mentioned in a stage whisper. "Several pairs of nosy eyes are going to be spying on you through the living-room window."

"In other words, we'd better not sit outside in his car and neck." Sara chuckled as she dried her hands on a convenient dish towel. "I'll scandalize the boys."

"The boys nothing!" Mick boomed. "Jean'll have her binoculars out."

"In that case I'll be very discreet," Sara noted as she headed for the door. "Thanks for supper, Jean."

"I hope it goes well," Jean said, giving Sara's arm an affectionate squeeze before opening the door for her. "Give me a call when you've got a chance. Fill me in."

Sara left the boisterous house for her own quiet home next door. Usually the peaceful silence of her house relaxed her, but tonight she felt mildly edgy, almost missing the rowdy atmosphere of the Sharkey home. She switched on the floor lamp and studied her living room with objective eyes, wondering what Randy would make of her minigreenhouse along the sill of the bay window, the worn sofa barely rejuvenated by the crocheted afghan she'd spread across its torn upholstery, the birch rocker, the colorless braided rug she had purchased at a rummage sale last October, the rows and rows of books arranged on shelves along one wall. There was a starkness to her furnishings, an austerity she liked because it reminded her of homes like the Willoughby House. But... it *was* austere. Most people would probably find it distasteful.

Well, she certainly couldn't redecorate the house in

fifteen minutes. If Randy didn't like it, that was his problem.

She strolled past the stairway, which led to a partially finished attic, and entered her bedroom. Her hairbrush rested atop the bureau, and she gave her hair a vigorous brushing. It had completely dried and hung in a thick, glistening fall down her back. The striking blue-black color of it set off her porcelain complexion and pale eyes. Usually she braided her hair for convenience but tonight she let it hang loose.

She heard the doorbell sound. Setting down the brush, she surveyed herself in the mirror above the bureau, feeling a bit like a teenager about to embark on a blind date. Randy Zale was almost a blind date, she mused. She knew nothing at all about him. Except what he looked like. Except that he was uncompromisingly handsome and funny, his eyes sparkling with humor and something else, something more dangerous, more intriguing.

Unnerved by the thought, she abandoned her bedroom and strolled to the front door. She took a deep breath to bolster herself, then swung the door open.

"I'm early," he announced.

He seemed to fill the doorway. It wasn't that he was so big, although Sara's height made most men seem big to her. No, it had something to do with his presence, an aura of strength and certainty emanating from him as he followed her into the living room. He wore corduroy slacks of a rust color that matched his hair, and a wool shirt featuring a brown-and-gold plaid. It, too, matched his hair. His hair had too many colors in it, she contemplated as the light from the lamp caught glimmers of copper and gold in its luxuriant depths.

He scanned the compact living room, then crossed to her plants. "Green thumb," he murmured.

It occurred to Sara that he was searching her house for clues about her, and that the plants offered an obvious one. "I'm trying," she granted.

"Looks like you're succeeding. What is all this stuff?"

"These are tomatoes," she said, pointing to an egg carton, each compartment of which held a tender green sprout. "These are cucumbers, these are zucchini, and these are radishes. Carrots. Parsley. This is supposed to be an herb garden," she said, sighing, pointing to a forlorn collection of weedy stalks emerging from the loamy soil of a foil-lined shoe box. "I don't think it's going to work out, though."

His silence when she finally stopped speaking convinced her that she must have been rambling. Abashed, she cast a quick nervous glance at him. He was staring at her, his eyes barraging her with unreadable green light, his lips curved in an enigmatic smile. "You think I'm nuts," she guessed.

"I think it's a beautiful herb garden," he declared softly. In spite of his spreading smile, he didn't sound as if he were teasing.

"Do you know what I'm doing wrong with it?" she asked, turning back to the feeble stalks.

"Me? I don't know the first thing about gardening," he admitted. "Except that these little brown things..."

"Dill," she identified them. "They're supposed to be green."

"They look sort of like filaments. You know anything about electronics?"

Her heart dropped, settling in a leaden lump against her diaphragm. Electronics? First hockey, now electronics. The evening was doomed. "No," she answered sadly. "Nothing at all."

"Then I won't bore you," he cheerfully closed the

subject. "Go get your coat. We've got to drive to Uniondale."

"It's not that cold out, is it? You're not wearing a coat."

"I left mine in the car. You'll need one at the game."

Why, she wondered. Wasn't hockey played indoors? She wouldn't reveal her ignorance by asking him, however, and she fetched her blue wool pea jacket from the closet.

He casually took her hand as he escorted her down the front walk to his car. Sara couldn't resist a hasty glance at the Sharkeys' house. She noticed the living-room curtains fluttering, and smiled.

Her smile faded when Randy drew to a halt beside a sleek black sports coupe. "What kind of car is this?" she asked as he helped her into the low-slung leather passenger seat.

"An Alfa," he told her, closing her door and then strolling around to the driver's side.

"An Alfa," she echoed dubiously as she took in the posh dashboard, the leather-wrapped steering wheel, the complicated stereo and mother-of-pearl-trimmed gear stick. It seemed to be an expensive car. Sara was unimpressed. To her, an automobile was transportation and little more. The used Chevrolet she'd bought after moving to Levittown was a necessity. Given her druthers, she'd much prefer a horse to a car, but horses weren't allowed on the Long Island Expressway.

"An Alfa-Romeo," he added, as if this were all the clarification she needed. He ignited the engine and revved it; it issued a roar before subsiding to a gentle purr as he shifted into gear and eased away from the curb. He drove in silence for several minutes, then asked, "Would you like some music?"

"Sure," she said.

He reached across her to the glove compartment, his arm brushing lightly against her knee. Purely by accident, she told herself, though he let his elbow rest on her leg as he groped for a cassette tape in the glove compartment. The pressure of his limb against hers seemed curiously personal, more personal than his deliberately having taken her hand on the front walk. She wondered if he was even aware that he was leaning on her, if he was aware of the havoc he created in the nerves of her thigh.

Finally he plucked a tape from the compartment, risked a rapid look at it, and asked, "You like Bach?"

That was a relief. At least Randy liked good old-fashioned classical music. "I love Bach," she told him.

She caught the glimmer of his smile as they cruised beneath a streetlight. He inserted the cassette into the tape deck, and music spilled forward from speakers behind their seats. It was Bach, all right, but not any performance of Bach Sara had ever heard before. "What is that?" she asked.

"Hmm? 'Switched-on Bach,'" he identified the recording. "Bach played on a Moog synthesizer. Don't you like it?"

She listened for a minute to the tinny, cartoony sound of the Bach Two-Part Invention. "I think I prefer his music played on a real instrument," she confessed grimly before pressing her lips together in distaste. The one thing she thought they might agree on turned out to be another miss. Bach on a Moog synthesizer indeed!

Randy was evidently unconcerned. "A synthesizer is an instrument," he affably argued. "What's a musical instrument but a tool through which sound is created by human intervention? In any case, the music exists through the organization of vibrations. The guy who made this record was merely trying to present an old composition on a new instrument so we can hear it from a fresh perspective." He paused in his dissertation, slanting an amused smile at her. "You don't have to like it if you don't want. I think it's kind of refreshing to hear old things new ways myself. Now the guy performing, Walter Carlos...I take that back. He's Wendy Carlos now."

"What?"

"He had a sex change operation a few years ago."

"I...see." She didn't, but she thought she ought to pretend she did.

Her hesitant tone bothered Randy. His brow creased in a thoughtful scowl; he did a quick mental assessment of the woman beside him, trying to forecast the evening. He was by profession a problem solver, and ever since he'd left the Willoughby House that afternoon he'd been thinking of Sara Morrow as the most fascinating problem he'd ever want to solve.

It wasn't merely her beauty that attracted him, though he couldn't deny that she was exceptionally beautiful. She was unusual in her beauty, so unlike most of the women he knew. There was a freshness about her, a sheer naturalness. He hadn't expected that she'd be wearing cosmetics at her job, given the period costume and all, but she wasn't wearing any now, either, and that appealed to him. There was something so clean and basic about her looks, as if she had washed in spring water and castile soap.

Maybe he'd asked her out simply because she was so different from the sort of women he generally socialized with, women he met at clubs, at bars, at parties, through work. Women who were loud and lusty, ambitious, chic—women who, like Randy, were out for a good time. Sara wasn't like that, and this date might have been a very bad idea, but... but what the hell. He liked a good puzzle.

Her house had surprised him; it looked as if the only creatures inhabiting it were those motley plants along the window. Perhaps Sara hadn't lived there long; perhaps it was all she could afford. But the house was idiosyncratic in its very lack of idiosyncrasies. Whatever Sara owned was right there—the shabby furniture, the plants and little else. Not that Randy was inclined toward rich women, but he'd been looking for something at the house that might have given him a hint of what sort of person Sara was. Plants. That was the big hint.

Plants. Growing things. Nature girl, he decided. Especially with her wholesome looks, with her hair hanging like a sheet of silk down her back. "I love your hair," he commented. "Thank you for wearing it down."

"I... I'm glad you like it."

"I do," he murmured. "Very much. I'd like to run my fingers through it."

His abruptly stated desire shocked Sara. She wasn't used to a man so straightforward. Stu was the only man she had ever been seriously involved with, and he had never said anything directly. What she had learned about him she learned from others, or from inference. What she had learned of his feelings for her she learned through his actions, which were sometimes loving and sometimes not. But never once in the three years they had known each other—in the nearly two years they had lived together—did he compliment her hair.

It was more than Randy's words that astonished her. She was also stunned by the thought that she would like to have him run his fingers through her hair.

He didn't, of course. He kept both hands safely on

the steering wheel, carefully piloting the powerful sports car through the increasing Saturday night traffic. To distract herself, she asked, "How was your dinner with Petey?"

"Noisy," he replied. "He enjoyed it."

"But you didn't?"

He shot her a fast glance. "During the whole meal I kept thinking I'd rather be with you. It made me feel a bit disloyal to the kid, but... it's the truth."

"You don't even know me," Sara objected.

"I know that the minute I walked into that old house this afternoon I didn't want to leave."

"Because it smelled of baking bread," she suggested helpfully.

"Because you were in it," he corrected her.

Sara was grateful that he didn't elaborate. His attention was drawn to the crowded parking lot outside the huge Nassau Coliseum. He prowled the rows of parked cars, reluctantly settling for a space far from the door when he was unable to find any closer. He shut off the rinky-dink synthesizer music, locked his door, and glided around the car to fetch Sara.

At least he's chivalrous, she thought as he slipped her hand through the bend of his arm and led her toward the brightly lit building. Granted, his comments about her hair and about wanting to remain in the Willoughby House with her weren't exactly chivalrous. But she had already discovered that afternoon that Randy wasn't subtle. At least, she believed, he was frank.

Inside the door, he handed a ticket-taker two tickets and then led Sara up a flight of stairs to their seats, which were located about twenty rows above the ice and nearly midway between the two ends of the arena. "Great seats, huh?" he enthused.

Sara nodded vaguely as she unbuttoned her jacket.

She started to remove it, then realized why Randy had suggested that she bring it. The arena was blustery cold. She left the jacket on.

Boisterous fans were seated on either side of them, above them, below them. In the glaring arena light, Randy turned to her, his tranquil smile a welcome oasis amid the hubbub. Sara couldn't help relaxing in the warm glow of his presence, her gaze taking inventory of the healthy golden tone of his skin, the clear green irises of his eyes, the sturdy line of his nose, his angular jaw. "Are you an electrician?" she asked, thinking of his comment about electronics at her house.

He grinned, seemingly oblivious to the activity surrounding them. "Something like that," he replied.

"That's an evasive answer," she scolded him.

"If you're asking what I do for a living, I'm a professional whiz, I guess."

"A whiz?"

"I work with electronics, computers...." He apparently realized that that, too, was an evasive answer, and he tried to come up with something more concrete. "I customize computer systems for industry. I write programs to meet clients' specifications. Sometimes I help them to define their specifications. I design office systems, transportation systems—I'm currently working on a project for Grumman Aircraft. A computerized navigational system."

"It sounds interesting," Sara muttered. Actually, it sounded repugnant to her. It sounded complicated and convoluted and not at all to her liking. Computers were the antithesis of the simple life she revered.

Her realization that Randy was devoted to something beyond her understanding, something she had no desire to understand, deflated her. She didn't know why it should. This was just an evening, a one-shot date. So they were poles apart professionally. She could still make the best of the evening.

But she couldn't shake her sadness. She wanted to like Randy, she admitted to herself. She wanted him to run his fingers through her hair....

A flurry of activity on the ice steered her attention away from her troubling thoughts. Two strings of men dressed in bulky, colorful uniforms and shining helmets skated out onto the ice, holding their sticks. The crowd exploded in a deafening cheer as the players skimmed the ice. Most of them skated to the side of the rink, taking seats behind a Plexiglas window. The remaining skaters arranged themselves in formation on the ice, and a referee dropped a small black puck between two players.

The game began, accompanied by more screaming from the fans surrounding Sara and Randy. Sara quickly realized that each of the two teams was trying to get the puck into the other team's goal, but they moved so swiftly that she could scarcely keep track of the puck. It was much too tiny to see against the glittering plane of ice.

She was grateful that Randy, while absorbed by the game, wasn't shrieking like a maniac the way the people around them were. He sat back in his seat, his arm draped over the back of hers, and watched, his gaze fastened to the puck.

Two players skated convulsively into each other and skidded across the ice, slamming into the side boards of the rink. Sara gasped at the sickening thud of their bodies colliding with the wood, but nobody else paid much attention. The game didn't even stop. "Are they okay?" she asked Randy, her eyes round and glistening.

He seemed puzzled by her concern. "Sure," he said.

"But they... they were moving so fast."

"They're well padded," he reassured her.

She turned back to the game. A referee had blown a whistle, and while some of the audience hooted and booed, the players took up a new formation and the referee dropped the puck between two players near a goal. Sara was curious about what had happened, but to ask Randy would have been to proclaim her ignorance, so she kept her mouth shut.

The play continued. Two players in a corner began swinging their sticks at each other's heads. One threw his gloves to the ice. All the players swarmed around them, clustering like ants about a cookie crumb. The referee blew his whistle, unscrambled the players, and sent two to a small Plexiglas-protected seat and announced a penalty. "The penalty box!" Sara exclaimed, excited to recognize an aspect of the game.

She felt Randy's eyes on her, and she turned cautiously to find him gaping at her. "You've never been to a hockey game before, have you?" he guessed.

She caught her lip between her teeth, then shrugged and resigned herself to letting her ignorance be known. "No, I've never been to a hockey game before."

"Why didn't you say something?" Randy asked.

"What should I have said?"

A low, husky chuckle rumbled up from his chest. "Do you know what's going on?" He angled his head toward the ice.

"I know that that's the penalty box," she declared proudly.

Laughing, he shook his head in amazement, letting his arm slip from the back of her seat to her shoulders as he leaned conspiratorially toward her. "Okay, that was offsides," he explained a break in the game. "That means that one of the Oilers skated over the blue line ahead of the puck. It's against the rules."

"A penalty?"

"No, just a face-off. That's what they're doing now," he patiently lectured her as the players squared off and the referee dropped the puck between them. "When the Oilers go offsides, the face-off occurs near their goal, which benefits the Islanders." He hesitated. "Do you want me to go into all this?"

"Yes," Sara instantly replied. She did want him to. She wanted to understand something that interested him. And she didn't want him to remove his arm from her shoulders. It felt good there. Surprisingly comfortable. So comfortable that she wasn't immediately aware of his fingers toying with the silky black strands of her hair. When she did realize that he was running his fingers through her hair, she felt a warm blossom open inside her, uncurling like a new green leaf, pale and delicate, reaching for life.

"That's icing," Randy explained as the game halted again for another face-off. She listened to his simple, clear description of the infraction, her brain keenly attuned to what he was saying even as her soul followed the progress of the bud opening inside her. She wondered if what she was feeling now resembled anything Randy might have felt earlier that day when she had lectured him on the history of the Willoughby House. He had seemed genuinely interested in what she had to say, yet his admission in the car of his attraction to her made her wonder whether that afternoon he had been listening to her words with his brain while his soul had been listening to something else, to its own secret unfurling.

The skaters vanished from the ice. Only twenty minutes had elapsed since the start of the game. "Is it over?" she asked.

"Just the first period. There are three periods." He

stood up, stretched, and helped her to her feet so she could also stretch. He was over a head taller than she, she noted, feeling absurdly short next to him. He peered down at her, his green eyes glowing curiously. "Why didn't you tell me you didn't know anything about hockey?" he asked.

"Just because I don't know anything about it doesn't mean I can't watch a game," Sara answered. "Anyway, I'm learning."

"What do you think?" he questioned her. "Are you enjoying it?"

I'm enjoying your hand in my hair, she almost replied. *I'm enjoying the light in your eyes when you gaze down at me.* Somehow she forgot that he was a computer buff, an electronics whiz enamored of synthesizer music and fancy cars. All she could think of was that his hand felt glorious in her hair. It felt as if it belonged there.

She remembered that he was awaiting an answer, and she said, "Very much."

His smile expanded. The sight of his dimples made her smile as well.

The game resumed, and Randy's explanations grew less and less frequent as Sara began to make sense of the sport. After a while, he spoke only if she asked him about something that had occurred on the ice, and soon she had developed a rudimentary grasp of the action below her. When the skaters fell she still cringed, but they always picked themselves up and rejoined the game. And although there was one other fight, which, she told Randy, struck her as infantile, she wouldn't exactly have called the sport violent.

At the end of the game, the Islanders emerged victorious over their archrivals. Randy, while pleased, didn't make a fool of himself like the rejoicing fans surrounding them. He deftly steered Sara through the swarming throng, down the stairs to the door, and outside into the dark night.

They walked in silence to his car. He unlocked her door, assisted her into the seat, and then joined her, taking his place at the wheel. He twisted to face her in the bucket seat, and even in the darkness she felt the warm glow of his eyes upon her. "So tell me, Sara," he murmured, his voice a low, husky hum. "Are you wearing a chastity belt?"

"What?"

He issued a soft laugh. "Should I take you out for a drink, or should I take you back to your house and ravish you mercilessly?"

Her mouth flexed as she tried to unscramble her thoughts. "Are those my only two choices?" she managed.

"I don't know," he mused. "Can you think of a better idea? My place, I suppose..."

"Randy, I..." What had she resolved at her house? The "chastity belt" she was going to use was a verbal one. "I'm not going to invite you back to my house," she declared. "And I'm certainly not going to go back to yours."

"Any particular reason?" he asked.

"Any particular reason?" she echoed incredulously. "I've known you all of, what, six hours? And you want to make love to me?"

"I wanted to make love to you after knowing you only five minutes. But if you don't want me to, that's okay. I can take it."

"How very generous of you," she said with a sniff. "Haven't you ever heard of discretion, tact, diplomacy, subtlety?"

"Do you want me to play games with you?" He sat up straighter, surprised by her charge. "I'm not really good at playing games. I was hoping you'd prefer honesty."

"I do," she confessed, lowering her eyes to the pearl-inlaid gear stick between them. "But Randy... you're a little bit blunter than I'm used to."

He shrugged. "Well, give it back to me between the eyes. Nice and blunt. You hate my guts? I've offended your sense of modesty? You think I don't respect you?"

"I should think you'd want to get to know me better first," she pointed out.

"Hmm." He weighed her comment, then nodded. "Fair enough. Let's get to know each other better." He leaned over to her seat and touched his lips gently to hers. Then he settled back in his own seat, started the engine, and steered out of the parking lot.

Chapter Three

"You're right," he said.

They were seated in a cozy corner booth at a dimly lit, unpretentious bar. Sara faced Randy, her hands folded primly in her lap as she studied his attractive face. His eyes were a muted green, the soft, delicate color of her tomato seedlings. "Right about what?" she asked.

"About coming here to talk. Mind you, even if you had invited me back to your house, I would have wanted to get to know you better. Two people can get to know a lot about each other by making love, don't you think?"

Sara was relieved by the approach of a waitress carrying their drinks—a glass of the house Chablis for her, a Campari on ice for him. *Blunt,* she thought. Randy was certainly blunt. "They can get to know some things, I suppose," she allowed. "But I—I'm not really interested in pursuing a serious romance."

"You think sex is serious?" he asked, his eyes sparkling whimsically.

She lifted her glass and sipped. It seemed easier than answering his provocative question.

He leaned back against the vinyl banquette and scrutinized her, his expression thoughtful despite his smile. "You, Sara Morrow, are a very solemn woman."

"No, I'm not," she objected. "Just... reserved."

"Old-fashioned. I bet you never kiss on the first date."

"I don't date much," she told him.

"That's a surprise. You're incredibly beautiful. I've told you that already, haven't I?" He fingered his glass, then raised it to his lips and consumed a mouthful of the rosy liquor. "All right, I'm game. Tell me all about yourself."

"What do you want to know?"

"Start at the beginning," he coaxed her. "Were you born or hatched?"

More hatched than born, she admitted to herself. "I... sort of arrived," she informed him, striving for honesty.

He threw back his head with a low, smoky laugh. "Oh, Lord, you *are* old-fashioned. Didn't your mommy ever tell you where babies come from?"

Sara smiled, then decided to explain her enigmatic remark. "I was kind of an experiment for my parents," she said. "My mother thought pregnancy and childbirth would be interesting experiences. She's very big on experiences."

"And was she right about pregnancy and childbirth?"

"I guess." Sara shrugged. "Motherhood didn't interest her very much, though." She drew the tip of her index finger about the dewy rim of her glass and smiled pensively.

Randy waited patiently for her to continue, but when she remained silent he prodded her with a question. "Where do your folks live?"

"My mother lives in Marin County, north of San

Francisco. My father lives near L.A., in Malibu."

"Ah." He nodded knowingly. "That's how come you were so attuned to Petey." At her quizzical glance, he explained: "Child of a broken home."

She nodded. "How about you? Why are you so attuned to Petey? Are your parents divorced, too?"

"My parents," he declared, "are disgustingly happily married. Going on thirty-eight years now. Very traditional, devoted to each other. They finish each other's sentences, call each other pet names, keep school graduation photos of my brother and me in silver frames on top of the television set. Currently enjoying the leisurely life of retirement in Florida."

Sara sighed enviously. "Then why do you empathize with Petey?" she asked him.

"Petey and I go back a long way," he said. "His father was my roommate at MIT. We work together now. His mother was at Wheaton College when we were at MIT—they were a college romance, so I've known her almost as long as I've known Larry. I knew Petey when he was just a twinkle in their eyes and all that." He exhaled grimly. "I was their best man."

"Why are they splitting up?"

"Who knows?" he grumbled, then drank some Campari to quell his disgruntlement. "Larry tells me his side at work, Renee her side over coffee at their house. I don't think they quite know themselves. They're bored, frustrated, stale... not as happy as they think they have a right to be. I'm sure they aren't any happier apart than they are together, but they aren't interested in hearing my words of wisdom. So I just listen."

"Are they already divorced?"

"Just separated at the moment," he informed her. "She's got the house; he's renting a place a couple of miles away. They don't seem terribly cheerful about it." He eyed Sara curiously. "You know more about these things than I do. Can you explain it to me?"

"No," she honestly replied. "No, I can't explain it. I don't understand my parents at all." She addressed the clear gold-white fluid in her glass. "A year ago, my mother remarried some twenty-three-year-old guy she met in a human potential class. My father lives with two other men and three women in a beach house, and I'm not sure I want to learn the details of that arrangement."

Randy's penetrating gaze settled on her. "Where, in a mess like that, did you come from?"

"Didn't your mommy ever tell you where babies come from?" she teased, deliberately echoing his phrasing.

He laughed. "Okay. So you were—arrived. In California?"

She nodded. "I went to school in New England, though. Well out of my parents' way."

"And then when you finished your schooling, you started working at Old Harkum Village?"

She shook her head. "No, I taught for a few years first. American history at a public high school in Brooklyn."

"No kidding? A history teacher?" He angled his head to appraise her. "You don't seem the type?"

"Oh?" She grinned. "What's the type?"

"Someone with a little bun on the top of her hair, about ninety-three years old, with a nasal voice and spectacles on the tip of her nose. My American history teacher was like that. Mrs. Dunkel. The most boring teacher ever to walk the earth."

"If that's the type, I'm glad I don't fit it," Sara admitted, chuckling at the ridiculous image he had described. "Your Mrs. Dunkel wouldn't have survived a week at the school where I taught. It was in one of the slummier parts of Brooklyn. We served a pretty rough clientele."

His eyes flickered with interest. "*Blackboard Jungle*," he said, alluding to the classic book and movie about a slum school. "I hope they didn't scar you too badly."

She responded by rolling up the right sleeve of her sweater, displaying the faint red scar an inch above her wrist. Randy seemed shocked by her having taken his comment so literally. "How'd that happen?" he asked.

"I was trying to break up a fight in the corridor," she replied, rolling the sleeve back down. "I didn't realize that one of the kids had a knife. Worse things happened in that school, believe me. Kids got mugged, robbed; teachers got attacked. There was a rumor a girl was raped in one of the bathrooms, but it never went to court, so I don't know if it actually happened."

"I can see why you'd want to leave that job," Randy noted sympathetically.

She shook her head again. "It wasn't the violence that bothered me," she revealed. "It was..." She paused to consider her words. "Differences with my superiors." His fascinated gaze encouraged her to continue. "We had different philosophies about education. When I got my master's degree in education, I was offered several jobs, but I specifically took the one in Brooklyn because I thought that I could affect more students that way, that I could really *teach* them something about America's history." A sardonic laugh slipped past her lips, expressing her disillusionment. "Unfortunately, that wasn't the modern approach to education. My supervisors wanted me to pass the students into the next grade whether or not they had learned anything. They didn't like it that I was always flunking my students, holding them back because they hadn't learned the material. They thought I didn't understand their practical, up-to-date methods."

"I thought the schools were all embracing a more rigorous educational philosophy these days," Randy commented.

Sara chuckled scornfully. "On paper, sure. But in reality, they get edgy when the ninth grade is full of eighteen-year-olds. They don't like it when the kids resent them, and if you leave a kid back, he certainly resents you. Our principal operated on the assumption that the violence in the halls was a product of resentment over low grades and harsh teachers. He told me that I should loosen up, that by being overly strict I was trying to compensate for the fact that all the students were bigger than me. So when my three-year contract was up, I didn't ask to have it renewed. Much to the principal's relief, I'm sure."

"And then you came to Old Harkum Village?"

"Then I came to Old Harkum Village," she confirmed. "What a change! How much more thrilling to *live* the history instead of simply teaching it! Being an interpreter is the ideal job for someone like me."

"An interpreter?"

"That's what we're called. We interpret the mode of life of the period for the visitors."

"You love it," he guessed. Her radiant grin offered proof that he was correct. "That's great. I'm glad you found a job that suited you better."

Randy could only begin to know how well it suited Sara, but she refrained from indulging in rapturous effusions about the delight she took in the antiquated world in which she functioned every day. She knew that if she tried to describe the joy she felt at pretending that she was actually living in another era, she would sound foolish. Instead, she turned the spotlight on him. "And you? You went to MIT and majored in computers?"

"Something like that," he affirmed. "After I graduated, I worked for a while in computer systems design, then picked up an M.B.A. and started my own company here on the Island."

"Any particular reason for Long Island?"

"I grew up here, and there's a lot of work for a firm like mine in the area." He shrugged. "It was home. My brother and his wife live on Roosevelt Island in New York City, so we can see each other reasonably often."

"You're close?" She sighed wistfully. How she had longed to have a sibling to share her misery with!

"Yeah, we're close. There are few people I enjoy getting into screaming fights with as much as Artie."

She gave Randy a reflective perusal. "Given the sterling example of your parents and your brother, how come you aren't married?"

He seemed momentarily taken aback that she could match him in tactlessness, and then he seemed pleased by it. His cheeks creased with dimples as he considered his reply. "Too young?" he speculated.

"How old is too young?"

"Thirty-four." He considered his age, then shook his head. "Not too young. I'm sure I'll get married when I find the right woman. In the meantime, bachelorhood has its rewards."

"Yes, you were going to tell me about your fetishes," she teasingly reminded him.

He laughed. "I'd rather demonstrate them than talk about them," he said, returning her playful taunting.

"You're not going to demonstrate them on me," she warned.

"Your loss." He shrugged, then grew serious. "Now you tell me, lovely Sara. Why don't you date much?"

"I..." She stalled, toying with her glass and sipping some of the crisp, cold wine. "I guess I'm not that interested."

"Try again," he ordered her, his gentle tone failing to conceal his disbelief.

"It's the truth," she insisted. "I prefer being alone to being with men."

"Hmm." He leaned back again, his eyes locked on hers. When she let her hand slide from her glass, he covered her fingers with his. "Is this allowed?" he asked, angling his head toward their hands. "Or do you prefer not being touched?"

Sara opened her mouth to reply, but no words emerged. The warm pressure of his hand on hers felt both soothing and arousing. Her fingers relaxed into the curve of his hard palm and a slow-moving warmth climbed her arm to her chest, where it spread in radiating waves through her flesh. Right now, she decided, she preferred to be touched. By Randy.

His thumb traced the slender length of hers. "You have beautiful hands," he observed softly. "I noticed them when you were kneading the dough this afternoon. All I could think of was how it would feel to get a back rub from you."

"A back rub? Is that one of your fetishes?" She hoped the joke would ease the trembling warmth that continued to filter through her body, fed by the quiet caress of his thumb.

"Bull's-eye," he confessed.

"It sounds relatively safe."

His eyebrows lifted. "Should we find out?" he invited her. She laughed at his audacity and shook her head. He grew silent for a long moment, scrutinizing her in the atmospherically gloomy light of the bar. "What happened? Did someone break your heart?"

Her eyes flashed so brightly, so suddenly, that they both flinched. She didn't confirm his suspicion; she didn't have to. He clearly knew he had guessed right. "Recently?" he asked.

"About a year ago."

"Long recovery."

"Long relationship." She sighed.

He nodded, lowering his gaze to their hands meshed together on the small table. He seemed to be debating with himself whether to release her, ultimately deciding against it. Another moment's consideration compelled him to lift her hand to his mouth and kiss it.

The gentle friction of his lips against her knuckles shocked her, fanning the eddying warmth he had instilled within her into a dangerous flame. She tried to withdraw her hand from his, but although he lowered it from his mouth he refused to let go. "Sara," he murmured. "I won't force things between us if you aren't ready. But...I like you. I want to see more of you, spend time with you."

"You want me to rub your back."

"Definitely." He briefly smiled, then reverted to his earnest tone. "You aren't like any other woman I've ever known. I don't know what it is about you, but you're different."

"I bet the other women you know understand hockey."

Again he smiled briefly, hesitantly. "Some. But that's not what makes you different."

"I'm old-fashioned," Sara reminded him. "A modern woman would have taken you to her house and let you ravish her mercilessly."

He weighed her reasonable suggestion. "Maybe."

"Then I'm just a challenge." She succeeded in pulling her hand from his, and when she did she realized that he hadn't been holding it tightly at all. It had been her own reluctance to lose physical contact with him that had prevented her from breaking free of his grasp earlier.

The green light in his eyes narrowed into two sharp points, laser beams piercing her skin. "No, you're not a challenge," he refuted her soberly. "You're an enigma. You're a mystery."

"There's nothing mysterious about me," she protested with a nervous laugh.

"Yes, there is. You seem..." He ran his acute gaze over her face, seeking, searching. "You seem otherworldly."

"A spirit from the grave?" She laughed again.

"Detached. Not a part of the world around you. In the world but not of it, or however the quote goes." He assessed her, puzzling over her and over his words. "Then there's something about you that seems utterly earthy, something completely different from that detachment, that lets you tune into the things around you. At the hockey game, for instance—the way you watched it, the way you started moving with the rhythm of the game..."

"What?"

"You just seemed to take it in, to make it a part of you. After a while, you were anticipating things, watching where you knew the puck would be before it got there."

"I didn't do that," she argued.

He nodded. "Perhaps you weren't even aware of doing it. But I noticed. I was watching you as much as the game." His hand shifted on the table, as if longing to fit itself around hers again. "And the way you read

Petey's story so quickly. You're keyed into the world around you, even while you're busy trying to distance yourself from it." He let his hand settle on his glass, which he lifted and drained. "All right, I'll admit it, Sara. You're a challenge. Not *just* a challenge, but yes, a challenge."

She considered his words intently, astounded that he had pinpointed her so well. He hadn't completely solved the riddle of Sara Morrow, but he had come surprisingly close. He knew that she was in love with the earth but reticent about the civilization that occupied it. He knew that she was sensitive to individuals, to rhythms, even as she endeavored to escape the reality of contemporary society.

She couldn't think of anything to say. Her mind was overcome by the understanding that Randy was possibly more sensitive than she was—certainly more sensitive to her than anyone else she had ever known. And that made *him* different, too.

The waitress broke through the cloud of silent thought that had enveloped them and asked if they wanted to order another round. Randy shook his head and settled the bill. Then he shrugged on his leather jacket, helped Sara into her pea jacket and ushered her out of the bar.

The sleek car didn't bother her as it had at the start of their date. Nor did Randy's choice of music, or his career. As he drove back to her house, Sara sat in the mellow darkness of the bucket seat awash in the realization that she and Randy had much more in common than she had initially suspected, though she wasn't quite able to put her finger on exactly what it was that they shared.

Randy, too, was immersed in thought, his eyes following the flow of traffic around his car while his mind pursued its own interests. Sara's reaction to his thumbnail analysis of her indicated that he'd been pretty accurate. Yet defining the puzzle didn't necessarily solve it. He'd discerned Sara's earthiness the moment he saw her kneading her bread dough at the Willoughby House that afternoon. Of course, baking bread was an earthy thing to do, but Sara's attitude, her motions, her mood... he couldn't quite put a name to it, but it had struck him forcefully. She understood bread, and children, and loneliness.

He tried to imagine her childhood, her lackadaisical parents. It just didn't seem possible that she could have come from such a background. He wanted to be able to put it all together, but it wasn't coming clear to him. If he punched Sara's data into one of his computers, he'd probably come up with zilch. DOES NOT COMPUTE. NEED MORE INPUT. That was it. Randy needed more input.

The houses along her block were dark when he pulled the car up to the curb in front of her home. He climbed out of the car and jogged around to her side to accompany her up the walk. On the front porch they stopped awkwardly. "I—I don't think I'm going to ask you in," she stammered, too confused to risk complicating matters further.

"Don't," he replied. "If you did, the temptation would drive me crazy." His lips spread in a poignant smile, and then he lowered them to hers.

His kiss was light, tentative, patient. There was nothing demanding in it, nothing expectant. He seemed to be waiting for guidance from her. Her mouth moved hesitantly against his, her teeth pressed into her inner lips, longing to offer him entry. But her mind held her back.

Randy slipped his hand beneath the shimmering black cloak of her hair to the nape of her neck. His fingers were warm as they roamed tenderly across the skin. He drew back, then kissed her again.

This time her mouth overcame her mental misgivings. It softened, and she could almost feel his smile as his tongue toured the breadth of her lips and then the pearly surface of her teeth. Then he ventured farther, into the trembling recess within, searching. Their tongues touched almost shyly, but the meeting melted something inside Sara, causing her mouth to open more fully for him.

It was the invitation he had been waiting for. His fingers arched firmly about the base of her head, holding it steady beneath the building intensity of his tongue's assault. Suddenly she was swamped again, as she had been swamped by his subtle fragrance at the Willoughby House. But this time what swamped her was something that transcended Randy's spicy aftershave. It was the aroma of Randy himself, of his virile essence penetrating her senses, urging her small body more intimately against his long, hard one.

Her arms reflexively reached for his shoulders, and he adjusted his lean frame to her petite shape. His free hand slipped beneath her jacket to her waist, hugging her close, sketching a tantalizing route along the edge of her sweater before exploring the satiny skin beneath it. "No double-knotted camisole," he whispered.

She sighed weakly and edged her mouth from his. "We're putting on quite a show for the neighbors," she murmured, hazily recalling Jean's teasing after Sara had eaten dinner with the Sharkeys.

"Then let's give them their money's worth," Randy recommended, steering her mouth back to his.

His hand moved higher beneath her sweater, his fingers describing a mysterious pattern along the delicate ridge of her spine. If she had given herself the opportunity to think, she would have been astonished by her body's organic response to him. She would have been shocked by the pulsing tension in her legs as they rocked her closer to him, by the dangerous pitch of her heartbeat as his chest mashed her breasts through her clothing, by the imperative throbbing in her hips as they sought refuge in the cradle of his thighs. "Randy," she breathed, her words springing not from her mind but from somewhere else, somewhere she couldn't identify. "Randy—maybe you should come inside."

He hovered on the edge of indecision, and then his arms released her and he stepped back. "No," he said, although the refusal obviously pained him. "No, not tonight. I...we..." He paused to control his ragged breath. "I want you, Sara, I want you—but not tonight, not now." He expelled his breath in a hoarse sigh. "I'm going to hate myself in the morning," he said, chuckling. "But we both know, Sara, we both know what would happen if I walked through your door. And you aren't ready for that yet, are you?"

She lowered her eyes. Her gaze rested on his chest, on the neat row of buttons fastening his shirt. If she were a more reckless person, she would tear the buttons off, parting the cloth to expose the splendid chest she imagined lurking behind the protective stretch of plaid wool. But Randy was right. He was more sensitive to her than she was to herself. She wilted against him, her cheek relishing the scratchy fabric separating her skin from his. "No," she reluctantly conceded, her voice muffled by his jacket. "No, I'm not ready yet."

He squeezed her tightly, then relaxed his arms. "I'll call you, Sara," he promised. "I'll see you soon."

She watched him pivot and stride briskly down the walk, his shoulders hunched forward as if they alone could propel him to his car. Once he was ensconced behind the wheel, she turned and let herself into the house.

Her nerves rippled disturbingly beneath her skin. She had wanted Randy, wanted him in a way she could hardly fathom. She had wanted him more than she had ever wanted Stu—and she had known Stu for almost a year before their relationship had become intimate. Stu had been handsome, too, dark and manly, a skillful kisser. But with him she had never felt the sublime communion that she had just felt with Randy.

Shaken by her shattering response to him, she removed her jacket and hastened to her bedroom. She undressed, tied on her flannel bathrobe, and crossed to the bathroom to wash for bed. She didn't want to think. She didn't want to feel. She just wanted to sleep, to wake up in the morning knowing once again who she was.

She didn't hear the chiming of her doorbell until she left the bathroom. Frowning, wondering whether Jean was so nosy she couldn't wait until morning to get a report on Sara's date, she scampered to the front door and opened it.

Randy stood on the porch, leaning against the doorjamb and smiling sheepishly. "This is going to sound like the line of the century, but my car won't start," he announced.

"Oh." Her hand drifted to the lapels of her robe, modestly holding them shut below her throat. "Do you—have you any idea what's wrong?"

"Probably a short in the wiring," he surmised.

"Do you want to use the phone?" she stupidly asked.

He laughed. "Sara, it's midnight on a Saturday night. What garage is going to be open at this hour?" When she remained standing in the doorway, staring dumbly up at him, he added, "If it's an electrical problem I'm sure I can fix it myself. In the daylight."

"You want me to put you up," she stated dully.

"I was hoping you'd offer," he said, gliding past her into the living room. His gaze dropped to the sofa and his lips twisted wryly as he predicted what she would request.

"Of course." The words reflected both her letting him spend the night and her relegating him to the couch. She couldn't let him stay in her bed. She had only just met him; she hardly knew him. She wasn't ready. They both knew that. "I'll . . . get some linens."

The errand offered her a needed excuse to leave Randy. She abandoned him in the living room, heading for the linen closet beside the bathroom. She rummaged through her meager supplies, yanking a towel and two sheets from a shelf. The only pillow she owned was the one on her bed, and she sneaked into the bedroom to fetch it. She suspected that Randy would object if he knew she was giving him her own pillow.

When she returned to the living room, he had already removed his jacket and kicked off his loafers. He truly was going to spend the night in her house, she realized as her eyes focused on the shape of his toes visible beneath his dark socks. What had he said about the temptation driving them crazy?

Shaking her head clear, she concentrated on making up the sofa, removing the afghan to spread the bottom sheet directly over the tattered upholstery, then adding the top sheet and finally the afghan as a blanket. She handed him the towel, directing her gaze to his chin so she wouldn't be snared by his mesmerizing eyes. "Anything else I can do for you?" she asked.

He sighed. "What a question," he muttered wistfully. "Go on to bed, Sara. I'll be fine. Thanks for putting me up."

Obediently she turned and padded to her bedroom, shutting herself inside.

She didn't sleep. It wasn't because of the absence of her pillow—she could easily forgo that small comfort. It was because even as she willed her mind to relax, her soul refused to relinquish its consciousness of Randy asleep in the other room. If he was asleep. Objectively, she hoped he was resting better than she was, but subjectively, she suspected that he wasn't. And she found the thought oddly flattering.

She arose early, put on her robe, and tiptoed to the living room. Randy appeared to be slumbering contentedly in the curtained room, the afghan drawn up to his chin. His clothing was piled neatly on the rocker. The thought of his nakedness beneath the cover unnerved her, so she turned her back on him and walked to the kitchen. She filled her stove-top percolator with water, spooned some ground coffee into the metal basket, and set the pot on the gas stove, twisting on the flame beneath it. Then, succumbing to curiosity, she drifted back to the doorway to spy on him as he slept.

Only he wasn't sleeping anymore. He was seated on the couch, his magical green eyes wide open and fixed on her, the afghan skittering down to his waist. She caught a glimpse of his chest, a golden expanse of sinew and ribs adorned by an enticing shadow of tawny hair across the upper portion, tapering down to his flat abdomen. His shoulders and arms were muscular, beautifully sculpted, implying strength and power. Obviously his torso matched his face in sheer attractiveness.

"Good morning," he greeted her before she could turn away.

"Good morning." The coffee water had the good grace to start boiling at that moment, and she excused herself. "I've got to adjust the heat under the percolator," she explained as she hurried back into the kitchen.

She lowered the flame, then riveted her attention to the window as she tried to ignore the sounds of Randy emerging from beneath the covers and getting dressed. The sun broke through a few residual clouds, and she scanned the horizon in search of a rainbow. She didn't find one.

Hearing Randy come into the kitchen, she slowly turned around. He was wearing his corduroy trousers and was slinging on his shirt. His chin was shaded by a light bristle of beard, and his lids drooped lazily, shielding the sleepy humor in his eyes. "Did you sleep well?" Sara asked politely.

"Terribly. How about you?"

His honesty forced the same from her. "Not too well," she admitted.

"Uh-oh." He chuckled. "Did you hear me?"

"Hear you?"

He ambled to the refrigerator and peered inside, then shut it. "I made several abortive raids on your bedroom door last night," he confessed. "The third time I actually got my hand on the doorknob before chickening out and returning to the couch."

Blunt. "Am I supposed to say thank you?" she asked softly.

He laughed. "Why not just say three cheers for willpower?" He swung open the refrigerator door again. "Have you got any orange juice?"

"No, but I've got oranges. I'll squeeze some fresh."

"Fresh-squeezed?" His smile broadened, reflecting his delight at the treat. He stepped out of her way so she could pull three oranges from a lower shelf. She sliced them in half, then twisted one of the halves over the textured core of her glass orange juicer. He watched her for a moment, a frown darkening his features. "You know, they make electric orange squeezers."

She lifted the pulpy orange rind and set it aside. "This works fine for me."

"Can I give you a hand?"

She shook her head and concentrated on wrenching the juice from another orange half. "Why don't you sit down and make yourself comfortable."

He did so, lounging in a chair by her table and buttoning his shirt. She checked the coffee, priding herself on her ability to time it by instinct. It would be ready when the orange juice was, she calculated as she resumed squeezing the halved fruits. After placing the empty rinds in a bag of compost she was saving for her garden, she poured the accumulated liquid from the bowl of the juicer into two glasses. She extended one to him.

He stood up to accept it, but instead of grasping the glass he curled his hand around her wrist and drew her to himself. "Good morning," he whispered before covering her mouth with his.

Her lips instantly flowered open for him, and his tongue delved daringly inside her mouth. Fortunately he had the presence of mind to take the glass from her trembling hand and set it safely on the counter. Then he folded his arms around her and deepened his kiss.

She felt as if her bones were thawing, softening into jelly, as his tongue engaged hers. *Blunt,* she thought. Forward. Not good at playing games. But virile, incredibly virile. She savored the stunning force of his kiss, the brazen claim his mouth made on hers, the possessive grip of his arms about her slender shoulders. Her soul coiled down into her like a tightened spring below her abdomen, straining for release.

As he allowed his mouth to lift to her brow and higher, into her hair, he slid one hand over her shoulder to her throat and beneath the soft flannel of her robe. His hand traveled gingerly over her smooth, pale skin before capturing the warm fullness of her breast. His fingers discovered her already rigid nipple, and she gasped.

"I ran out of willpower last night," he murmured huskily, his lips close to her ear. "Whatever we've got left between us is your supply." His teeth tested the curving flesh of her lobe.

"Please..." She was breathing erratically, unsure of what she was pleading for. "Please, Randy..."

"Tell me."

"Stop."

He immediately did, his hand slinking out into the air, his mouth lifting from her temple. Sara turned to the sink, dragging air into her lungs, feeling her cheeks grow feverishly crimson. She forced her quivering fingers to tighten her robe protectively around herself.

"I'm sorry," he offered softly.

"No...don't be," she managed.

"Okay. I'm not sorry."

She spun around to find him still close, his expression a blend of disappointment and grudging acceptance. His gaze took in her flushed, breathless condition, the play of doubt and shock and desire in the depths of her gray eyes. Before she could speak, before she could think of what to say, he lifted the glasses of juice and carried them to the table.

She stilled her quaking nerves by keeping busy, pouring the coffee, then cutting into slices half a loaf of bread that she had baked at the Village earlier that week and setting it on the table. In the refrigerator she located a stick of butter and a jar of strawberry preserves. Annie, one of her colleagues at the Village, had made it; she had promised Sara that this year during the berry season she would teach her how to preserve fruit.

Sara set the table with plates, knives and spoons before warily taking her seat across from Randy. He eyed the bread, then her. "Have you got a toaster?" he asked.

"No. I can brown the bread in the oven if you'd like."

"Not necessary." He took a slice, then skimmed her counters with his gaze. They were clear, devoid of the modern gadgetry found in most kitchens. "Don't you believe in appliances?" he asked.

"I can live without them," she replied, smearing jam unevenly across a slice of bread. "When you've got them, you become dependent on them, and then when they break you're up the creek."

"Not if you know how to repair them," Randy pointed out. His statement tweaked his memory, and he added, "I'll fix the car as soon as I'm fully awake."

"Cars, too," Sara remarked. "You become dependent on them, and then they break down and complicate your life. Back in the old days, before the invention of the Long Island Expressway..." Sara bit her lip to stifle herself. She realized she was sounding off, reverting to her nostalgia for a time that was long gone.

She peered at Randy, who was watching her, amused and curious. "Before the invention of the Long Island Expressway...?" he cued her.

"Suburbs weren't so prevalent. People lived in towns, near one another, near the things they needed. They could walk. They didn't have to depend on newfangled things like cars, which, as you well know, have a ridiculous tendency to break down."

"You're mad because I spent the night," Randy suggested.

"No, but..." She sighed. If he hadn't spent the night, he would never have kissed her that morning, never have held her, never have approached her soul with his potent touch. And she might have been much better off not having to deal with the overwhelming effect he had on her. "I suppose you're thrilled that your car broke down," she chided him. "As you said, it's the line of the century."

"It really refused to start," Randy defended himself. "Face it, Sara, you *did* invite me in last night. I didn't have to invent some stupid story about a short circuit in the electrical system just to get through your door. I could have simply accepted your invitation."

"In other words, you're honorable and trustworthy," she said dubiously, thinking that no matter how honorable and trustworthy he was, his kiss had still had a devastating effect on her. "Do you think you'll be able to fix the engine?" she asked to distract herself.

He shrugged, then nodded. "I'm very handy when it comes to gizmos and gadgets. And now I'll be able to see what I'm doing, rather than trying to find the problem using a flashlight at twelve-fifteen at night. If I'm right about what's malfunctioning, it shouldn't take too long to fix."

"You've got until eleven-thirty," Sara granted him. "Then I've got to leave for work."

"You work weekends?"

She nodded. "The Village is open all day Saturday and half a day Sunday. I get Monday and Tuesday off."

He glanced at his wristwatch and shrugged. "Eleven-thirty. No problem."

They ate in compatible silence, Sara one slice of bread and Randy three. He leaned back in his chair with his coffee, extending his legs beneath the table until his bare feet came to rest beside hers. She relished their nearness, his nearness. She was glad his car had broken down, just for the pleasure of seeing his face across the table from her over breakfast. She was glad he was with her. She had stopped his loving assault by the sink only because she wasn't ready—she wasn't ready to let him sweep her away. He could, she mused as she eyed him surreptitiously above the rim of her mug. Randy Zale could definitely sweep her away if she let him.

He watched her, his eyes darkening as if he could read her thoughts. Lowering his mug, he ventured, "Can I ask a personal question?"

She braced herself for it, then nodded.

"The guy you used to be with—what happened? What did he do to you?"

A personal question indeed. Yet she couldn't blame Randy for asking. He and she both knew that they were on the verge of something, and that her disaster with Stu was standing in her way. She stood up, playing for time to collect her thoughts, and refilled their mugs with coffee. Then she lowered herself back into her chair and inhaled. "He didn't do anything, really," she began. "He was a pretty normal, typical man."

"Uh-oh," Randy ominously intoned. "You've got something against normal, typical men?"

"Maybe." She shrugged.

"What's your definition of normal and typical?"

"He... lied to me. He was dishonest."

Randy seemed relieved. "Then I guess I don't qualify as normal-slash-typical," he said with a grin. "What did he lie about?"

"His marriage, for starters."

"He was married?" Randy appeared incredulous.

Sara nodded grimly. "When we first met he was. He told me he was already divorced, but I later found out that his divorce wasn't final until after I'd known him a year and a half. I—I was already living with him by then."

Randy's eyebrows arched slightly. "You don't seem like the sort to get mixed up in something like that."

"I was pretty naive," she admitted. "And Stu was awfully attractive. He was handsome, dynamic.... He was an artist."

"Oh, Lord—you had to support him, too?"

"No, he was professionally successful. He made his living as an illustrator. We met right after I was hired at the high school. I was assigned to a textbook committee. He illustrated textbooks, among other things." She paused to sip her coffee. "He was an exciting man, I suppose. Being with him was never boring. And I had been raised by my parents to believe that the First Commandment was 'Thou shalt not be bored.' Stu wasn't boring." She sighed morosely as her memories weighed on her. "And eventually he did get divorced. But...it was worse than his just not telling me he was married when we met. He never told me had a son."

"Ah." Randy straightened in his chair and listened attentively, his long fingers draped about his mug.

"I found out one day last spring," Sara continued, "when his wife—his ex-wife—showed up while he was out and dumped this poor little boy on me. She had some stringy young man in tow and said they were going away for a while and Stu had to take care of the child. The details of his divorce—that was bad enough. But then to neglect his child that way... In the years I knew Stu, he had never even mentioned that he had a child."

"So you left him?"

"Emotionally, yes. I moved into the spare room. But I couldn't leave the apartment, not with this sad little child there and no one to look after him. I took care of him, took him to Prospect Park, read to him. He was five years old, and I don't think anyone had ever read to him in his entire life." She sighed again, her heart swollen with sympathy for the pathetic waif she had briefly taken under her wing. "After a month, his mother returned, without the stringy man, and took the boy back. By then the school term was winding down, and I secured a position to start at Old Harkum Village in September, after the summer help left. And I moved out of Stu's place, out of his life."

Randy seemed to hang on her every word, the green of his eyes softening to the color of the sea. "You moved here?"

"No, I couldn't move into this house until August." More bitter memories infused her, causing an involuntary shudder to grip her spine. "I decided to fly to California to visit my mother and meet her new husband. After I was there a week, he made a pass at me."

"Oh, Lord!" Randy's eyes widened in disgust.

"I shouldn't have been surprised. He was younger than I, to say nothing of my mother." She drained her cup and set it on the table with a dismal thud. "What absolutely threw me was that when I told her about it she didn't care. 'Oh, we have an open marriage,' she assured me. 'That's the only way to be these days.' She's very modern, my mother. I'm not. I left."

"What did you do?"

"I went south to see my father. The weather was hot—I could spend most of my time on the beach, returning to his little menagerie just to sleep. I counted the days until I could return here and settle in."

"Forgive me for sounding judgmental," Randy

drawled, sweeping back a heavy lock of chestnut hair from his brow as he studied Sara. "But it all sounds pretty sordid to me."

"It is sordid," she agreed sourly. "They're happy with their lives, and I guess Stu is, too. I suppose it's none of my business. Nobody's getting hurt by these things."

"Except Stu's son. And your parents' daughter."

"And Petey," she concluded, her eyes meeting Randy's across the table.

"And Petey," he agreed softly. He released his mug and tapped his fingertips together as he summed up what Sara had told him. "I can see why you're skittish around men."

"I'm fine," she asserted firmly. "I just think I can do a whole lot better without them."

Randy studied her thoughtfully before getting up and carrying his mug and plate to the sink. "Well, dear lady," he murmured as he crossed the room to the doorway, "I hope I can prove you wrong." He left her, vanishing into the living room. She stared at the plates in her sink, at the space by the door where she had last seen Randy, wondering about him, wondering whether he would—or could—prove such a thing. The possibility frightened her a bit. She liked the serene life she had been living lately. She wasn't looking for a change.

Shrugging, she finished clearing the dishes and washed them. Once the kitchen was clean, she moved to the living room, where she found Randy stepping into his shoes. He smiled at her, then reached for his jacket. "I'm going to go have a look at the car," he said.

"If you need anything, come get me," she offered. "I'll be in my bedroom, getting ready for work."

"Hmm. Talk about temptation," he muttered under his breath as he sauntered to the door and out.

Unable to suppress a smile, Sara walked to her bedroom, selected a pale pink frock to wear at the Village, and donned blue jeans and a ribbed white sweater to drive to work in. Then she braided her hair, wrapped the braids smoothly around her head and pinned them. When she was satisfied with their evenness, she roamed to the living room, trying not to think about what she had told Randy over breakfast, about what he had told her, about the challenge implicit in his words and actions. She wandered aimlessly to the window to check her bedraggled herb garden.

But she was distracted from her plants by Randy's figure, visible through the window, bowed over the engine of his sports car. He looked so graceful, even laboring on his car. His broad shoulders were bent beneath the raised hood, his sleeves rolled up, to reveal his strong golden forearms. The sun glanced off his hair, lifting its fiery highlights to the surface. So handsome, she thought. So incredibly attractive. And the way he had kissed her, the way his hand had felt on her skin...

She wanted to believe she could do without men. She wanted to believe that the peaceful world of Old Harkum Village and the basic chores of survival were all she needed to fulfill her. No matter how enticing Randy Zale was, she didn't want the sort of excitement he could bring to her life. She didn't need it. She was better off without it.

But maybe, she thought, trying not to acknowledge the hope that rimmed her soul, just maybe Randy would manage to prove her wrong.

Chapter Four

Randy didn't drive directly to his house in Cold Spring Harbor. Instead, he headed into the center of the small village nestled around a cove on Long Island's North Shore. He cruised past the huge Victorian sea captains' houses lining the route into town, then parked by the small park that abutted the water. He climbed out of his car and strode across the grass, which was spongy and damp from the previous day's downpour, toward the placid gray water of Long Island Sound.

Cold Spring Harbor was charming the way Old Harkum Village was. Its ancient buildings bespoke a grand history. Randy settled on a sun-dried bench, stared out at the water, and began to reflect. He'd chosen to build his house in Cold Spring Harbor because the area was pretty, heavily wooded and not yet overdeveloped. But he'd never really thought about the historical beauty of the village before.

Sara was having an unexpected effect on him, he realized. He wasn't sure he liked it. She was too complicated. Life was far simpler when he'd pick up a woman at a bar, swap one-liners for an hour, and retire with her to bed. He figured he'd get serious and settle down someday, but right now all he wanted was some free-spirited fun.

So why bother with Sara Morrow? Why waste his time trying to figure her out?

Maybe he was no longer interested in simplicity. Or maybe, as she'd accused him last night, he was chasing her only because she was a challenge.

No, it had to be more than that. Randy had plenty of challenges in his life. His work was a constant challenge. Satisfying his customers, providing solutions to their various industrial problems, keeping one step ahead of his competitors and two steps ahead of innovations in technology—these were the challenges that constituted his every working day.

Yet the challenge Sara offered was quite different. It had to do with breaking out of his complacency, viewing the world through different eyes. It had to do with seeing the proud houses around him and remembering that the world began long before he had ever discovered the power of a silicon chip.

Her past was so unlike his. He'd grown up in a stable middle-class family, always knowing he was loved and wanted. He'd never really considered it before, but what Sara had told him about her childhood filled him with appreciation for his own. She was giving him a new perspective on things.

Sure, he was physically attracted to her. Spending the night on her couch had been a mild torture for him. He'd lain awake, picturing her in her bed, alone, untouched. The fact that she'd lived with a dishonest man couldn't shake Randy's bizarre perception of her as a virgin. She was purer than any woman he'd ever met before.

He wanted her, but he wanted more than that. He sensed a wisdom in Sara that he envied. The challenges she'd faced in her life made his own challenges seem paltry by comparison. He wasn't satisfied by the means she'd developed to cope with her challenges, but he respected her for having survived them. If only he could show her that there was room in her world for someone like him, that she needn't write off all men simply because she'd gotten caught up with one bad one.... He wanted to do this for Sara. It was vitally important to Randy.

He'd call her. They'd get together next weekend, go out for dinner, do something more romantic than attend a hockey game. He'd prove to her that a "normal, typical" man like himself wouldn't hurt her, but would only enhance her life. If they made love, fine; if not, fine. All he wanted was to open her up, to get her to relax and enjoy herself and not let the demons of her past prevent her from experiencing the joys of the present. That was all he wanted for her.

Then he remembered that he might be stuck with Petey for the weekend. Renee and Larry had mentioned the possibility of attending a marriage encounter weekend, and Randy had generously offered to baby-sit Petey for them if they went away. Anything—he'd do anything to get them back on track. He didn't want them to split up. They were his closest friends, and it tormented him to see them risking a marriage that seemed completely salvageable to him.

Okay. He'd wait until he knew what their plans were for the weekend, and then he'd call Sara. He'd play the weekend out one way or another. Just as long as it included time with Sara. Maybe they could do something together with Petey, take him to a movie or a roller rink. For some reason, Randy was willing to bet that spending time with Petey would appeal to her. They were kinsmen in the world of broken homes, casualties of the modern family. Randy adored his young friend Petey; perhaps it was no wonder that he'd found himself taken by someone like Sara. The thought that he might be spending the following weekend with two such special people pleased him immensely, and as he stood and then loped back to his car, his face was illuminated by a buoyant smile.

"GREAT NEWS, SARA. We're getting married."

Sara turned to find Ira Lipton, shoemaker for Old Harkum Village, framed by the open upper half of the Willoughby House's Dutch door. She exhaled and turned back to the group of Italian tourists congregated before her table. She was too weary to react to Ira's preposterous remark.

The past several days had drained her. Sunday afternoon the Village had been jammed with visitors, not only those who had intended all along to visit the Village on Sunday but also those who had planned to visit on Saturday but had been discouraged by the rain. And when she had gotten home after her hectic afternoon, she found Jean on her doorstep, demanding to know about the sleek black Alfa-Romeo that had remained parked outside Sara's house overnight. Jean swore she believed Sara's explanation that the car had broken down and that Randy had spent the night on the sofa, but Sara didn't think her neighbor *really* believed the contrived-sounding story. As if Sara cared. She was an adult. She was entitled to have a man spend the night in her house without explaining or justifying her behavior.

Perhaps the reason she had responded so peevishly to Jean's needling curiosity was that she knew how close she and Randy had come to...to what? Making love? What would have happened if he hadn't chickened out, if he had followed through on his third assault on her door and barged into her bedroom? Would she have thrown him out? She didn't think she would have. And the thought shook her.

How could he be destroying her resolve so easily? How could she be letting him threaten the equilibrium she had so carefully cultivated since leaving Stu? She absolutely did not want a man in her life. She did not want excitement. She just wanted peace, tranquillity, stability.

And Randy... Randy wanted to prove her wrong.

If he were so eager to prove her wrong, though, why hadn't she heard from him? His failure to call her on Monday or Tuesday, her two days off, both relieved and roiled her. Maybe, after calm deliberation, he had decided that she wasn't worth disproving. She tried to convince herself that she was glad he had reconsidered his interest in her. But as the days elapsed without a word from him, she began to grow edgy and moony like a silly adolescent.

She *did* want him to call. As troubled as she was by him, she couldn't shake certain images from her mind. Not the ones of his mesmerizing eyes; of the clean lines of his face as he had hovered over her at her sink, kissing her, touching her; of the confident smile he'd tossed her way when he had announced that he hoped to prove her wrong about men; but... an image of him and Petey outside the Willoughby House on a rainy afternoon, playing in the muddy red puddles of the dirt road by the farm. He was a man who cared about a lonesome child. That was why she wanted him to call her.

But he hadn't. In fact, the only telephone call she got was a totally unwelcome one from Hattie, one of the secretaries at the high school where Sara used to teach. Sara liked Hattie and was pleased to hear from her, but not pleased by Hattie's message: Would Sara reconsider the failing grade she had given one of her students the previous year? Vincent Chesler was an intelligent boy; he had scored high on the standardized tests. Granted, he hadn't attended Sara's class religiously, and when he had he was surly, nasty and uncooperative. Granted, he hadn't turned in all the assignments. But if Sara submitted a revised grade, he could graduate this year. Wouldn't she think about it?

Of course Sara wouldn't. She remembered Vincent Chesler, nicknamed Turk, or, when he was really strutting, *The* Turk. She had given him a failing grade, she informed Hattie, because he had earned a failing grade. She wasn't going to lower her standards to accommodate him.

Hattie expressed her respect for Sara's principles, commented that Turk Chesler would be furious, and promised to keep Sara informed. *So Turk would be furious,* Sara raged inwardly after bidding Hattie good-bye. Well, she was furious, too, furious to be pressured into changing his grade so it would reflect not his performance but the school's eagerness to get rid of troublemakers.

The past few days had been difficult enough for Sara. And now this: Ira leaping over the lower half of the Willoughby House Dutch door to propose marriage to her.

She didn't have the energy to fend off his out-of-the-blue flirtation. She had spent the past fifteen minutes trying to share the history of the Willoughby House with the Italian tour group, all of whom insisted that they understood English, although their questions indicated that they didn't comprehend much of what Sara was saying. When she explained that the ceiling was low to conserve heat, they all nodded and smiled and said, "Heat. Like summer." When she told them that

Josiah Willoughby had been a farmer, they all nodded and smiled and said, "Farmer. He makes farms." Then each of them had demanded to pose for a photograph alone with Sara. They had traded their cameras and taken turns, Sara's smile becoming progressively more cramped with each photo. By the time Ira sprang into the kitchen, her vision was impaired by two dozen purple dots, the result of staring into two dozen burning camera flashes.

"Married?" she asked him, not bothering to conceal her astonishment.

"You heard right. Next month, sweetheart. You and me down the aisle to the altar."

She glowered impatiently at Ira. He was tall, gangly and rather underweight, his knee breeches and vest slightly baggy on his reedy frame. Her acquaintance with him extended only to the few staff functions at which they'd chatted casually. Annie had suggested that Sara befriend Ira because his skill at shoemaking was quite impressive, and he frequently made authentic pairs of period farm shoes for his friends. But Sara hadn't had much opportunity to get to know him. She certainly had no intention of marrying him! "I don't know what you're talking about," she said softly.

His wicked smile melted into a congenial one. "Here in the Village, every spring we stage a nineteenth-century wedding. This year you and I were chosen to portray the bride and groom. Gil will explain it to you, I guess," he added, referring to their boss, the head curator of the Village. He noticed the half-sliced loaf of bread on her table and helped himself to a piece. "I think it's considered an honor, by the way, so be pleased."

"Why me?" Sara asked, surprised.

Ira shrugged. "Well, there aren't that many young

women to choose from. Kitty Stanhouse has been a bride twice already. So. Will you marry me, Miss Sara?" He dramatically dropped to his knees before her.

The European tourists tittered and elbowed one another excitedly. "Marry?" one asked. "You and him marry?"

Playing to his audience, Ira rose to his feet, grabbed Sara's hand, kissed her knuckles, and then wrapped his arm about her narrow waist. "That's right, ladies and gentlemen," he announced proudly. "This pretty little lady and I are going to tie the knot."

"Tie the knot," the foreign visitors repeated, debating quietly among themselves as to precisely which knot Ira was referring to. One of the men who seemed a bit more proficient in English explained, "Marry. They shall marry." His colleagues were thrilled, and they insisted on taking numerous additional photographs of Sara and Ira—the happy young couple—standing by the fireplace, on the porch, next to the bed.

At last the tour group left, and Sara dropped wearily onto the mattress. "Please, Ira—could you explain this whole thing a little bit more clearly? I still don't understand."

Ira watched through the open half of the door as the group of tourists wended their way around the Village's farm. Then he turned back to Sara. "I told you, we're getting married. It's a lot of fun. Someone will be picked to play your parents, someone else to be the minister—usually that's Gil himself—and you'll have a bridesmaid and I'll have a best man. We go through the ceremony at the church, and then there's a bridal supper in the garden behind the Boodner House—weather permitting—and then we ride off in the carriage, hopefully with Ginger pulling us, because Tomtom is a bit too frisky these days," he noted, naming two of the Village's horses. "The wedding gets announced in the press beforehand. We always get a huge crowd. You'll see, it's fun."

"Uh-huh." Sara nodded vaguely.

Ira studied her. "I guess they'll have to sew a new dress for you. Kitty and Roseanne Galiano were close enough to the same size so that they could both use the same dress, but you're so much smaller than they are, Edith'll probably have to sew you one from scratch. I don't know." He shrugged. "See what Gil says. The wedding's a month off. That's enough time to get a dress made up."

Sara nodded again. In the eight months she had worked at the Village, there had been other special events: a nineteenth-century-style clambake, a magic lantern show, a portrayal of a Revolutionary War training camp that had existed not far from the site of Old Harkum Village. Evidently a nineteenth-century wedding was another regular enactment. If Sara ever returned to the even-tempered, well-balanced person she had been before Randy invaded her life, she thought she would enjoy playing the part of the Village's bride very much.

"I tell you what," Ira continued, clearly thrilled to have been chosen as the groom. "As a wedding present, I'll make you a pair of shoes. Would you like that?"

"You'd really do that?" Her eyes sparkled gratefuly.

He grinned. "Stop by the shoemaker's shop when you've got a chance this week or next, and I'll measure you. You must have tiny feet. It won't take me long."

"How lovely!" She eyed the flat cloth shoes she had bought for the job—they were just barely acceptable as nineteenth-century shoes, and then only because the sweeping hems of her dresses hid them. Having a genuine pair of handcrafted leather period shoes would complete her sense of belonging in the ancient settlement. "And I'll bake you a wonderful wedding cake," she vowed in return.

"Nope." Ira shook his head. "The bride doesn't bake her own wedding cake. But if you've got an extra loaf of bread lying around, I wouldn't turn it down."

She hastened to the oven to check the loaf within. It was done, and she proudly slid it from the chamber and, wrapping it in a cloth so Ira wouldn't burn his hands, presented it to him.

"Bless you, Sara," he crooned. "This is going to be a fattening engagement, I can tell."

"You could use a little fattening," she said, clucking playfully.

"Spoken like a true wife." Tucking the bread beneath his arm, he leaped over the bottom portion of the door and shambled back to his shoemaking shop.

Late that afternoon, Sara was still thinking about portraying a young farm bride at the Village when she removed her gingham frock in the dressing room in the main building and slipped on her jeans and sweater. She drove home wondering what besides a loaf of bread she might give Ira. After all, he was going to make shoes for her. Perhaps she would bake him a fruit pie. She supposed she could cheat a little and buy apples at the local supermarket—the Village orchard hadn't even begun blossoming yet, so apples wouldn't be dropping from the trees for a good five or six months. The real challenge, of course, wouldn't be obtaining the apples but timing a pie in a fireplace oven. Sara thought it would be a worthwhile skill to master, and a delightful gift for her groom.

She was mentally reviewing what ingredients she

would need for her pie when the telephone rang. "Hello?" she answered it.

"Hello, Sara, it's Randy."

Randy. The cheerful smile that had shaped her lips while planning her wedding was replaced by a warm, slightly giddy smile at the thought that the man she wasn't sure she wanted in her life had decided to brave reentry into it. "Hello, Randy," she greeted him.

"Sara, I'm sorry I didn't call you sooner—"

She cut him off. "Don't be silly." Had the previous three days felt like years to him, too, she wondered. That was all it had been—three days.

"Well, I'd like to see you this weekend, but by now maybe you've got plans."

Plans? Sara didn't date. Surely Randy remembered that. "This weekend," she repeated noncommittally.

He seemed to be laboring over his words. "I wanted to take you out to dinner Saturday, someplace a bit more romantic than the Nassau Coliseum.... I don't know, maybe I can hire a baby-sitter," he mumbled to himself.

"A baby-sitter?"

"I've got custody of Petey this weekend."

"Oh?" Sara rested against the counter and felt her smile expanding. This was why she liked Randy, she reminded herself. His concern for his young friend Petey.

"Larry and Renee have decided to attend a marriage encounter weekend at a hotel in the Catskills, and I offered to take care of Petey while they were gone."

"A marriage encounter weekend?" Sara groaned, her smile gone. "Are those things still being held?"

"What do you know about them?" Randy eagerly grilled her.

"My parents went to one once. My father wound up seducing the wife of one of the other couples there. Both my parents decided it was an interesting experience." Sara continued dispiritedly, "I don't know why your friends want to waste their time and money on that nonsense."

Randy didn't respond immediately. "I don't know, either, Sara," he finally admitted. "But whatever they're willing to try is all right with me. At least they're making an effort to get back together again. Meanwhile," he added, his tone transforming to a humorous lilt, "I'm playing bachelor father this weekend. Do you know anything about baby-sitters?"

"You can't leave Petey with a baby-sitter," Sara complained on the boy's behalf. "His parents are ignoring him; you can't ignore him, too."

"In that case," Randy declared, sounding oddly victorious, "will you have dinner at my place Saturday night?"

Sara got the distinct impression that Randy had planned to invite her for dinner all along, that he had known she would refuse to let him abandon Petey even for a few hours. "Your place, huh?" she murmured, both pleased and apprehensive.

"With a snoopy eight-year-old chaperon. What could be safer?" Randy asked teasingly. Then his voice grew solemn as he added, "I'd love for Petey to get to know you. You're right, Sara—he is lonely. Maybe you and he would hit it off. What do you think?"

What Sara thought was that Randy was uncannily accurate in locating her emotional reflexes and stimulating them. But she didn't give herself a chance to resent his accuracy. "Of course I'd like to get to know Petey," she agreed.

"Then you'll come for dinner," Randy decided for her. "Not romantic, but edible. I live in Cold Spring Harbor. Do you know where that is?"

"Sort of," she replied.

Randy patiently gave her directions to his house, and Sara dutifully jotted them down. They contained numerous unmarked turns and "difficult-to-find" forks and "if-you-go-too-far-you'll-see" landmarks. "It's a long driveway through the woods," he concluded. "So don't give up when you don't see the house right away. You work Saturday, don't you? What time can you get here?"

Sara did a quick mental calculation. If she left the Village at five, got home by five-thirty, changed her clothing, showered, and drove to Cold Spring Harbor... "Six-thirty, maybe?"

"Fine. If you can make it earlier, do. By Saturday evening we lonely boys will be sorely in need of womanly companionship."

"Thanks for the reminder," Sara parried. "I'll be wearing my double-knotted camisole."

Randy laughed. "I'll see you Saturday, Sara," he said before hanging up.

Good Lord, it *was* like adolescent dating, Sara thought as she anticipated her evening with Randy. No matter where she was or what she was doing, whenever she thought of him her pulse jumped, her cheeks darkened in a girlish blush, and a crazy smile teased her lips.

She had never dated as an adolescent, having gladly buried herself in the all-girl boarding school where her parents had sent her and the all-woman college where she continued her education. Although boys occasionally expressed an interest in the pretty young girl with the striking black hair and white skin, the Dresden-doll daintiness, the haunting, haunted gray eyes, Sara had kept her distance. All she knew about male-female relationships was what she had seen in her parents' marriage and divorce. Love was fleeting; sex was its own justification; commitment was meaningless. Sara had reacted by completely shrinking from relationships with men. As a teenager, she hadn't thought she was strong enough to handle such relationships. After her one big mistake with Stu, she decided that she wasn't weak enough to need such relationships.

So Randy's attentions, his courtship, his politely asking her for dates, had a certain old-fashioned charm about them, and Sara couldn't help responding to the novelty of being courted. Maybe it *was* girlish and goofy, but she didn't care.

She knew, too, that her fledging relationship with Randy wasn't, in truth, adolescent. She knew that the passion that burned between them when they kissed, when they touched, was the passion of a man and a woman, all the more dangerous because it was real and powerful and because she and Randy knew how to act upon it.

When I'm ready, Sara reminded herself as she drove to Randy's house Saturday evening. He would tease her, he would tempt her, but she knew that the minute she said no, he would back off. He had proven his trustworthiness last Sunday morning in her kitchen.

Whether or not she would be ready tonight was a moot question, she acknowledged as her eyes flitted back and forth between the road and the sheet of paper on which she had written the verbose directions he had given her over the telelphone. Tonight she and Randy would be taking care of Petey. An eight-year-old chaperon, she thought with satisfaction. She had chosen her clothing accordingly: a pair of gray corduroy jeans, a man-tailored pink blouse, loafers and her pea jacket, in case the night grew chilly. Nothing at all suggestive about her attire, she knew. A double-knotted camisole would be more appropriate to her outfit than the lacy lingerie she was actually wearing.

The roads were picturesque, winding up and down hills, through dense forests. As Randy had predicted, Sara missed one turn and came to an unwanted landmark. She made a U-turn, found the street she had overlooked and steered onto it. More snaking roads, more easy-to-miss veers and forks, and at last, the driveway to his house. It was longer than she had expected, and she was glad he had warned her not to be discouraged when his house didn't instantly loom into view. In fact, the forest-lined driveway was so long that she found herself pitying him for having to shovel snow from it in the winter. She decided long driveways were impractical, because one had to drive forever just to reach a street. In Old Harkum Village, the houses snuggled up to the road. People wouldn't have needed cars even if they had been available in 1791.

Eventually she saw the house, although in the encroaching darkness it blended in well with its sylvan surroundings. It was a sprawling modern structure composed of wood, fieldstone and glass, nestled in a rock-strewn clearing in the woods. No place for a garden, Sara mused as she parked beside Randy's sports car and strolled up the slate walk, which was lit by knee-high lanterns, to the front door. She rang the chime and waited.

The door swung open, and Randy swept her into the foyer. "Hello," he whispered before brushing his lips over hers.

His light kiss was interrupted by Petey's piping voice: "Is she here, Randy?" Then his approaching footsteps, and Randy and Sara sprang apart as the wiry, dark-haired boy appeared in the foyer. "Hi," he said in his high, clear voice. "You're Sara. Randy says I know you from that old place he took me to."

"Old Harkum Village," Sara reminded Petey as Randy slid her jacket from her shoulders. "I was the lady who baked the bread, remember?"

He scowled and tilted his head slightly. Evidently he didn't recognize Sara in twentieth-century clothing and with her long hair loose. "I remember the bread," he told her.

"Good enough," she reassured him, allowing him to grasp her hand and drag her into the spacious living room.

The room was angular, walled in glass, stone and wood, and much larger than any living room needed to be. Its vaulted ceiling sloped over a second-story loft, and its furniture comprised brown and beige leather blobs of indeterminate shape and geometrically irregular marble tables. An abstract wood bas-relief hung on one wall, and a canvas splattered with angry streaks of paint hung on another. A free-standing elliptical fireplace, with hearths on both sides, stood between the living room and the adjacent dining room.

Sara hated the room.

She quickly hid her distaste when she felt Randy's hand on her shoulder. "We've got a mess in progress in the kitchen," he told her. "You want to come and contribute to it?"

Turning to him, Sara felt the mysterious radiance of his green eyes reach something inside her, softening it, making her forget about the repellent decor of his living room. Her smile matched his as she followed him through the dining room, with its glass-topped table and chrome-and-leather chairs, to a large kitchen.

Sara halted in the doorway, transfixed and horrified

by his kitchen. Every modern convenience—and then some—cluttered the counters, hung from the ceiling, nestled beneath the polished cherry-wood cabinets: a microwave oven, a countertop grill, a food processor, a blender, an electric drip coffee-maker, an electric coffee grinder, an electric Crockpot, an electric skillet, currently filled with ground chopped meat, an electric timer buzzing by the microwave oven....

She recoiled slightly, trying to absorb the abundance of gadgetry. Part of one wall was covered by a dizzying display of knobs and dials that resembled the cockpit of a spaceship. "What—what's that?" she dared to ask.

Randy turned from the meat, which he had been stirring, and followed her extended finger to the panel of controls. "Sound system," he explained. "The stereo's upstairs in the loft, but I can turn it on from here if I want, adjust it, decide in what rooms I want to hear what. Do you want to listen to anything?"

She shook her head, dazed. She took solace in Randy's familiar appearance, clad in evenly faded blue jeans and a pale blue shirt with white pinstripes. His sleeves were rolled up to his elbows and she focused on his graceful, sinewy forearms. How natural Randy seemed, surrounded by so much mechanical garbage.

"Randy!" Petey was tugging at his arm. "Didn't you hear? The chips are ready."

"I heard the timer," Randy assured the boy as he crossed to the microwave oven. He removed a tray of golden taco shells. "Do you like tacos?" he asked Sara. "Petey was insistent."

"Tacos are fine," she said weakly, her eyes drifting around the kitchen, noting the electric can opener, the electric knife, the electric knife sharpener, the electric dough kneader, the huge refrigerator across which Randy waved his hand, magically opening the door without touching it. Sara jumped. "How'd you do that?"

"Hmm?" He turned to her, a platter of shredded lettuce and minced tomatoes in his hand. Then he grinned. "Electric eye. I rigged it up myself. Come on." He beckoned her. "Give it a try."

She nervously approached the refrigerator. Randy pointed out the electric eye, nearly hidden by the door handle, and she cautiously waved her hand across it. The door swung open.

"Cute, huh?" Randy laughed.

Sara didn't reply. She was too spooked by the weird door latch. Cute, perhaps, but spooky. Weird. It made her think of invisible rays, air currents, futuristic things over which she had no control.

"Randy, show her the spinning bar!" Petey urged him.

She didn't want to see the spinning bar, but Petey was already dragging her to an assortment of liquor bottles on a semicircular tray attached to a wall. Before Randy could stop him, Petey hit a switch and the bottles rotated out of view. She glanced anxiously at Randy. "They're in the den now," he told her. "Would you like a drink?"

"No, thank you," Sara managed, although Petey thoughtfully rotated the bottles back into the kitchen in case she changed her mind.

It was all nonsense, she meditated as she carried platters of spiced meat, vegetables and grated cheddar cheese into the dining room. Nonsense, junk, gizmos and gadgets, as Randy might call them. Inane gadgets designed to complicate one's existence. Randy's house was antithetical to everything Sara considered important in a home, in a life; simplicity, serenity, independence. His kitchen literally hummed with electricity. If ever there were a power outage that lasted more than a couple of hours, Randy's universe would come to a complete halt. The electric eye in his refrigerator wouldn't work. He wouldn't be able to brew coffee. He wouldn't be able to bake. He wouldn't be able to open a can of soup to eat cold. He wouldn't be able to function.

Subdued, she took a seat next to Randy, facing Petey. Randy carried out a brimming pitcher of sangria for the adults and a cola for Petey. The sangría was garnished with translucent circles of lemon, lime and orange. Sliced in the food processor, she wondered. Or maybe by the electric knife?

"Are you okay?" Randy asked her as he stuffed a tortilla shell with meat for her.

She snapped to attention. "Just tired, I guess," she mumbled. "Don't forget, I worked all day."

"My parents are gone for the weekend," Petey declared brightly. "They went to the mountains."

"And Randy's taking care of you for the weekend?" she asked, happy to turn her focus on Petey.

"Uh-uh," the boy crowed. "I'm takin' care of him. Isn't that right, Randy? You said I had to take care of you and Sara tonight so you wouldn't get in trouble."

Sara guffawed and turned to Randy, her eyes blazing with mock indignation. "You told him that?"

"It's the truth, isn't it?" Randy defended himself with a nonchalant shrug.

"In that case," Sara turned back to Petey, "you'd better do a good job. We don't want Randy getting into trouble, do we?"

"Or you either," Petey pointed out. Sara laughed again.

The conversation relaxed her. Petey's sad eyes notwithstanding, he was a bubbly youngster, apparently aware that his parents' outing that weekend might help to resolve his life in some way. He asked Sara point-blank whether her parents were divorced, and when she told him they were, he asked countless questions about what her childhood had been like. She tried to answer him frankly, though she refrained from going into detail about her parents' bizarre life-styles. She didn't want to shock or frighten Petey.

He warmed to her, and she to him. Randy occasionally intervened in the conversation, but mostly he sat back in his chair at the head of the table and watched Sara and Petey interact. Sara was always conscious of Randy's presence, his strong fingers grasping a collapsing taco, his cheeks creasing with dimples as he smiled, his watchful eyes guarding over the meal, replenishing dishes and glasses as they emptied. He had told Sara last week that she was keyed in to Petey. Yet during this dinner, he seemed keyed in to both Petey and Sara. He let them share their feelings with each other—Petey's justifiable fear and Sara's empathy and compassion—without intruding. Sara respected him for it.

At last the food was gone. "Tell her about dessert!" Petey whooped as Sara gathered several plates to help Randy clear the table.

"Ice cream," Randy revealed to Sara with an indifferent shrug. "Petey thinks ice cream is the Second Coming."

"I'm actually pretty full," Sara admitted, not interested in dessert. She handed two plates to Randy, who scraped them into the sink. He must have a food disposal, too, she reflected. Her guess was confirmed when he turned a switch and the scrapings—just what Sara would have saved for her compost heap—were swallowed by the drain with a repulsive gurgling sound.

Before he continued cleaning up from their dinner, Randy prepared a pot of coffee for Sara and himself and then scooped a small portion of ice cream into a bowl for Petey, who gleefully sat on a stool eating it while Randy worked. With the food disposal and the trash compactor, and the sink dispenser that provided instant boiling water, and the dishwasher to accept the rinsed plates, the task of cleaning up was less than arduous in a kitchen like his.

Sara tried to still her antipathy to Randy's gadgets. She had no right to judge him, she scolded herself. He was an electronics whiz, a computer nut. It made sense that he would take pleasure in accumulating gadgets.

Her gaze alit on the dough hook attachments for his electric mixer. "Do you bake bread?" she asked.

Randy glanced over his shoulder to see what had inspired her question, then turned back to the dishwasher to load the last of the dishes. "I've tried," he conceded. "It didn't come out too well."

"You should have kneaded the dough by hand," she crisply informed him, fingering one of the dough hooks disapprovingly and then setting it down. "You have to feel the dough to know when it's ready."

"Maybe that's what I did wrong," Randy admitted with an unconcerned shrug. "Your bread tasted infinitely better than mine, so I'll defer to you on that."

By the time he had finished wiping the counters, the coffee was ready—in the same amount of time it would have taken her old-fashioned stove-top percolator to brew, Sara estimated. Randy set Petey's bowl in the sink and poured two cups. "Can I show Sara your Zinger?" Petey asked.

Sara's eyebrows shot up. Randy laughed. "I don't know," he said slyly before facing Sara. "Do you want to see my Zinger?"

"I'm afraid to ask what your Zinger is," she muttered, her eyes glinting as mischievously as his.

Petey grabbed her hand and tugged her out of the kitchen. "It's neat. Come on. I'll play with you—you'll love it!"

He towed her to the den, which was furnished a bit more traditionally, with raw stone walls and built-in bookshelves, a leather couch shaped like a couch and several chairs shaped like chairs. Standing before one wall was a six-foot television screen, a video recorder beside it on one side and a computer terminal of sorts on the other. Petey released Sara's hand and nudged her onto the couch. Then he carried over the computer box and two control levers wired to it.

Randy leaned over her from behind the couch to set her coffee on the table in front of the couch. "Just say the word and I'll kick him out," he whispered.

"No—no, I'll play with him," Sara said, sympathetic to the small boy.

He placed one of the control levers in her hand, then started the computer. The screen filled with a multicolored splash, and then the word "Zinger." "Is this one of those games?" she asked tensely. She had never played a video game before.

"Randy programmed this one himself," Petey bragged. "You've got to zing me before I can zing you. I'm the green one," he said, pointing to two nondescript creatures, one green and one yellow, wandering around the screen through a maze of red lines.

"What do I do?" Sara floundered, gaping at the screen.

"Use the joystick," Petey explained.

"The what?"

Randy settled on the arm of the couch beside Sara. "The joystick," he said, indicating the control lever in her hand.

She glared at him. "It's really called a joystick?" she

mumbled, flabbergasted by the implications of the term.

Randy's eyes sparkled with lewd laughter. "I swear, Sara. Go ahead." He angled his head to her control lever. "Play with that little joystick in your lap. Wrap your hand around it. Move it around. See what happens."

Sara couldn't prevent a blush from flooding her cheeks as she manipulated the stick. The yellow creature began to move around the screen, running into walls, spinning in circles. Eventually she began to discover the relationship between the lever and the creature, and she maneuvered the creature about the screen with greater finesse.

She fingered a red button on the tip of the stick and cast Randy a naughty smile. "What happens if I press this?"

"Fireworks," he warned her, managing to keep a straight face.

Challenged, she pressed the button. The screen filled with an explosion of mind-boggling color, then reverted to the yellow and green creatures wandering through the maze. "You weren't kidding," she muttered, unable to stifle a giggle.

"That's the way it is with joysticks, lady," he deadpanned.

Although she continued to feel awkward playing the game, she found enjoyment in the delight Petey took in "zinging" her. Clearly she lacked the killer urge needed to excel at the game, but the silly little creatures wandering around their maze tickled a smile from her. When she did finally manage to "zing" Petey, she felt a surprising rush of satisfaction.

"I think I'll quit while I'm ahead," she announced, handing the joystick to Randy and rising from the couch so he could play the game with Petey. She squeezed onto the couch beside Randy and sipped her coffee, laughing at the antics of the two of them as they aggressively combatted each other on the screen. She wasn't sure she liked the game; a quiet, somber chess match would have been more to her taste. But she liked the feel of Randy sitting beside her on the couch. She liked his sexy sense of humor, and the variegated hues of his hair illuminated by the colorful lights emanating from the screen, and the clean, spicy scent of him. She liked watching his graceful fingers manipulating the joystick, though she thought it best not to say so. She knew if she said anything it would come out sounding very wrong. So she remained silent, watching him, his eyes intense on the screen, his rousing laughter filling the room whenever Petey "zinged" him.

Eventually he set down his joystick and pointed Petey toward a digital clock on one of the shelves. "What time is it, tiger?"

"Eight fifty-one," Petey reported.

"Which means you've got exactly nine minutes to put on your pj's and wash up and get into bed," Randy reminded him.

Petey appeared reluctant, but he obediently left the room. Randy stored the computer and the joysticks on a shelf and clicked off the screen. "Would you like some more coffee? Or something stronger?" he offered.

Sara shook her head. She was thinking about how she detested digital clocks. She much preferred the sweep of hands around the circular face of an analog clock, simulating the sweep of the earth on its axis. Perhaps children knew how to tell time much more easily in this day of digital clocks, but she was certain something had been lost in the translation.

She accompanied Randy to the kitchen, where he added their coffee mugs and Petey's ice-cream bowl to the dishwasher. Then he took her hand and guided her down a hall to the bedroom where Petey was to sleep.

The boy was wearing pajamas resembling a striped baseball uniform, and his face was freshly scrubbed. "Will you tell me a story, Randy?" he asked.

"Sure thing, tiger," Randy said, settling himself on the edge of the mattress after Petey had arranged himself beneath the covers. Sara remained in the doorway. She didn't know if she was intruding on a private moment between Randy and his young friend, but she wanted to hear Randy's story, too.

He waited until Petey stopped shifting before beginning: "Once upon a time there was a robot named Petey," he said. "This robot looked just like a boy. He acted a whole lot like a boy. He even had a scar on his knee that looked an awful lot like the sort of scar you get when you fall off your roller skates, which happens to a lot of boys." Petey laughed, and Sara could imagine the scar on his knee. "But this Petey was a robot, which meant he could do all sorts of things that kids couldn't do."

"Like what?" Petey asked.

"Well, for instance, he could fly, because he had a little jet engine implanted behind his ear. And he could see through walls, because he had an X-ray lens built into one eye. And he could find lost dogs and cats, because he had a heat-sensing device in one finger."

Petey looked toward Sara. "You finish the story," he begged her.

Her gaze shifted to Randy, who nodded his encouragement, and then back to Petey. Randy could weave his little fantasy about robots, she thought, but she could just as easily unravel it. "One day, Petey the robot broke," she picked up the thread. "He didn't work. And he realized that all he really wanted in life was to be a real boy. Being able to see through walls and fly wasn't as important as being able to climb trees and play ball and go roller skating. So he went to sleep, and while he was asleep a wonderful thing happened—he was turned into a real live little boy. And when he woke up he was so happy that he never had anything to do with robots ever again."

Randy eyed her curiously, trying to fathom the undercurrent in her words. Petey, however, seemed satisfied. "Thanks," he said. "That was okay for a story."

His small soprano voice attracted Randy's attention. He stood, tousled Petey's hair, and turned off the lamp beside his bed. "Sleep tight, tiger," he whispered before joining Sara at the door.

He led her back down the hall to the living room, adjusting a globe lamp to a low light before folding his arms around her. "Alone at last," he purred, gently grazing her brow with his lips. "Not exactly the romantic dinner of my dreams, but..." His mouth dropped to her eyes, whispering across each tissue-thin lid, and then to her cheek.

Sara reveled in the understated strength of his embrace, in the teasing caress of his lips across her skin. Her soul wanted to blossom open for Randy. But her mind held back. She liked Randy, she wanted Randy... but things weren't right.

He immediately sensed her reticence and pulled back. "What's the matter?"

"I hate your house," she announced.

He stared at her, a perplexed frown creasing his brow. "You hate my house," he repeated, as if certain he must have misunderstood. At her dismal nod, he considered her intently for a long moment, then burst out laughing. "So what?"

"I'm not joking, Randy," she said falteringly. His robust laughter wasn't at all what she had expected, and it disconcerted her, leaving her off-balance and unsure. She tried to revive her negative feeling about his home. "I'm serious. I don't like it."

He examined her upturned face, her eyes troubled and turbulent, and exhaled. He led her to one of the shapeless pieces of leather furniture and drew her onto it beside him. It was soft and downy, arranging itself comfortably beneath her. He gazed around them at the strange living room. "Okay, I'll bite. What don't you like about my house?" he asked.

"It's..." She would be honest, she resolved. She would be as honest as Randy was. He deserved her honesty. "It's too modern. You've got it all cluttered with—with gizmos and things."

"My toys, you mean?" He smiled hesitantly. "I just like playing around with that stuff, Sara. Anything that saves me five minutes of work..." He turned back to her, perusing her face, his puzzlement still evident in the dark tinge of her eyes. "Why does it matter?"

"A house is a reflection of the person who lives in it, don't you think?"

He considered her statement. "Nothing personal, Sara, but your house is pretty—" he groped for the right word "—grim."

"I don't like my house, either," she admitted. "But it's all I can afford at the moment."

"What's your idea of a good house, then?" he asked.

"The Willoughby House," Sara told him.

"Where you work, you mean?" He laughed again, apparently finding her taste in houses ludicrous. "Sara, that house has its historic charms, but come on! This is the twentieth century."

Sara sighed. She watched Randy reach for her hand, study it, run his bronze-hued fingers along the pale length of hers. He was waiting for her to speak, and she reluctantly obliged. "I don't much care for the twentieth century, Randy. I don't feel at home in the modern world. Sometimes I think...I think I would have been much better off living Mrs. Willoughby's life."

"You said she wasn't very happy," Randy reminded Sara.

"But at least...at least she had her life simplified, down to the basics. She loved her husband, she raised her sons, she baked her bread and tended her garden and swept her hearth. She knew what her life was about. She was content."

Randy continued to examine her hand, then settled back against the cushions and guided her down beside him so they were more lying than sitting, facing each other. His eyes probed hers. "Is that what you want? Contentment?"

"More than anything."

"I don't believe that," he argued gently. "There's much more to life than being content."

"Oh? What?" she asked him.

"Happiness," he suggested. "I bet Mrs. Willoughby would rather have been happy than content. She'd rather have had her children survive and grow and father healthy grandchildren for her. Maybe she'd rather have had a few gadgets to make her chores less tedious. She might have preferred to spend less time baking bread so she could go to law school or something. Maybe she would have loved computers. I bet she would have enjoyed a good game of Zinger every now and then."

"That silly game?" Sara scoffed.

"Silly?" Randy protested. "Oh, come on, you got a kick out of playing with Petey. I saw you smile, so don't deny it."

"I enjoyed playing with him, yes, but—"

"And you enjoyed playing with the joystick. Don't deny it, Sara. You loved pushing that joystick's button. I've got your number, woman. You can't fool me."

His easy humor touched Sara. How could she be so pious, rejecting his gizmos and gadgets, when he was so downright good-natured? "Okay," she conceded. "Joysticks do have their appeal."

"That's what I like to hear," he murmured with a seductive grin. "But enough about that." He brushed a lock of hair back from her face. "You look tired. Did you have a rough week?"

She shrugged. "It had its ups and downs," she commented.

"What were the downs?"

"The high school where I used to work wants me to raise the grade of a student I flunked, to a pass so he can graduate this spring."

Randy snorted and shook his head. "What were the ups?"

"The up..." She smiled, relaxing against the cushion, pleased by the fact that she could see nothing but Randy, his fine, open face, his beautiful eyes. "The up is that I'm getting married."

"What?" He flinched.

"At the Village. We're staging a nineteenth-century wedding next month, and I've been picked to play the bride. You can come and watch if you want."

"Watch you get married? Remind me to mark it on my calendar," he muttered sarcastically.

"It's just an enactment," she emphasized. "I think

it'll be fun to dress up and recreate...a time when a marriage really meant something. When people married back then, they truly did it for better or for worse, till death did them part and all."

Randy digested her words. His expression grew solemn as he absorbed their underlying message. "And that's why you hate my house," he guessed. She could almost see him mentally making the connections between his modern house and her parents' modern marriage, his electronic "toys" and the games people played with each other in lieu of commitment.

"Oh, Randy..." She sighed. "I don't want to hate your house, but..."

"Can I make it better?" he murmured, his lips a breath away from hers. "Would it help if I kissed you?" His eyes locked onto hers for a moment, penetrating, trying to see her soul.

He didn't wait for her to answer.

Chapter Five

His lips touched hers, covered them, gently coaxed them apart. She closed her eyes and leaned toward him, losing herself in his quiet embrace, in his loving kiss, losing her awareness of the house, the futuristic living room, the undefined down-filled leather cushions that absorbed their weight.

Randy reached around her shoulders to the back of her neck, pulling her even closer as his tongue sought and found hers. Kissing him *did* make it better, she thought. No matter where he lived or what he did, his kisses were more powerful, more intoxicating than anything she had ever felt with a man before. Stu's kisses had never permeated her entire body as Randy's did. Stu's kisses had never drawn her out of herself as Randy's did, had never made her reach for him, had never made her yearn for more.

Her tongue followed Randy's to the edge of his teeth and then into his mouth. He groaned, thrilled by her mild aggressiveness. Letting his fingers float down her back, he took delight in the varying textures of her—her damp, eager mouth, her silky black hair, the fragile ridges of her ribs through the smooth cloth of her shirt, the angles of her knees bending to his, the satin softness of the skin of her cheeks and throat, the feminine roundness of her hips. His hands explored her with a quiet relentlessness, determined to know every part of her, to become acquainted with every cell in her body, every nerve, every impulse.

"Sara," he whispered, easing his head back and lifting one of her hands to his mouth. He kissed her palm, then cupped it over the sharp edge of his jaw. Sara realized that he wanted her to learn him as he was learning her, to touch him, to introduce herself to his body.

His skin was harder than hers, coarser, darker. His bones were broader, sturdier. His hair was slightly thicker than hers—or at least it felt thicker—soft and dark underneath, where the sun couldn't reach, and silky and copper-gold on the surface, fringing his ears and brushing against the collar of his shirt. She loved his hair, she admitted. Maybe more than he loved hers.

She let her hands drift over his collar to his back, its broad, muscular strength evident in its firm contours. Closing her eyes, she conjured up a picture of his naked chest as she had seen it last Sunday morning at her house. She wanted to touch his skin, to feel his heartbeat through the glittering mat of hair. She wanted to touch him, to forget everything but the feel of him, as fundamentally male as any man of any century.

Timidly she drew her hands forward to the front of his shirt and pulled a button out of the slit strip of cloth that held it. Randy's gaze hardened, and he wrapped his long fingers around hers. "Sara?" he murmured. "Are you ready for this?"

She felt as startled as he looked. Her hand closed into a fist inside his grasp, and an embarrassed flush of pink stained her cheeks. "It's...it's just your shirt," she stammered. "If you don't want me to..."

His lips curved in an indolent smile. "Are you kidding?" he chuckled throatily. "I want you to tear all my clothing off and...oh, ravish me mercilessly for starters." His smile waned and his green luminescent eyes wistfully perused her face. "What I don't want is for you to rush into something you aren't ready for."

"Are you always this solicitous about your women?" she asked, astonished by Randy's concern for her. Hadn't she undergone a zillion wrestling matches with Stu when he had tried to rush her, refusing to wait for her to be ready? That was the way modern men were, wasn't it? It was the way all men were—grasping, pushing, struggling to score.

Randy laughed. "Do you really want to discuss my past affairs at a time like this?"

"I didn't mean..." She wasn't sure what she meant, and she shut her mouth and stared at his hand enveloping hers.

"Sara, I care for you. I want you, I want you very much. You know that." He sighed, his fingers stroking hers, melting the fist. "But you're special. You really are old-fashioned."

"I'm not a child," she argued. "I lived with a man, for heaven's sake...."

"And you were hurt by it," he reminded her. "You're sensitive, Sara. You're a sensitive, special woman. I don't want to hurt you."

She measured his words, unsure of exactly what he *did* want. He wanted her, but not to hurt her. Did he think that by making love to her he would hurt her? Did he think she was incapable of deciding what she was ready for? "Should I leave?" she asked. In spite of her tense words, her hand softened in his, opening, welcoming his thumb against her palm.

"No." He lifted her hand to kiss it, then lowered it to his buttons. "You should take off my shirt."

With his assistance she did, unfastening the buttons

and pushing the cloth back over his shoulders, down his arms. She let her hands travel lightly across the warm stretch of his chest, the velvety tendrils sweetly inviting her to comb through them to his skin and the hard muscle beneath it. He watched her as she touched him, his eyes shining with amusement as they shuttled between her adventurous fingers and her expressively rapt face. When she allowed herself to rove down to his navel, he sucked in his breath and groaned again, passion overcoming amusement.

"Sara." He countered the tender scratching of her fingernails with a feverish assault on her mouth, thrusting his tongue deep inside her, gentleness replaced by a ravenous longing, a conquering strength. His hands scrambled down the front of her blouse, opening it and yanking it from the snug waistband of her slacks. He shoved the cloth out of his way, flinging it over the side of the leather furniture and onto the floor. His hands engulfed her narrow waist, then slid up to the pink lace cups of her brassiere. "Double-knotted camisole indeed," he growled as he massaged the full mounds through the alluring semisheer fabric, clearly excited by her revealing undergarment.

He located the clasp of the bra and undid it, depositing the lacy scrap of material on the floor with her shirt. Then he pressed her back into the yielding cushions, sliding partly onto her, and buried his face in the valley between her breasts.

He was kissing her sternum, but her body responded elsewhere, a taut coil of desire twisting deep inside her, in the cradle of her hips. They arched to him, and she felt his arousal, full and eager against her inner thigh. She was ready, she thought, readier than she had ever been before, as ready as she would ever be.

No. Not as ready as she would ever be. Randy

seemed compelled to make her readier. He devoted himself to feeding her desire, causing it to build to greater proportions, until it seemed too large for her tiny body to contain. His mouth skirted the shapely white mound of her breast before centering on her nipple, stimulating it with shocking jabs of his tongue, delicate nips of his teeth. She moaned, clinging to his head, wanting more. He tightened his lips about the swollen tip and sucked, setting loose a primal pulse inside her.

Her hips rose to meet his again. She wanted him, wanted him to find and quell that pulse, to share it, satisfy it, vanquish it. She was ready, and while she was too dazed to shape the words, her inflamed, writhing body was telling him that she was unbelievably ready for him.

"Oh Lord, Sara," he breathed, lifting his lips from one breast only to plant them on the other. "You're so beautiful, so incredibly beautiful." His hand slipped down to the snap on her jeans, sliding beneath it, discovering the lace-trimmed edge of her panties.

"Randy?" A distant, high-pitched voice, muffled, calling. "Randy?"

He froze, his hand pressed into the concave stretch of her abdomen, his mouth rigid against the pliant flesh of her breast.

"Randy?" Then the sound of a door opening, and approaching footsteps padding rapidly along the plush carpet of the hall. Randy somehow managed to slide higher on Sara, covering her naked chest with his own. In spite of Petey's intrusion, Sara couldn't keep herself from responding to Randy's weight upon her, the scratchy tangle of his chest hairs tantalizing her already engorged nipples. When she inhaled her breasts rose up against him, feeding her arousal. She held her breath.

"Randy, I'm thirsty." Petey's voice was quite close now. Sara couldn't see him—she couldn't see anything but the dark shape of Randy's shoulder shielding her. But she could picture Petey at the edge of the hallway where it opened into the living room, in his baseball-uniform pajamas, gawking at the two half-nude bodies locked passionately together on the unstructured leather sofa.

Randy didn't turn to look at Petey. Clearly he was loath to move, afraid that if he did Sara might be exposed to the little boy's view. "Go back to bed and I'll bring you a glass of water," he ordered, his voice gruff and uneven.

Petey said nothing for a moment, and then, "Are you kissing Sara?"

He's no fool, Sara thought wryly. Randy's hand gently brushed her arm, as if he could sense her edgy reaction to the boy's question. "Yes, I'm kissing Sara," he replied as calmly as possible under the circumstances.

"Like my daddy used to kiss my mommy?"

Randy swallowed. "Something like that. So back to your room, Petey. Go back and wait. I'll bring you some water." He shifted slightly against Sara, his erection still evident. "As soon as I'm able to walk," he whispered slyly, his breath tickling her ear. Sara's laughter was smothered by the warm cave of his armpit.

At last the sound of footsteps receded down the hall. Slowly, cautiously, Randy lifted himself from Sara, his eyes sparkling mirthfully. "Remind me never to have children," he murmured, feigning annoyance.

Sara herself was unable to speak. She was stunned by the fiery yearning in her body, the unfamiliar seething hunger, and by the unexpected intrusion of Petey, like a messenger sent to interrupt her, to allow her to regain her bearings before it was too late. If Petey hadn't come along, Randy would have made complete love to her. She knew that. He did, too. Her body wanted it. It still wanted it, even as she numbly put on her bra, which Randy had located on the floor and handed to her, along with her shirt.

Her body had been ready, but her mind? She didn't know. She needed this break, this pause to assess what was happening.

Randy tugged on his own shirt, then bent to kiss her brow. "To be continued," he murmured. "Don't go away." He sauntered into the kitchen.

Sara listened to the swing of a cabinet door on its hinges, the gush of water in the sink, Randy's footfalls down the hallway, the hiss of Petey's bedroom door ruffling the plush carpet as Randy opened it, the muffled voices of man and child talking in the bedroom. Her quivering fingers fumbled with the buttons of her blouse, but ultimately she managed to close them. Should she have bothered, she wondered. Wasn't Randy going to return in a few minutes and unbutton them again?

She stood, trying to clear her head, trying to think, trying to determine what she wanted. Anxiously she prowled the room, drawing to a halt in front of the carved oak bas-relief. Its strange, jagged shapes made no sense to her, no sense at all.

She liked art; living with an artist, how could she help but like art? But she liked at least remotely representational art, paintings or sculpture in which she knew what the artist was trying to express—what he wanted his work to communicate to her—without her having to read a pamphlet or locate a title. She stared at the random wood bulges hanging on the fieldstone wall of Randy's living room and couldn't even decipher what emotion the artist had been trying to convey when he had carved them.

She didn't like the piece. But Randy obviously did. He wouldn't have hung it in his house if he didn't like it.

He liked the bas-relief and the abstract painting across the room. He liked shapeless furniture and gadgetry. He liked expensive cars that broke down, and Bach played on synthesizers. He liked computers, Zinger, joysticks, large-screen televisions. Things. The very things Sara abhorred were the things with which Randy filled his world.

How could she love him? How could she make love to him? It wasn't enough that her body responded insatiably to his. Sara *was* old-fashioned in her way, and her way meant that there had to be commitment between people, devotion, understanding, love. Sex, no matter how physically glorious, wasn't enough.

She wasn't so reactionary that she thought people had to marry before they could indulge in sex. In fact, marriage struck her as an utterly useless institution; as far as she could tell, whether people were married or not seemed to have little bearing on their commitment to each other. But there ought to be love to accompany lovemaking, she thought. There ought to be "love, honor and cherish."

She liked Randy. She liked his kindness, his humor, the rapturous effect of his body on hers. But she didn't love him. She couldn't. He was a modern man, and she was not a modern woman.

Hearing Petey's door being shut, she turned from the bas-relief and folded her arms. She watched Randy's approach down the hall to the living room, his gait relaxed and his cheeks dimpled. He strode directly to

Sara, cupping his hands beneath her elbows, and smiled down at her. "Sorry about that," he said. "Maybe we should repair to my bedroom. It's got a door. With a lock."

She was tempted. Having him stand so near her was almost more temptation than she could resist. She deliberately focused her eyes on the abstract painting behind him. "I..." Her voice sounded weak and uncertain to her. "I don't think so, Randy."

He accepted her words, considered them, digested them. His hands remained on her elbows, gently stroking the soft flesh of her upper arms. "Do you want to talk about it?" he asked.

"I...don't know what to say," she muttered, hating herself for refusing him after having encouraged him so boldly.

His fingers continued their soothing massage. "Is it something I did, or something Petey did?"

"Neither, Randy. It's me." She sighed glumly, easing out of his grip, hoping that she would be able to think more clearly if he weren't touching her. She prowled restlessly around the living room, pausing before the bas-relief and grimacing.

"It's my house?" he asked, his tone heavy with dissatisfaction.

She turned bravely back to him. "It's us, Randy. I'd...I'd enjoy making love to you, but I...I don't love you."

His eyes radiated a thoughtful, muted light as he studied her across the room. He let his gaze wander slowly over her, trying to puzzle her out. A line formed across his brow as he absently ran his fingers through his disheveled hair. "In other words, you're not ready," he guessed.

"I'm ready, Randy," she corrected him. "But I don't love you."

"You want to get to know me better."

She shook her head. "I don't think I *can* love you," she noted softly. "We're too different. I look at your house and it tells me what's important to you. You like things, toys, junk. Your life is cluttered with... with electric Zingers. That's what you like, that's what you want. I'm completely different, Randy. Your silly toys repel me. You knead bread dough with automatic dough hooks. I knead bread dough by hand. Don't you see?"

He ruminated. "Let me see if I've got this right," he muttered caustically. "I don't knead bread dough by hand, so you can't love me."

"That's just... I only used that example to illustrate a point," Sara defended herself. "Randy, I'm lost here in your world. I belong in a simpler world, where the greatest challenge of life is to live, not to keep an Alfa-Romeo's electrical system from shorting out. Maybe it's easier to knead bread dough with electric dough hooks, but easier isn't always better. And video games... well, maybe they're an interesting experience, but I don't want interesting experiences. I want simplicity. I want basics. I want to know that I can survive through the simple routines of living—baking, gardening, building a fire, toting water...."

"And excluding men," Randy grunted.

"No, not... not necessarily. But if I were to share my life with a man, he would have to appreciate the simple sort of life I want. He couldn't be enamored of all this twentieth-century garbage."

Randy stiffened slightly, sensing condemnation of him in her words. "You know what your problem is,

Sara? You don't want to face reality. You'd rather live in a drafty, creaking hovel like the Willoughby House, without any conveniences—"

"That's right!" In spite of his stern tone, Sara was relieved by his understanding of her.

"Sara, the purpose of my 'garbage,' as you call it, is to free me to do more important things. I can either spend an evening washing dishes, or I can load the dishes into the dishwasher and spend the evening doing something more important."

"Like playing with your joystick?" she snapped.

"Like making love to you." He exhaled, then turned away, disgusted. "All right, leave," he said, sighing wearily. "Go enjoy your little fantasy world, Sara. I don't want to argue with you."

Sara could tell that he was furious. His shoulders were slightly hunched, his hands clenched, the line of anger across his brow seemingly indelible. "Randy," she tried to placate him, "I don't mean to pass judgment on you, but—"

"But that's exactly what you're doing," he said, snorting and spinning around to face her. "You don't approve of the way I live. I'm not humble and rustic enough for you. I derive more enjoyment from programming computer games or rigging electric-eye switches on my refrigerator than from sweeping the fireplace. Fine. Don't approve. I think you've got a screw loose, but that's your business, not mine."

"I'm not made of screws," Sara retorted. "Robots are made of screws. And when they've got a screw loose, they die."

He caught her reference to the bedtime story he and Sara had told Petey. His eyes fixed themselves on hers, his frown dissolving into a soft, disappointed smile. "Sara," he murmured, hazarding a step toward her, then another. "Oh, Sara... what am I going to do with you?"

"Say good-bye?" she suggested quietly, her voice hoarse with sadness. "Forget about me?"

He chuckled. "If I were a robot, I'd just reprogram myself. But I'm not. I'm a man."

I know, Sara thought morosely. She knew she wouldn't be able to forget about him any more easily than he'd be able to forget about her. But she also knew that they were wrong for each other, and that it would be best for her to leave before they both succumbed to the physical passion that burned so imperatively between them.

Afraid her voice would crack if she dared to speak, she strode to the foyer and fetched her jacket from the coat closet. Before she could put it on, Randy had it in his hands and was lifting it over her shoulders for her. "Sara," he said pensively, watching her hand as it reached for the doorknob. "I'm sorry you feel this way."

"I'm—I'm sorry, too," she confessed, her eyes trained on the floor. "But I'm sure about this, Randy. We're all wrong for each other."

"We felt pretty right for each other on the couch a few minutes ago," he refuted her.

Her cheeks warmed with color. "I desire you, Randy—we both know that. But it's not enough." Unable to speak further, salty tears filling her throat, she turned the knob and heaved open the door. "Good night," she whispered. Before he could stop her, she raced down the walk to her car.

ASSURING HERSELF that she had done the right thing didn't help much. Sleep eluded Sara Saturday night, and she walked through her Sunday afternoon shift at Old Harkum Village like a zombie, barely able to concentrate on the tasks by which she claimed life's meaning was defined. Kneading her bread dough wasn't sensuous—it was laborious. Repairing her broom didn't gratify her—it stymied her. If she hadn't been seated before a captive audience of visitors, she would have cursed aloud at the recalcitrant bristles as she wove them back into shape.

The smell of baking bread cloyed. The sun caused her eyes to water. When Edith, the Village's chief costumer, stopped by the Willoughby House to take Sara's measurements for a new dress for the wedding, Sara felt dizzy and dismal as she lifted her arms to accommodate the tape measure, sucking in her waist and arching her back for an accurate measure of her torso. Every time she moved her head, a few hairs braided too tightly pinched the nape of her neck.

If she was right about Randy, why did she feel so out of sorts? Her decision to leave him Saturday night had been the only fair thing to do. Sure, she could have stayed and had sex with him. But she wouldn't have emerged satisfied from such a physical encounter. And Randy, realizing that she wasn't satisfied, wouldn't have been pleased, either. She believed him when he claimed that he didn't want to hurt her, that he wanted her to be ready. If her soul hadn't been ready to make love with Randy, despite her body's demands, he would have sensed it. And then they both would have been disappointed.

She was old-fashioned. They both knew that. She wouldn't sleep with someone she didn't love. Since she wasn't sure she would ever find a man she could love, she was willing to forgo sex—even sex with Randy. She would rather abstain than to become intimate with someone she couldn't love, no matter how exciting a man he was.

She had been correct. She had done the right thing, the best thing. She had followed a wise course in leaving him Saturday night. So why did she feel so dreadful about it?

Sunday night she tried not to think about Randy. She ate a light supper, read, took a hot bath, and crawled into bed early, exhaustion overtaking her. After a solid night of sleep, she arose feeling a bit better on Monday. It was an unseasonably warm day, and Sara decided to celebrate the spring sunshine and her day off by working in the garden.

Her labors were interrupted by the sound of her telephone, audible through the storm door of her open back door. Her hands were covered to the wrist with moist soil, and her braid was hanging in an uneven rope down her back. Callers always seemed to have a sixth sense about the most inopportune time to phone.

She didn't care. She slapped her muddy hands against the legs of her denim overalls as she raced to the house. She didn't even let herself consider why her heart was drumming anxiously, her pulse pounding in her veins in response to the telephone summons. She didn't care to think of how much she wanted to hear from Randy. "Hello?" she breathed anxiously.

"Sara Morrow?" a deep, guttural voice spun through the wire. "This is Donald Corcoran."

The principal at the high school where she used to teach. Sara felt the air escape her lungs in a tortured sigh. She tucked the telephone between her ear and her shoulder and shoved her dirty hands beneath the spout of her kitchen sink, rinsing off the clods of soil and trying to ignore the disappointment that gripped her spine. "Hello," she politely greeted him. "How are you?"

"I'm fine, Sara," he said, all business. "I've just had

a meeting with a former student of yours, a young man named Vincent Chesler."

"Turk," she grunted.

"Turk?"

"That's his nickname. Or at least it was his nickname last year."

"Well, whatever," Donald mumbled. "Sara, this young man is very eager to graduate with his class this year. The only thing standing in his way is the failing grade he received in your class last year."

"He got a failing grade because he deserved one," she dryly maintained. "He was a terrible student."

"Be that as it may..." The principal cleared his throat. "I hate to hold him back just because of this one grade. He isn't a stupid kid. It seems to me he ought to graduate."

"You want to get him out of your hair?" she complained. "Donald, he was a mean-spirited, lazy boy. He had plenty of opportunity to make up the failed work. I offered to help him. He could have taken a summer-school course. He could have repeated American History this year. It isn't my fault that he waited until his final term at school to protest the grade."

"Sara." Donald's voice indicated forced patience. How many times during her three-year tenure at the school had they had similar fights about her strict grading policies? "I'll grant you, he seems to be a troublemaker. I don't really care to have him around for another year. But beyond that, I'm thinking of him. What good can possibly come of our holding him back?"

"He might learn something about discipline and responsibility," Sara suggested. "To say nothing of the course material."

"If he hasn't learned anything about discipline and

responsibility by now, I fail to see how our holding him back will teach it to him at this late stage."

"That's your problem," Sara noted. "I'm not teaching anymore."

"Sara, if you care about this boy at all—"

"I care enough to think he ought to develop a sense of pride in his accomplishments," she declared. "I care enough to think he ought to earn the grade he gets. I care enough to think he might benefit from learning about the history of his own country."

"Sara—"

"He'll be eligible to vote this fall," she added. "Do you want someone who doesn't even know what the Constitution says or what the American Revolution was all about to choose your elected officials? I don't."

"Sara." Donald sighed. He had heard her views many times before. "As you say, you're not teaching anymore. It really isn't your obligation to save this one young man from his own ignorance."

"Then pass him. Go over my head and change his grade," she flippantly advised. "What do I care?"

"I can't do that without your signature," Donald reminded her. "Would you be willing—"

She cut him off. "I would not. I won't sign anything I don't believe in. You know that."

Donald sighed again. "You won't budge on this?"

"I won't. You do with Turk Chesler what you want to do. But I'm not going to push him through the door just to save your skin and erase a failure from your records. Turk's your troublemaker, not mine."

"I'm not so sure of that," Donald said ominously. "He holds a terrible grudge against you."

"Well, too bad for him." Sara sniffed. "If he wants to graduate into adulthood, perhaps he ought to grow up."

Donald was silent for a moment. "I'm sorry you feel that way, Sara," he ventured. "I know you're very committed to what you feel is right. But in this day and age, we sometimes have to make decisions based on pragmatism."

"It's your decision," she agreed. "Do what you want. Just don't ask me to endorse something I don't believe in."

"Then you won't sign a change-of-grade form?"

"I won't."

Another sigh. "All right, Sara. If that's how you feel about it."

"That's how I feel," she asserted.

"All right." He floundered for something to say, then gave up. "Take care. I hope you're enjoying your new career at that restoration village."

"I am," she told her former boss, adding silently, *Nobody expects me to abandon my principles there. Nobody expects me to be modern and pragmatic for the sake of convenience.* "Thanks for calling, Donald. Tell Turk I'm sorry, but I'm not going to bail him out."

"I'll tell him." Donald complied. "So long."

She dropped the receiver back into its cradle and felt her shoulders go limp. She couldn't help resenting people who counted practicality as a more worthy determinant of behavior than principle. If the school wanted to ignore the values and standards of education to pass a troublemaker through their doors, that was their choice. But Sara wouldn't be a party to such pragmatism. She wouldn't sell out for the convenience of the school. She hadn't sold out during her career as a teacher, and she certainly wouldn't sell out now.

THE DAYS DRAGGED BY. She heard nothing from Randy. She considered calling him, but she didn't know what she would say if she reached him. She didn't know what she wanted from him.

Yes she did. She wanted him to understand her. She wanted him to embrace her world view. She wanted him to declare, "You're right, Sara, the simple things in life are the most important. Video games are a waste. Luxurious automobiles are foolish. An electric-eye refrigerator door is cute, but cute isn't worth much." She wanted him to admit the genuine beauty of simplicity, of honest labor, of pure living. It wasn't enough for him to relish home-baked bread; she wanted him to renounce electric dough hooks.

But he wouldn't. She knew he wouldn't. And she wouldn't call him. There was no point in attempting the impossible. He liked his toys and she despised them. She was better off without him.

Jean Sharkey was sensitive to the desolate mood that overcame Sara. She invited her for dinner several times, and the rowdy disorderliness of the Sharkey family was a necessary diversion for Sara. One evening she helped Pipsqueak construct an old-fashioned kite out of two laths of wood and a worn linen bed sheet. Together they sawed and clamped the wooden sticks, forgoing nails for more authentic wooden pegs, and they stitched the cut sheet by hand about the frame. They fashioned a tail out of shreds of cloth tied together, and Pipsqueak frantically ran about the living room, trying, he said, to test the aerodynamics of the kite. Jean made him stop when he came dreadfully close to knocking over a lamp.

Making the kite was a good distraction, Sara decided. So was researching how to bake a pie in a fireplace brick oven for Ira Lipton, her Village intended. When the Willoughby House was empty of visitors, she practiced rolling pastry dough into thin strips and weaving a lattice with them. She brainstormed with the Village's tinkerer about converting some of her hand-hammered baking pans into ovenworthy pie plates. She perused some of the books in the main building in search of period recipes.

Other than a number of school groups on class trips, the Village's attendance during the week was sparse. Saturday it bustled with visitors, and Sunday, an even warmer day, the Village was jammed. Sara repeated her lecture on the Willoughby House so many times she no longer needed to think about what she was saying. The explanation about the low ceiling, the bed in the kitchen, the prevalence of springhouses, the sorry fate of the Willoughbys' offspring, tripped from her tongue in a rote litany.

"How come the ceiling is so low?" a young man in the umpteenth group to swarm into the Willoughby House's kitchen asked. "Were the people short in those days?"

Sara's eyes were glazed as she focused on the man's face, one of about thirty crowded into the small room. "According to Julia Willoughby's diary, a photocopy of which is on display in the main building, Josiah Willoughby was nearly six feet tall. The people were not markedly shorter in 1791 than we are today."

"Well, you're a shrimp yourself," the man ribbed her.

She grimaced and pounded on the yeasty lump of dough before her. "The ceilings were built low to conserve heat," she explained, her voice remaining unemotional though she vented her irritation on the hapless dough.

"Isn't it true that the people somemtimes got into bed in pairs and bundled together for warmth?"

Sara subliminally recognized the voice, but she instinctively began her routine answer without giving the voice much thought: "Since Josiah and Julia Willoughby gave birth to four children, we can safely assume that they—" And then her gaze discovered a pair of striking green eyes through the crowd of visitors and she stopped.

"That they figured out a way to keep warm on a long winter's night?" Randy completed for her.

Her fingers dug convulsively into the dough, and she bowed her head to avoid looking at him. What was he doing here? Why had he decided to contact her after avoiding her for the entire week? Why was he ignoring what she believed was her sound decision to break off things between them?

Someone else called out a question concerning the sleeping arrangements of the Willoughby sons, and Sara answered automatically, "They slept in the loft. You can't go up there now because the floor beams need reinforcement," she warned, intercepting a curious young girl who had started toward the ladder leading to the attic. "When our capital grant is approved we hope to repair the beams and open the attic to the public, sometime this fall. The four boys slept in the same bed, head to foot. Eventually, two of the boys passed away, so that by the time the remaining two Willoughby boys reached maturity the bed wasn't uncomfortably crowded."

"What became of the sons?" a woman asked.

"The elder son, also named Josiah, inherited his father's farm and settled here with his wife. The younger son became an itinerant lay preacher."

"Wasn't he the one who was shot by a jealous husband?" Randy spoke up.

The mass of visitors turned to look at him. Sara felt her cheeks reddening. From the sun, she thought, the sun beating through the window behind her, warming her. The sun and the roaring fire in the fireplace... "Any other questions?" she asked, eager to squelch Randy.

Unfortunately, there weren't. The crowd filed out, all except Randy. Dressed in jeans and a yellow oxford shirt with its sleeves rolled up against the heat, he looked utterly gorgeous to Sara. She cringed at his approach. "Here I am again," he announced in a soft, husky voice.

"Why?" She kept her eyes on her dough, which she twisted and fidgeted with, trying to knead out her nervousness. The faint spicy scent of Randy's after-shave stymied her attempts to stay calm.

"Because," he explained, "I can't stop thinking about you."

"Randy, I'm sorry about what happened last week—"

"So am I," he murmured. "Why don't we put it behind us and try again?"

Her head jerked up; her gray eyes sparked with silver light. "Whatever for?"

He let his gaze wander languidly down her body, taking a keen interest in the way her blue linen frock hugged her ribs and waist, accentuating her fragile figure with its wide skirt and lace-trimmed bodice. Sara sensed that, like the robot of his bedtime story, Randy had an X-ray lens implanted in his eye, and that he was seeing her naked body beneath the prim dress, that he was seeing the soft white skin that had once responded so wildly to his caresses.

She struggled to breathe, to keep her pulse under control, to keep her cheeks from flooding hot and scarlet and giving her away. She focused on her dough, smashing it, folding it, plunging her fingers into its warm heart to keep them from trembling.

"I was here yesterday, too," Randy confessed.

"You were?"

"I spent hours walking around the Village. I visited every building but this one. I watched someone make a pair of shoes, someone else make a felt hat. I watched two men plow the farm." He paused. "It's a beautiful village, Sara. It's so peaceful here. A person can really think in a place like this."

Her fingers stopped toying with the dough. She lifted her eyes to his, seeing in them the churning shadows that indicated a mental struggle. "What did you think about?" she asked softly.

"About you. About why this place means so much to you." He sighed. "Sara, I want to understand. I do." He sighed again. "You hate my house," he drawled. "So we'll keep our distance from my house."

"Keep our distance?" she muttered. "Keep our distance when?"

"Tonight."

She was pleased by the constant flow of her tone, despite the fact that the muscles in her throat were contracting spasmodically. "And what did you have in mind?"

"Sara," he whispered. "Sara, you're so special, so different. I've started to call you a dozen times this past week, but I didn't know what to say. I thought maybe if I came here I'd be able to figure out the words." He circled one floury wrist with his long fingers and pried it from the gooey dough before her. He studied it intently, rubbing the dusting of flour from her smooth skin with his thumbs. "Sara, I can't lie and say I'm madly in love with you. But... but I can't stop thinking about you, and that must mean something. Maybe I don't understand you, but I *want* to, and that's more than I've ever felt for a woman before. And I know you must feel something for me. Maybe you don't love me, either. Sara, but you must feel something. I think I know you well enough to realize that you wouldn't have responded to me at all if you didn't feel something."

"Well yes, Randy . . . I . . ." She wished he would stop caressing her hand. With each gingerly stroke of his thumb against the inside of her wrist, her blood pressure spurted higher. "Of course I feel something for you, Randy, but . . . I just don't see the future in it."

"The future?" He latched on to the word, his eyes glittering as he lifted them to her face. "Since when did you care about the future? I thought you were all wrapped up in the past."

"You know what I mean," she complained.

"Sara, nobody can see the future. Back in your beloved nineteenth century, a lot of charlatans probably claimed they could. Another generation of charlatans is undoubtedly at it now. But you and I don't believe that stuff The only way you can see the future is if you take a chance and walk into it and let it become the present." His grip tightened snugly around her hand. "What do you say, Sara? Will you take a chance with me and see what happens?"

"Oh, Randy." She sighed. He already knew her answer. He knew—by the faint pink hue spreading along her delicate cheekbones, by the subtle rise of her breasts, by the undeniable softening of her hand in his. molding to his shape, to the strength of his hold on her—what her answer would be. She wanted to understand him, too. She wanted to understand the sort of man who was so brilliant he couldn't keep himself from inventing new gadgets, new toys. She wanted to understand the sort of man who had such faith in the future, and in her ability to face it.

She didn't have to answer his question. He could tell, just by looking at her, that she would have to take a chance, that she would have to say yes.

Chapter Six

He told her he would pick her up at her house at six. She tore out of the Village as soon as she was able, irked by the ten-minute delay changing her clothes caused her. She was overcome by excitement, an emotion she had thought didn't mean much to her. She was excited by the realization that she and Randy would be spending another evening together. She was excited by Randy himself.

At her house, she raced to the bedroom to hang up her Village costume and undress, then hastened to the bathroom to shower. As she shampooed her hair, she wondered what sort of evening Randy had in mind. She wondered exactly how they were going to march into the future together. She hoped he didn't dream of a future cluttered with banal electronic paraphernalia.

Once she had dried herself and brushed out her wet, shimmering hair, she returned to her bedroom. What to wear? Something special, she decided. Something special for facing the future.

She selected a Victorian-style blouse with a high, lace-trimmed neck and long, blousy sleeves. Not exactly futuristic, she mused, but pretty and feminine and becoming on her. Then she chose a calf-length flowered dirndl skirt to wear with it. She rummaged through her drawers for fresh underwear, and her fingers located a white silk camisole edged in champagne lace. It was old-fashioned in a sexy sort of way. She had bought it, and matching panties, a year ago, thinking to surprise Stu with it—thinking to add some excitement to their lives, she recalled ironically. She remembered vividly the day she had bought the elegant lingerie. She had brought it home and found Stu's ex-wife, with her stringy escort and her son, standing in the foyer of the brownstone, waiting for someone to arrive and take the boy off their hands. Sara had never worn the camisole.

She slipped it over her head and adjusted the narrow straps on her creamy shoulders. Her firm breasts held the sensuously textured fabric taut across her chest, leaving it to drop loosely to her hips. She felt deliciously feminine in it.

Randy would never see it, though. They weren't going to make love tonight. She knew that, and she knew he knew. She believed he understood her feelings about love being a part of sex, and he had candidly announced that he wasn't in love with her. But it didn't matter that he would never know what undergarments Sara was wearing. All that mattered was that *she* knew, and that the dainty articles of clothing made her feel wonderfully naughty, old-fashioned yet exotic.

She pulled on the blouse and skirt, added a pair of nylons and shoes, and brushed her hair again, protecting the shoulders of her blouse from the excess water with a towel.

Randy was early, ringing for her a few minutes before six. She spun around in front of the bathroom mirror, adjusting the slenderizing waistband of her skirt before removing the towel from her shoulders and heading for the living room to answer the bell.

So handsome, she thought as he stepped over the threshold. He, too, was dressed slightly more formally than usual, in black wool twill trousers, a crisp white shirt and a herringbone-tweed blazer. His awesome green eyes took her in, appreciation of her appearance registering in their shimmering depths. "Hello," he purred, giving her a light kiss on the cheek.

"Hello." For some reason, she felt as if this were their first date. Shyness tinged her cheeks with pink and caused her large gray eyes to sparkle.

"I guess you're not exactly sorry I imposed myself on you again," he said, his gaze continuing to course admiringly over her. "You look lovely."

"Thank you."

"It's warm out—you won't need a coat," he advised. "I'd hate for you to hide that pretty blouse from me."

She laughed, and the trilling sound of her laughter erased her shyness. "Then let's go, shall we?" she suggested.

He reached for her hand, but stopped at the raucous, intrusive pealing of her telephone. Groaning softly, she excused herself to answer it. She left him and went to the kitchen to pick up the receiver. "Hello?"

"Sara?" A woman's voice crackled through distinctive long-distance static. "It's Mom."

Sara groaned again. Her mother began to prattle, a long, involved verbal essay on her life. Sara shifted her weight impatiently from one foot to the other, rubbing her fingers listlessly over the laminated counter, eyeing her seedlings along the windowsill. She remembered to insert "uh-huh's" at the appropriate times, an occasional "No!" when necessary. Her mother went on for twenty minutes, with Sara silently calculating the cost of the call and taking satisfaction that it would appear on her mother's phone bill instead of hers.

By the time her mother had run out of steam, Sara was exhausted by the mere chore of listening. She bade her mother good-bye, hung up, and rejoined Randy in the living room. "All set?" he asked.

"All set," she replied limply, moving directly to the door.

Randy let her stew in silence as they strolled down the walk to his car. He helped her onto the seat, then took his own seat behind the wheel. "Music?" he offered as he started the engine.

Sara shrugged uninterestedly. A bit of Moog synthesizer noise would suit her mood just perfectly, she thought sullenly.

He reached over her to the glove compartment and pulled out a tape. He inserted it into his tape deck, adjusted the volume, and then steered away from the curb. The compact interior of the car filled with one of Bach's Brandenburg Concerti. Played on *real* instruments, Sara reflected. Real seasoned violins and cellos, real polished wood recorders and harpsichords. She turned to Randy, her face glowing with gratitude that he had chosen this tape to play for her, that he was showing his respect for her taste. But his gaze was fastened on the road, and she decided not to say anything.

When he reached the eastbound ramp of the Northern State Parkway, he rolled down his window to allow some of the mild evening air to waft over them. "Would you like to talk about it?" he asked.

"About what?"

"The telephone call. It's put you in a funk, hasn't it?"

She sighed and rubbed her fingers over her soft flowered linen skirt. "It was from my mother," she revealed.

Randy nodded and waited for her to continue.

"She's getting a divorce," Sara said.

Randy cast a swift glance at Sara. "The younger man?" he asked. "How's she holding up?"

Sara shrugged. "She seems quite pleased about it, actually," she explained. "She said they were great friends and expected to continue their relationship on a different plane. I think that translates to mean they're going to continue to sleep together but not monogamously."

"I see," said Randy. "Were they monogamous when they were married?"

"Who knows?" She snorted, then corrected herself. "No, they weren't. But things fell apart when Al—her husband, or rather her ex-husband—slept with a man. He said he thought it would be an interesting experience." She groaned softly. "Mom agreed that it must have been an interesting experience for him, and though she could respect his wish to try new things, she didn't want to be married to someone who was gay. I don't know that one interesting experience makes him gay, but I guess it rubbed Mom the wrong way." She shuddered. "Mom told me Al is goinng to be in New York City for a couple of weeks. He wanted my telephone number. I told her not to give it to him." Sara sighed again. *Sordid,* she thought, remembering Randy's word for her parents' living arrangements. The last thing she wanted in her life was the attentions of her mother's suddenly bisexual ex-husband.

Randy considered her tense silence for a moment. "Are you upset?"

"No," she replied, then changed her mind. "Yes, I am. They go through such vicissitudes just for a cheap thrill every now and then. It's such a waste." She exhaled morosely. "I don't know where I came from—

other than what my mommy told me about how babies are made," she added.

"You're obviously reacting to them," Randy noted. "A little two-bit psychology here, Sara, but obviously your personality is just a negative reaction to your parents."

"I suppose so," she agreed.

He extended his hand to hers and gave it a gentle squeeze. Then he let her ruminate in silence as he continued driving east. He exited the parkway somewhere in Suffolk County and steered north toward the water. Although Sara couldn't see the Sound, she could smell its salty fragrance tingeing the breeze that spilled through Randy's open window.

He coasted into the parking lot of a large old clapboard house with a sign hanging before its door: Devon Inn. "I think you'll like this place," he said hopefully as he guided the car to a parking space and turned off the engine.

Tucking her hand into the crook of his elbow, he escorted her around to the front and inside the building. The inn was a restored nineteenth-century structure; Sara didn't need the plaque displaying the date beside the front door to tell her that. She took note of the brick foundation, the settled glass in the twelve-pane windows, the uneven, pegged wood floor of the entry. A hostess led them to their reserved table in the vast dining room, which was decorated with Americana—oil-lamp centerpieces, Colonial-style place settings, pewter pieces displayed on the mantel.

Sara smiled. Randy was trying, she realized. He had played genuine Bach for her, and he had chosen this restaurant because he knew it would appeal to her. He had clearly planned this evening to avoid the conflicts of their last evening together. "Is this going to be a romantic dinner?" she asked him, a teasing grin shaping her lips.

He shook out his linen napkin before spreading it across his lap. "I sincerely hope so," he replied, mirroring her grin. His eyes circled the quaintly decorated room and his grin expanded. He liked the inn, too. He liked the classic simplicity of it. He liked the way Sara looked in it, the way her surroundings enhanced her beauty. Although he'd never been to the restaurant before, he'd spent the morning combing a restaurant guide, anxious to find just such a place to take Sara. It amazed him that he wanted to go to such lengths to please Sara, but he did. Her obvious pleasure touched him deeply.

The hostess lifted the hurricane glass from the lamp to light its wick, then handed them menus and departed. They perused the restaurant's offerings. Sara selected bluefish, Randy prime rib and a bottle of Burgundy for them to share. Once he had given their order to the waiter, the waiter disappeared, leaving them in the relative privacy of their corner table.

"So what are your mother's plans?" Randy asked.

Sara quirked her eyebrows. "Who knows? I'm sure she doesn't. I don't want to talk about her, Randy." She honestly didn't. She wanted to forget about her crazy parents and think only of Randy, of his kindness and sensitivity in arranging their evening. She watched him across the table, the amber glow of the lamp casting his face in a soft golden light. "How's Petey?" she asked.

"I didn't thrash him too hard last week." Randy chuckled sardonically. "In fact, I've completely forgiven him."

"How generous of you," Sara said, joining his laughter.

"I suppose it was just as well that he interrupted us when he did," Randy quietly commented, surprising Sara. She leaned forward slightly, curious. "You weren't ready—*we* weren't ready. I don't want to rush into anything with you."

"You're content just to have a nice dinner?" she asked, seeking confirmation of her own feelings.

He nodded. "You're special, Sara. I want everything to be special for you."

She let his gentle compliment warm her, soaking through her flesh and deep into her. He wasn't madly in love with her, but...but she didn't need him to be madly in love with her. She needed only for him to understand her. And tonight he was trying. He was coming very close.

"How are Petey's parents?" she asked.

Randy waited while the waiter deposited their salads and poured their wine. He clinked his glass against hers before drinking. "They seemed to have differing opinions about their marriage encounter weekend," he related.

"Oh?"

"I got Larry's side Monday at work. He plopped himself down in my office and rambled for three hours. It's amazing that I can stay in business," Randy commented wryly. "Larry said they spent a lot of time sitting in circles on the floor and talking about meaningless things in contemporary jargon. He said the best part of the weekend was sleeping with Renee. Apparently the physical aspect of their marriage isn't the problem. He said it was terrific to share a bed with her for a change."

"Did she think it was terrific?" Sara asked.

Randy shrugged. "I had dinner with her and Petey on Tuesday. She couldn't go into too much detail with him around—he's developing into a real problem that way," he joked. "But she said she thought the discussions were the best part. She said she vented her spleen and felt much better afterward."

"If she vented her spleen to Larry, it's no wonder he didn't enjoy the discussions," Sara pointed out.

"Good point." Randy toasted her. He sipped his wine, meditating. "Petey was in a petulant mood. I think he expected the weekend to solve all his parents' problems and bring them back together again. He was disappointed when his father took off for his apartment Sunday night."

"Poor child." Sara sighed sympathetically. "I know what he's going through. I used to pray every night before bed that some miracle would happen and my parents would get back together. Of course, sometimes they did get back together, and then they'd separate again. It was even worse that way, having hope and then losing it over and over again."

Randy gave her a wistful smile. She wondered if he was pitying her. She carefully absorbed the nuances of his expression, his steady gaze and dimpled cheeks and defiantly angled jaw. She saw no pity there, just compassion, and she relaxed in her chair. "What was it like to live in a stable home?" she asked him.

Their entrées arrived, and Randy waited until they were alone again before speaking. He tasted his succulent beef, smiled, and then considered Sara's question. "Boring, I guess," he told her. "Of course the nicest things can seem boring when you're living through them. I took my parents' happiness for granted. It never occurred to me that other kids grew up in different sorts of situations." He ate, mulling over his memories. "We were very middle-class, very traditional. My father went to work; my mother took care of the house; my brother and I fought and played together, joined the Little League, built a tree house in the yard, that kind of thing."

"What did you and your brother fight about?" Sara asked, fascinated. She gladly would have done anything to have a sister to fight with.

Randy laughed. "I was the younger brother, so I went through twelve years of public school walking in his shadow, being compared with him, being called Artie by my teachers, who had all had him in their classes two years earlier. He was brilliant, a very organized, competent guy. So I rebelled by being obstreperous, messy, radical. Instead of doing my homework, I fiddled with computers. Instead of running for school office, like he did, I ran the audiovisual squad. Instead of being the teacher's pet, I was a pain in the neck."

"But you must have done well," Sara argued. "You went to MIT."

"Naturally brilliant," he boasted self-mockingly. "Yeah, I did all right. Especially the last two years, when Artie was at Princeton and I didn't have his presence to contend with."

"So you were competitive with him," Sara summed up.

He nodded. "Once we parted ways, though, we became much closer. Nobody at MIT had ever heard of the famous Artie Zale, so I was on my own. He went on to law school, I went into business. Now that we've followed different courses, we can laugh and see how similar we are in a lot of ways."

"You aren't messy anymore," Sara observed, recalling his neatly maintained, if odd, house.

"Funny thing about that," Randy said, laughing. "As soon as Artie left for college, I became very tidy."

Sara laughed, too. She was captivated by Randy's tale of his childhood. It probably did seem boring to him, but it bordered on the alien to her. Even her friends at boarding school didn't have such normal, loving backgrounds. Most of them, like her, came from families where wealth replaced affection. They had all been sent away to school so they wouldn't get in their parents' way, whether their parents' way involved Junior League good works, world cruises or sexual hijinks. They were all lonely, abandoned, solitary and resentful of their elders. Their common ground was their shared sense of desertion.

She envied Randy's background. She envied the easy humor and confidence that such a close-knit family had created in him. And she was grateful to him for telling her about it, for letting her bask in its reflected warmth.

Sara felt herself brimming with Randy's thoughtfulness, his willingness to share himself with her on her own territory. To show her thanks, she asked him more about himself, specifically about his work. If he would take her to such an ideal restaurant, she would venture into his world as well. "How's your navigational system project?" she asked.

He seemed surprised and delighted by her interest. "Going well," he answered, keeping his reply simple.

"Is it going to be used in weaponry?" she dared to ask, aware that Grumman Aircraft held many military contracts.

"I hope not," he declared. "They tell me it'll be used in Coast Guard systems."

"What exactly do you do?" she asked.

Convinced that Sara seriously wanted to know, Randy told her. He explained, using lay terms, the way he approached a project, sitting with designers as they hammered out their needs, then returning to his firm's headquarters to work on various programs that would satisfy those needs. He described a recent project he had completed involving the computerization of a mass transit system, explaining how he analyzed the traffic patterns and commuting requirements and then devised a program to organize the city's fleet of buses to meet the demands of the commuters. "By timing the buses more efficiently and changing several routes, I was able to save the city a ton of money that it would have spent in purchasing unnecessary additions to its fleet," he told her.

So computers had their uses, she allowed silently. Through Randy's technical expertise he had been able to reduce a city's transportation budget and ease the travails of commuters. More commuters using mass transit meant fewer cars clogging the roads, less pollution and congestion, steadier tempers. Overcrowded cities were an undeniable twentieth-century fact, and Randy's gizmos and gadgets were able in some way to alleviate the plight of the people trapped in those overcrowded cities. Her judgment of his work softened considerably as she pondered its effects.

They topped off their meal with pecan pie—garnished with real whipped cream, Sara happily noted—and coffee. Once Randy had settled the bill and helped Sara out of her chair, he suggested a walk. "We're right by the beach," he told her. "It might be a little cool, but why don't we check it out?"

"I'd love to," she responded enthusiastically.

They left the inn and sauntered around behind the building to a walkway that abutted a pebbly stretch of shoreline. Without speaking, they held hands and meandered the length of the paved walk, gazing over the iron railing at the black water lapping peacefully against the sand. "Why don't we climb down to the beach?" Sara asked.

Randy glanced at her skirt, her shoes, her stockinged feet. "Are you dressed for it?"

She answered by bending over to remove her shoes.

"What about your stockings?"

"So they'll get wet," she said, shrugging. "Big deal."

Smiling, Randy stepped out of his loafers, tugged off his socks, and cuffed his pants halfway up his calves. He located a short flight of concrete steps descending from the walkway to the sand and ushered Sara down it, leaving their shoes on the lowest step. He took her hand again as they picked their way carefully among the stones and shells to the water's edge.

The humid fragrance of the sea washed over them as they stared out at the water. Phosphorescent sea life shimmered mysteriously in the silver light of the half-moon riding high above the horizon. "I wonder what the first person to see this place felt," Sara whispered, transfixed by the dark, beautiful vista.

"He must have been overwhelmed," Randy guessed.

"*She* must have felt as if the entire universe was water," Sara said softly, subtly correcting him. "She must have longed for a boat to explore the cosmos with. She must have dreamed dreams of water when she fell asleep."

Randy peered down at her, moved by her poetic imagining. She was so sensitive, he mused. Her perspective of the world broadened his own, made him see things and think thoughts he never would have entertained before. Once again he found himself contemplating how different she was from most of the women he knew, women who would never have meditated about dreaming dreams of water. Sara was different, and his soul celebrated her difference. He wove his fingers snugly through hers, savoring their slender coolness, and guided her along the sand.

A wave surprised them with its reach, splashing over their feet. Sara shrieked from the sudden chill. "Cold?" Randy asked.

Cold, she thought, but warm as well—warmed from within by Randy's presence. She shook her head and bent to pick up the tide-polished shard of a clam shell. It had been worn smooth, like mother-of-pearl, and it caught the moonlight in a clear white sheen.

"Pretty," Randy said when she showed it to him.

"Randy." She tossed the shell lightly back into the water and turned to face him fully. "Randy, why did you come to see me today? Why did you ask me to have dinner with you?"

Her question startled him. A salty gust off the water seemed to tangle her hair like damp, eager fingers, disheveling it. He took a moment to brush it back from her face with his hand. "I like you, Sara. Isn't it obvious?"

"But you aren't madly in love with me," she ascertained.

"I'm..." His eyes remained riveted on her pale upturned face. "I'm getting there," he admitted.

"How can you be?" she disputed him. "We're such a mismatch, Randy."

"Why do you say that?" He cut her off before she could answer. "Sara, I don't give a damn whether you like my house or not. That's not what brings two people together."

"But the things in your house, Randy—"

"My toys? I've got gadgets. You've got plants. So what?" He took her other hand in his and studied them both, clasped between his chest and hers. "Sara, what happened last week . . . it meant a lot to me."

"Having me walk out on you meant a lot?" she murmured in puzzlement.

He nodded solemnly. "You made me think, Sara. You made me sit down and think things through." His thumbs wandered over her knuckles as he studied her. "I've enjoyed the company of women in the past, but they've never made me think in quite the same way."

"What did I make you think about?" she asked, intrigued.

He remained mute for a long moment, collecting his thoughts. "When I saw Larry Monday morning," he began, "and he told me about the marriage encounter weekend . . . I sat there listening to him and nodding at everything he said. What was Renee's problem, he ranted. They were so good in bed together. Physically they were so compatible. They were two individuals; of course they had their differences. Renee had no right to expect Larry to understand every little thing about her. He understood the important things, didn't he? He understood what satisfied her, what made her feel like a wife, like a woman. What more did she want?"

Randy swallowed, his eyes drifting past Sara's face to the surging water behind her. "I sat there nodding, Sara," he continued, "and thinking about you, and how you stormed away Saturday night, just when we seemed so compatible. I didn't know what you wanted, what your problem was." A pensive laugh escaped him. "Another woman would have recognized that there was something pretty damned exciting going on between us, that when we kissed, when we touched, something spectacular exploded to life between us. And that would have been enough. But it wasn't enough for you."

"You were angry with me," Sara whispered.

"Livid. Furious. I spent nights pacing the floor. I never felt so frustrated in my life."

"No woman has ever said no to you before?" she asked.

Something flickered in his eyes, and he smiled. "Sure, women have said no to me. But it never left me so frustrated before. That should have told me something." His voice grew soft and contemplative again. "Then I saw Renee and listened to her complaining about how good sex was all Larry thought of, and how he refused to understand her, to try to see what was important to her, to climb inside her head and see what was going on in there. And once again, I thought about you. Renee was right, Sara. When you love someone you've got to get to know them that way. And I admitted that I really wanted to know you. I wanted to climb inside your head."

"Do you think you can?" Sara asked.

"I think I already have," Randy told her. "I confess I'm lost in there, but I'm trying to find my way."

"You think I'm wrong about your toys, don't you?" Sara hazarded.

"I think...I think you're seeing more in them than they really are. They're just something I use. Just like you use your broom and your fireplace and your table at the Willoughby House. They're what we do, not what we are."

"And what are we?"

"You're a woman who believes in love, honor and cherish," Randy claimed.

"And you?"

"I'm...I'm someone who thinks that a woman who puts that much value in such important things is a very rare person. Very special. Worth pursuing."

She measured his words, the husky, intense quality

of his voice convincing her that they came from his soul. "But you don't love me," she reminded him.

"I'm close," he swore. "Very close. Maybe I'm already there." He lifted her hands to his mouth and kissed each one tenderly. "If I did make love to you, Sara, it wouldn't be just because you turn me on, because I think you're unbelievably sexy. It would be because I... because I got into your head and learned my way around. Because I understood you."

"And do you? Do you understand me at all?"

He paused before answering. He thought about the time he had spent at the Village, the clean scent of the freshly turned farm acreage, the basic beauty of the rustic buildings, the hypnotic grace of Sara kneading her bread dough—creating nourishment out of flour, yeast, water and her own physical exertion—her love of what she was doing. "Yes," he declared. "I understand."

It was what she had hoped to hear, yet actually hearing it stunned her. She was afraid to look at him. Her gaze wandered to the glistening shells at her feet, to the water lapping the sand beside her, to the inn looming behind Randy's shoulders. His grip on her hand tightened slightly, and she felt his confession seeping into her, filling her. What he had revealed was more exciting than any "interesting experience" she could conceive of. "Then make love to me," she requested.

His eyes sharpened on her. "Here?" He scanned the public beach and the lit windows of the inn overlooking the water. "After last weekend, I'd think you'd be a bit concerned about nosy people barging in on us uninvited." He hesitated, then shook his head. "And I'm not going to take you back to my house. It obviously has a very unromantic effect on you."

"The inn," Sara suggested. "Is there a room at the inn?"

Randy's smile lit his face. He released one of her hands, clasped the other firmly, and led her across the beach to the stairs. They put on their shoes and walked around the building, through the front door and inside. Yes, there were rooms, the hostess told them, directing them to a lounge with a check-in desk. Randy hurriedly signed for a room, and they followed the quizzical young bellhop up a flight of stairs to a room at the end of the hall.

Sara absorbed the quaint decor—high ceiling, looming fireplace with carved mantel, flocked yellow wallpaper, chintz curtains and matching spread across the broad four-poster bed. She was hardly aware of Randy's tipping the boy, nudging him out the door, and hanging the DO NOT DISTURB tag on the brass doorknob before locking them inside.

He approached her eagerly yet cautiously, and curved his arms about her tiny waist. "Are you sure about this, Sara?" he whispered.

"Now that you've paid your money, I can't very well back out," she teased.

He remained sober. "I'm not kidding, Sara. I don't want to—"

She cut off his words with a kiss. She had to stand on tiptoe to reach him, but he quickly accommodated her, bending slightly to meet her avid mouth. As his kiss infused her body with its heat, she knew that this was right, making love with him was right. It transcended time. It was as primal, as fundamental as nature's design for man and woman. And it wasn't for sport, for entertainment, for the transient experience. It was a commitment between her and Randy, a commitment that at this moment they were both willing to make.

He understood her. Maybe not completely, but he understood her more than any man had understood her before, more than any man had even bothered trying to understand her. That was enough for now. It was more than enough.

His fingers worked their way down the small, cloth-covered buttons of her blouse, opening them. When he drew back the material and discovered her camisole, he sucked in his breath. "Oh, Lord, what is this?" he gasped, obviously thrilled.

"A camisole," Sara told him.

"Not double-knotted," he observed as he removed her blouse completely and indulged in an intense examination of the delicate silk garment. A slight frown crossed his face. "You were all set to make love to me all along," he complained. "I didn't even have to give you that long-winded speech."

She laughed and shook her head. "I wore this for me, not for you," she told him.

"Well, on behalf of whoever you wore it for, I'm very grateful." He left the camisole in place and turned his attention to her skirt, sliding it down over her narrow hips and letting it drop to the carpeted floor. Then he peeled off her sandy stockings, discovering the matching panties underneath. "Oh, Lord," he repeated. "Where in the world did you find this thing?"

She laughed again, an almost nervous giggle as she noticed the rapturous light in his eyes, the barely perceptible trembling in his fingers. "In a store," she replied weakly. "I thought it looked very old-fashioned."

"Uh-huh," he grunted. He shrugged off his blazer and unbuttoned his shirt, removing it with a solid purposefulness that mesmerized Sara. Simply looking at her seemed to arouse him fully, and looking at him aroused her as well. She reached for the hem of the camisole and started to lift it. He halted her. "Let me," he said.

His fingers reached the trimmed edge of the exquisite garment, then slipped beneath it to explore the softer silk of Sara's skin. She felt the heat of his body seeping through the smooth fabric to her breasts as his hands warmed her back, sliding up her spine, relishing the whisper of cloth against his knuckles, the whisper of her skin against his palms.

He opened his mouth to speak, but thought better of it and kissed her instead. His tongue probed hers, then retreated to taste her lips, her chin, her throat. Her head fell back as he grazed the slender white column of her neck, the graceful spread of her shoulders, the fragile projections of her collarbone. "Sara," he whispered. "Sara. I can't believe how much I want you."

She lifted her hands to his chest, relearning its strength and shape, her hands seeming to dance through the curling tendrils of hair that emphasized his masculinity. She let her fingers wander beneath his arms and down his sides, acutely aware of the wideness of his rib cage compared to her own dainty frame.

Randy eased a ribbon strap of the camisole off her shoulder, then let his hand dip beneath the slack lace trim to caress her breast. His lips followed his hand, pausing when the camisole blocked his path. Reluctantly, he lifted it from her shoulders and over her head. "Oh, Sara, Sara..." His voice emerged as a rough, rumbling groan as he gathered her against himself. "The best thing about wearing underwear like that," he whispered into her hair, "is that you can take it off."

"Is that so?" Her voice sounded airy and indistinct to her. Her hands had circled his back as his embrace obliterated the space between them, and now she stroked her fingertips along his skin, gently probing the muscles just above his belt. He sighed and leaned back into her hands. "Didn't I hear somewhere that you had a fetish about back rubs?" she asked, delighting in his immediate response to her massage.

"Sara, I've got a fetish about you. Whatever you do to me, that's what I've got a fetish about."

"Hmm." She pretended to consider various options. Randy caught her wickedly teasing glance and laughed, then preempted any ideas she might have had by wedging his fingers beneath the edge of her panties and sliding them down.

Sara sucked in her breath. She could no longer make jokes. The anticipation of Randy's lovemaking was rapidly approaching reality, and as the last bit of her clothing fell to the floor she could think only of him, of what it would be like to be loved by him, to be honored, to be cherished.

He stepped back to look at her, his gaze slowly, bewitchingly caressing her petite body. She longed for the feel of his hands on her, but instead he briefly turned his attention to himself, hastily shedding his trousers and shorts. Then he approached her, fitted her body to his, and commandeered her mouth with his.

She recalled the first time she had kissed him, in front of her house after the hockey game. She recalled how their bodies had molded together then, clothing and jackets notwithstanding. She recalled how amazed she had been that his huge frame could accommodate her small one so easily. Yet they fit, they fit perfectly. Randy's hips moved against hers, drawing her passion to the surface, inviting her to meet him, to share it with him.

Her reflexes accepted his invitation, matching his

movements, receiving his rhythm. Sara closed her eyes and buried her face against his shoulder, willing to make love to him standing up if he wanted. She couldn't bear the thought of releasing him long enough to cross the room to the bed.

She didn't have to. He lifted her into his arms and carried her, placing her on the mattress and lowering himself beside her. His lips ravaged hers, his hands ran the length of her body, his legs wove through hers. Sara's fingers raked across his chest in search of his heartbeat. She found it, rough, wild, primal, as fierce as her own.

This was what love was about, she knew: two bodies joining in the most old-fashioned union, the most elemental sharing. Her hands ventured down Randy's abdomen, then lower, mirroring his own hands in their journey down her body. He stroked her; she stroked him. He shuddered; she moaned.

Her hips rocked with his fingers, arching to him, longing for more intimate contact, yearning for the ultimate communion. She tried to lift him onto her, but he was much too big, too heavy. "Don't rush," he whispered, brushing her perspiration-damp hair from her face with his free hand, while his other hand continued to stimulate her. "I want this to last forever."

She closed her eyes and let her head sink into the pillow. Glorious waves of sensation seeped down through her, gathering in the well of her womanhood. He bowed to take her nipple into his mouth. At his tender sucking she moaned again, the sensation increasing to a precarious intensity. She wanted him. She needed him. She was ready for this, for him.

He seemed miraculously to sense her need—or maybe it wasn't a miracle. Maybe, she thought vaguely, it was that he was inside her head, understanding her, understanding her needs and wants. Or maybe it was simply that he was a man and she was a woman, and their bodies understood things that all the centuries of civilization could never change.

He rose up onto her, claiming her body with his, filling her with himself. Her hands clung to his shoulders, his head, his back, holding him, holding him as he drove them to a sublime moment of unity, when they were neither man nor woman anymore but something else, a single creature hovering on the brink of timelessness, waiting for heaven to shatter around them.

Sara cried out, her fingers digging deep into the muscles of his upper back as her flesh experienced that heaven, the throbbing release of ecstasy that overwhelmed knowledge, excitement, wonder. Randy accelerated his pace to reach her there, to share the splendor of it with her. Then he softened against her, unwilling to let go of her even as his muscles relaxed, as his spent body unwound.

Their chests clashed as they panted together. Randy gradually lifted himself up so that he could look at Sara. "Sara...I didn't plan this," he whispered hoarsely, some sort of apology.

"I know," she said, reassuring him.

"But I'm not sorry it happened."

"Neither am I," she said, smiling, reaching for his face, cupping her hand to his warm cheek.

He kissed her, then slid off her to regain his breath. They lay together on the rumpled bedspread, side by side, holding hands, assimilating what had happened. Sara knew that there had been love in this lovemaking, that it hadn't been a meaningless escapade, that Randy was as special to her as she was to him. She knew that he hadn't planned an elaborate seduction of her that evening. She knew that he was honest with her, that he was trying to understand her, that he was, if not madly in love, close.

She felt his hand moving languidly up her arm, dancing to its own private song. Maybe she loved him, too, she mused. If she didn't, she was close. Very close.

Chapter Seven

"Randy."

"Anything, lovely Sara," he whispered, lifting her hand to his mouth and pressing his lips into the yielding curve of her palm. "The answer is yes."

"Randy..." She sighed, relishing his tenderness, the liquid warmth that spread up from her hand through the veins of her arm to fill her entire body. "Randy, I'm not on the pill."

He grew still, continuing to hold her hand though his fingers seemed frozen into stone. He stared at the delicate white limb in his grasp, saying nothing for a long moment. Then, "What are you on?"

"Randy, I'm not—you must know me at least that well," she complained quietly

His fingers came to life again, slowly moving against her hand as he pondered her statement. He exhaled. "Why didn't you say something earlier?"

"Why didn't you?" she challenged.

"Guilty as charged," he muttered. He fell into deep silence, wrestling with his thoughts. Eventually he shifted onto his side and gazed down at her, a pensive frown darkening his expression. Exhaling once more, he released her hand and sat up. Still without speaking, he swung his legs over the side of the bed, stood, and crossed to his discarded clothing. He started to dress.

Sara gaped at him, aghast. Was this enough to shatter the closeness she felt toward him? Was this enough to smother the fragile love that had just begun to bloom between them? "Where are you going?" she asked nervously.

"Out in search of an all-night drugstore," he replied, sliding his arms through his shirt sleeves. He lifted his jacket and headed for the door. "Wish me luck."

Her worry faded. He would be back. He was upset but not angry. He would come back to her. "Good luck," she called to him as he vanished through the doorway, shutting the door behind him.

As she lay on the bed, her long black hair floating resplendently across the white pillowcase, she assessed what had happened, what would happen. Less than a minute passed, and already she missed Randy terribly.

When she was sixteen, her mother had dragged her to a gynecologist. "You have to be prepared," her mother had insisted. "You're a woman now." Sara hadn't felt like a woman, and her mother's concern had been absurdly premature. Later, again at her mother's insistence, she had started taking birth control pills, and when she met Stu, they finally served their purpose. However, she had stopped taking them the day she had returned to the apartment she and Stu shared, to discover his child standing in the foyer of the brownstone. At that moment she renounced men. There was no need to protect herself physically, as long as she protected herself emotionally.

She hadn't expected someone like Randy to enter her life.

She pulled herself up to sit, then reached with her feet for the floor. Restless, she prowled to the tiny bathroom that opened off the room. In the mirror above the sink she studied her face. Her eyes sparkled with silver light and her cheeks were touched with a rosy glow. Not a flush of embarrassment, but a flush of fulfillment. Her face looked changed to her. Was it happiness, she wondered, or was it something more? Was it the possibility that Randy had planted himself within her, that his seed had discovered a fertile place to flourish inside her?

The timing was wrong, Sara knew. That possibility was awfully slim. Yet the fact that the possibility appealed to her was itself a shock. There were more important gardens to sow, she realized, than the small plot in the yard behind her house.

She returned to the bed and waited. The minutes stretched out, each second lasting an eternity. She wanted Randy back. She wanted him with her. She wanted the excitement of his touch, his kisses....

Excitement? Had she suddenly been transformed into the sort of person who courted excitement? No. The excitement she felt in Randy's presence had nothing to do with the giddiness of "interesting experiences." It wasn't an outgrowth of boredom or frustration. It was a deeper, more intimate excitement, the excitement of two people daring to reach across a chasm of incomprehension, daring to step into the future together, daring to make a commitment.

At long last he returned. The time he had spent away from her had given him the opportunity to work through his thoughts, to remind himself once again that Sara wasn't like the women he usually socialized with. She wasn't the sort to be prepared for sex; after all, she hardly even dated. And even if she did, he suspected that she wouldn't do something as modern as taking birth control pills. Mrs. Willoughby never took birth control pills; Sara Morrow wouldn't, either.

The clerk downstairs had given him a perplexed stare when he'd inquired about a pharmacy. The inn had aspirin in stock, she assured him, if that was what he wanted. He'd mumbled something incoherent, and the clerk had directed him into town. Making his purchase, he'd felt like a teenager, as if he'd just embarked on his first sexual escapade. And in a way, it was a first time for him, the first time he'd ever lost himself so completely in a woman's love that he hadn't even paused to take precautions. It wasn't like Randy. He was always on top of things, modern, practical. Sara's mere presence had made him lose touch with reality.

It surprised him, but he wasn't sorry that it had happened. Beyond his concern about the consequences of what he'd done, he felt a strange, totally unreasonable thrill at acknowledging Sara's power over him. As completely irresponsible as it was, he didn't for a moment regret what they'd done.

He closed the door and locked it, undressed, and joined Sara on the bed. He gathered her into his arms, his hands moving tentatively over the smooth, pale skin of her back. She waited for him to speak, anxious to hear his reassurance, anxious for the music of his voice to wash over her. But he was still immersed in his own silent meditation.

"I should have said something," she apologized.

"I should have realized..." he refuted her, his own apology drifting off. "Sara, I'm inside, but I don't quite know my way around yet. You don't by any chance have a map, do you?"

She raised her face from his shoulder, bewildered. "A map?"

He eased her onto her back and studied her. "You know, like what they give out at Old Harkum Village, so people won't get lost or miss any of the points of interest." A wistful smile teased his lips as he tapped his index finger to her temple. "Here, for instance, is the Music Barn. A sturdy structure, representative of an earlier era. The barn isn't wired for electricity, so of course no Moog synthesizers can be played here." He lifted his finger, then pointed to the top of her head. "Here we have the Hockey House. One of Old Morrow Village's most recent acquisitions. As you can see, the frame is there, but the interior needs work before it's comfortable. And here—" he slid his finger to the base of her head "—here's the Old-Fashioned Church of Yesterday, where the residents of Old Morrow Village worship."

Sara laughed. "What an engrossing tour," she encouraged him. "Please continue."

Randy's smile grew poignant as he brought his finger forward, letting it rest at the center of her forehead. "Here's the Childhood House. It was built, oh, twenty-five, twenty-six years ago."

"Twenty-eight," Sara corrected him.

He nodded, then continued his tour-guide lecture. "You'll notice that the ceiling of the Childhood House is low, and yes, Miss Morrow was short. This house is much too small to contain all the sorrow and grief she stores here. But up in the loft she's got a special place for other children. She keeps sympathy there, and empathy." His smile broadened impishly. "And a game of Zinger to keep the kids occupied."

"No Zinger," Sara refuted. "Books and walks to the park."

"Hmm." Randy let his finger trace a line down to her cheek, then below the pucker of her pursed lips to the faint indentation above her chin. "I think there's a Stubborn House somewhere in the Village, too," he amiably complained. "In fact, I'm not sure where it is, but I think I've stumbled into it many times."

"It's not a house," she informed him. "More likely it's the road."

"Or maybe the ruts in the road," he readily agreed. His finger sketched the inviting curve of her lower lip. "Somewhere in this vicinity is the Man Place. Miss Morrow rarely uses this building. It's fallen into disrepair over the past year. As I understand it, Miss Morrow was planning to let it simply tumble to the ground, and then she was going to clear away the rubble and plow it into a farm."

"Is that what she was going to do?"

"According to her diary, a photocopy of which is on display in the main building..."

"You said she *was* going to clear it away," Sara murmured. "Has she changed her mind?"

"You tell me," Randy whispered, replacing his finger with his mouth.

Sara told him. Her kiss told him, her hands plunging into the velvet depths of his hair told him—her racing pulse, her rising desire, her body moving passionately against his told him all he needed to know about the place in the village of her soul that was dedicated to "Man."

SLEEPING IN EACH OTHER'S ARMS was simply too easy, too natural. Sara didn't remember the actual moment she fell asleep, but when a shaft of sunlight struck the bed she tried to sit up and discovered herself imprisoned by Randy's arm. His body was half draped over hers, his leg pinned her against the mattress, and his warm, dry breath brushed steadily over her shoulder.

She was able to move her head, and she turned to see his face close to hers. The sunlight struck his hair and ignited its blazing highlights. Sara realized that she had never really looked closely at Randy outdoors on a sunny day before. She hadn't known the multitude of tawny colors that lurked in the depths of his hair, requiring only the kiss of the sun to awaken them.

She watched him sleep, his face a peaceful mask, his body heavy and solid against hers. She hated having to rouse him. But it was Monday. Her day off, not his.

"Randy?"

He mumbled something indecipherable, then nestled his head deeper into the crook of her neck.

"Randy, you've got to get up." She struggled to free one hand and used it to shake his shoulder. "It's Monday."

"Monday." He flopped onto his back and opened his eyes, then rolled back to her. "Good morning," he whispered, gathering her up in his powerful embrace.

His mouth covered hers and his tongue slipped inside. Sara forgot about Monday, days off, obligations. To be kissed, to be held, to receive Randy's love was more important than anything else right now.

Slowly, reluctantly, he drew away, his eyes laboring to focus in the brightness. Sara's hands slid from his shoulders to his chest, tangling in the coppery hair that coated it. He groaned slightly, then yielded to the temptation of Sara's peripatetic fingers. He lowered himself onto her again, his mouth mining the sweetness of hers, his body blanketing hers. She ringed his waist with her arms and held him close.

"Monday," he gasped after breaking their kiss for air. "I wonder what time it is."

"You've got to go to work, don't you?" Sara guessed.

"Something along those lines, yes." His head dropped onto the pillow beside hers, his lips coming in contact with her ear. He couldn't resist the urge to run his tongue over the sensitive tip of the lobe

Sara moaned. She wanted him to make love to her again. Last night—time and again, long into the night—hadn't been enough Randy had teased her about trying to compensate for a year of abstinence, but that wasn't why she had responded so eagerly, so insatiably to Randy. It was him, Randy, she wanted Not just a man, but one man, one special man, the man who was determined to prove that she couldn't do without a man.

"I've got to go," he said, breathing into her ear "I've got a business to run."

"Then go," Sara teased him, her arms still gripping him firmly. "Who's stopping you?"

"You are and you know it"

She let her hands fall to the bed. Still he didn't move His lips grazed tenderly along the slope of her shoulder "I used to enjoy going to work," he groaned.

"You'll enjoy it again. Just be a big boy about it and get out of bed," Sara sternly admonished him.

"You first," he said.

"I can't. You're on top of me."

"Complain, complain, complain." He shoved himself up, and planted his hands on either side of Sara's head. His eyes showered her face with green sparks of joy. "All right. I'm going. Try to stop me."

"I won't," Sara swore, watching him lean back on his haunches, feeling a chill rush through her flesh now that he was no longer warming her.

He hesitated, giving her the opportunity to pull him back into the cradle of her arms. She laughed at his reluctance and kept her hands on the bed, away from his torso. "God, you *do* have willpower, don't you," he grudgingly conceded as he thrust himself off the bed. "Last night I never would have believed it."

Sara's cheeks colored but she didn't parry his affectionate needling of her. She knew they both would prefer to spend the rest of the century in bed together, but that wasn't a viable option. So someone had to take responsibility for getting them up and dressed. And since Randy wouldn't, she was forced to. She sat up and reached for his watch, which he had left on the night table beside the bed. "Eight-thirty," she told him.

He cursed.

"Does the boss get mad if you're late?" she asked with pretended innocence as she threw off the covers.

"I'm the boss, and yes, I get mad," Randy replied, trying to sound stricter than he obviously felt. "Eight-thirty." He reached for his trousers, pulled them halfway up his long legs, and then paused and cursed again.

"What?" Sara asked.

"I've got a nine o'clock appointment with some people from Grumman Aircraft." His movements shifted into high gear as he tossed Sara's clothing to her and then reached for his shirt. "We've got to get a move on."

Sara shook the sand from her now-dry stockings, then spread them out beside her and slipped on her camisole. She sensed Randy flagging behind her, and when she glanced over her shoulder she saw him watching her, his eyes radiating something closely resembling lust. He issued a ragged sigh and willfully marched himself into the bathroom so he wouldn't have to see her.

She smiled and finished dressing. The lacy blouse

and flared skirt seemed too dressy for a weekday morning, but it was all she had to wear.

Once they had groomed themselves—as well as they could without toothbrushes, hairbrushes, razors or combs—Randy spirited Sara from the room. They speedily checked out of the inn and scampered to the car. "We'll have to grab a bite on the way," Randy said contritely as he fired the Alfa-Romeo's powerful engine and steered out of the parking lot.

"I don't mind," Sara assured him.

'Do I look awful?" he asked as he cruised through the town in search of a fast-food joint. He found one and pulled up to the line forming at the drive-in window

Sara thought he looked utterly wonderful, but she forced herself to appraise him critically. "You could use a shave," she remarked, taking note of the pale stubble that had sprouted along his jawline overnight.

He nodded. "I keep an electric razor at the office, just in case."

"Just in case what?" she asked as they crept one car-length closer to their breakfast. "Does this sort of thing happen frequently?"

He shot her a quick look, but relaxed when he saw her teasing smile. "Sometimes, if I think I'm going to be spending the entire day tinkering in the lab, I'll skip shaving. And then if someone important shows up unexpectedly, I'm able to sneak back to my office and make myself presentable."

"Do you keep a tie there, too?" Sara asked.

He fingered his open collar as if he had forgotten about the requirements of business dress, then nodded. "I think I've got one somewhere. The jacket looks okay, doesn't it?"

"Fine," Sara told him, biting back the recurring urge to tell him how magnificent she thought he looked.

He steered up to a microphone protruding from the wall as Sara studied the menu printed beside it. "What do you want?" he asked her as he rolled down his window.

None of the items looked particularly appetizing to her, especially since she knew that they had all been cooked hours ago and miles away, and they would all be served in Styrofoam trays or wrapped in foil. Still, she had to eat something. "An English muffin," she finally decided. "And coffee."

"One English muffin," Randy hollered through his window at the lifeless microphone. "One egg-sausage sandwich. Two large coffees."

A disembodied metallic voice responded: "What do you want in the coffees?"

Randy glanced at Sara. "Black," she whispered, for some reason not wanting to be overheard by the microphone.

He nodded, then shouted through the window, "Two black."

The metallic voice recited, "One English muffin, one egg-sausage sandwich, two large coffees, black. Please drive to the pick-up window." A crackle of static, and the voice vanished. Randy dutifully drove ahead to the window.

Sara cringed. After the exquisite night she had spent with Randy in the restored inn, this breakfast was rocketing her back into the twentieth century with a vengeance. Microphones, speakers, plastic food containers, cars, lines, pick-up windows. No human contact. No sense of the food's having come from a natural source, from the earth's bounty. No feel of an egg in one's palm, its shell cracking, its contents being beaten, heated over a flame. No feel of the muffin dough being shaped from flour, water, yeast, shortening. When a uniform-clad youngster shoved a bag through the pick-up window to Randy, Sara entertained the notion that the food had begun exactly as it ended, taking shape right inside its logo-decorated wrappings.

While Randy paid and steered away from the window to the street, Sara unwrapped his egg sandwich, tucked a napkin between his thigh and the leather bucket seat, where it would be handy for him, and passed him his food. She nibbled her own muffin, which tasted rubbery and salty to her. Salted butter, she sniffed disapprovingly. She occasionally churned her own butter at the Village. Whatever had been spread across the limp muffin halves in her hand didn't much resemble the fresh butter she could make in her table-top wooden churn.

But this wasn't a meal to be savored. It was a modern meal for modern people on the run, people late for appointments, people who didn't have the time to taste what they were eating. Sara ate her muffin as if it were fuel necessary to keep her functioning. It was nothing more to her. It was simply modern, twentieth-century human fuel.

Once Randy had finished his sandwich, Sara removed the lid from his Styrofoam coffee cup and handed the cup to him. He navigated onto the Long Island Expressway, then took the cup and managed to take a long quaff without spilling any on himself. Sara sipped her own coffee, which tasted unfortunately weak to her, and stared out the window at the racing traffic on the dreary commuter highway. The Northern State Parkway, which they had used the previous evening to drive to the inn, was a much more picturesque road, bordered by mature plantings and lined with low wood fences rather than concrete and steel railings, but the Expressway was a more direct route. It was a modern road, Sara mused, a modern road for modern people in a hurry.

Randy drained his cup in a few long gulps. Handing the empty cup back to her, he said, "I think the best strategy is for me to drive directly to my office. I can arrange to have someone give you a lift home from there if you'd like. As it is, I'm going to be late for this meeting."

"Whatever is easiest for you," Sara generously offered. "If the meeting won't be too long, I could even wait until you're done."

He eyed her briefly, a pleased smile curving his mouth. "That would be nice, if you wouldn't mind. I don't know how long the meeting's going to take, though. We'll see how it plays." He reached past the gear stick to clasp her hand. "I'm really sorry about having to rush off to this stupid meeting. If I..." He hesitated.

"If you what?" Sara coaxed him.

"If I had known what was going to happen last night, I would have planned things out better. But—" he cast her another pleased smile "—last night exceeded my wildest fantasies. It was definitely worth oversleeping for."

Sara squeezed his hand. If Randy had planned last night, he would have arranged for a wake-up call or brought an alarm clock, and instead of awakening naturally they would have been roused by the noisy intrusion of some bell or buzzer. She tacitly agreed that it was better to oversleep. Reflecting on their breakfast and their breakneck commute to Randy's place of business, she mused that it would have been even better to have continued to oversleep, to have refused to answer the summons of the real world.

He turned off the expressway and followed a major thoroughfare to a recently constructed industrial park. He drove through the marked gate onto a newly paved road that meandered past one building and then another. The buildings were well spaced and modern, almost all constructed of concrete and glass and skirted by crowded parking lots. The only features that distinguished one building from the next were the identifying signs standing by their entrance driveways.

Sara observed the scene through her side window and played with the idea that the industrial park, with its flat, grassy lawns and its marked buildings, was an enclosed village, curiously similar to Old Harkum Village—a hermetic environment representing a specific era. Of course, the industrial park represented modernity, the present tilting toward the future. It was a village, but not one Sara would want to live and work in.

Randy coasted up a long straight driveway leading to a building favored by a bit of stone mingled with the concrete and glass. A sign reading Zaleco in bronze letters was fastened to the wall beside the glass double doors. The building was on the small side, one story high, with a flat roof. The few shrubs flanking the front walk and entry—yews, azaleas not yet blossoming, and huckleberry—were immature and scrawny-looking.

A parking space close to the walk was vacant, although nearly every other space in the lot was taken, and Sara quickly understood that the spot was reserved for Randy. He climbed out of the car, locked his door, and darted around to fetch her, chivalrous despite his being late. Taking her hand, he hurried with her up the walk through the door and into a spacious reception area. With a brisk nod to the woman seated behind the receptionist's desk, he tugged Sara down a side hall to its end. His greater height compelled Sara to jog to keep pace.

He shoved open a door and they entered a large, rectangular office. An attractive woman not much older than Sara sat at an enormous L-shaped desk, much of which was occupied by an elaborate word processor. Behind the desk stood a long counter that contained another computer. A window overlooked a flat stretch of dry grass to the rear of the building. A sofa and a coffee table covered with magazines stood against a wall.

The woman looked up from the screen of her word processor. She had short brown hair, a pixieish face and long fingers. A crisp beige suit with a dark brown crepe de chine blouse flattered her lean figure. "Randy!" she exclaimed as he entered. "Where in the world—"

"I know, I know," he cut her off, stalking across the carpeted floor to another door. Before opening the door, he said, "Sara, this is Charlotte Webster. Charlotte, Sara Morrow." Then he disappeared into his inner office.

Charlotte gaped at the open door through which Randy had vanished, then turned her perplexed gaze to Sara, whom he had stranded in the middle of the room. Charlotte appeared about to question Sara, but before she could, Randy was calling out to her. "Are the people from Grumman here yet?"

"I put them in the small conference room," she reported, having to shout over the grating buzz of his electric razor. "They're on their second round of coffee. Where the hell have you been?"

"'Call me irresponsible, call me unreliable,'" he crooned through the open door. The buzzing stopped and he appeared in the doorway, a pale blue striped tie wrapped around his neck. "This tie looks lousy, doesn't it?"

Charlotte pressed her lips grimly together. "Randy, if you keep those men waiting any longer, they're going to tie it into a noose and string you up." She stood and carried a stack of folders from her desk to him. "Shake a leg, pal. Time and Grumman wait for no man."

"We shall see," Randy countered, manipulating his tie into the semblance of a knot. He turned to Sara. "Charlotte, in case you haven't noticed, is Zaleco's salaried shrew. Is this knot even?" Before Sara could speak he gauged it with his hand, frowned, and took a long step toward her. "Please fix for me, will you?"

Sara felt awkward engaging in such a personal activity in front of Charlotte, but she didn't dare refuse. As she adjusted the knot and smoothed his collar, he lifted the top folder from the stack Charlotte held for him, opened it and scanned a page of figures in it. His eyes absorbed the multitude of numbers, and Sara could almost hear the calculations whirring in his brain as he assimilated them.

"There," she said shyly, letting her hands fall from the tie.

Randy bent down and kissed her lightly on the lips. "Thanks a million. I've got to run. If you get bored... Charlotte," he said, turning to his assistant, "if Sara gets bored, give her a lift home, okay? Her wish is your command."

"As is yours, Lord Zale," Charlotte said huffily. "Get out of here before you lose a few million in billings."

Randy blew out the door like a tornado, leaving the two women stunned in the sudden stillness of his absence. Charlotte gave Sara a careful examination—evidently disapproving of her loose, flowing hair and her alluring feminine attire—before returning to her desk. Sara opened her mouth to offer an explanation of her presence, but the woman cut her off before she could speak. "I don't want to know," Charlotte said brusquely. "It's Randy's business, not mine."

Sara wondered whether by business she meant Randy's reason for arriving at work fifteen minutes late with a strange woman in tow, or Zaleco itself. She offered a feeble smile to the gruff woman and lowered herself onto the sofa, where she hid behind a magazine. She hoped the men with whom Randy was to meet wouldn't be too irritated by his tardiness.

Yet his racing through the building, his frantic grooming, his abrupt disappearance all unnerved Sara. She was used to the more leisurely flow of life at the Village, where if she didn't have too many visitors at the Willoughby House she could stroll down the dirt road to visit Annie at the Boodner House, or Ira, her betrothed, at the shoemaker's shop. How bizarre, she thought, that Randy's work at Zaleco was hectic because millions of dollars were at stake, while people who lived a century and a half ago were so much more relaxed in their Old Harkum Village type of communities, where what was at stake in their daily toil was the very survival of their families.

That was what happened today, she thought, ignoring the magazine article before her as her mind pursued its own concerns. That was twentieth-century living: no longer striving for the essence of survival, the day-to-day struggle to put food on the table, to warm a house, to clothe one's children. Modern-day people invented their own struggles: prefabricated breakfasts eaten in moving cars in order to get to one's place of business—one of many ugly, modern structures with windows that don't open, in an ugly, modern industrial park off the Long

Island Expressway—in order to meet with a bunch of aircraft builders, all in order to earn a million dollars for one's company, and to pay the rent on the ugly, modern building and the breakfast bill at the fast-food drive-in. The epitome of modern life.

And that, the previous night notwithstanding, was the life Randy had chosen for himself. The inn, Sara admitted, was someplace special to him, someplace unusual, someplace for a dinner, for a night of love. But it wasn't an integral part of Randy's life. His life was Zaleco, selling computer systems to Grumman Aircraft, paying the salary of a gruff assistant who seemed completely at home with the two computers that graced her office. This was Randy's life, Zaleco and his house with its ridiculous contraptions, its doodads and doohickeys, its Zingers and joysticks. Last night, Sara thought, wasn't what Randy's life was all about. He might enter Sara's head, but he could visit there only as a tourist, unsure of the language, unable to handle the currency, fascinated by the alien world but certainly not at home in it.

He could visit, but he could never become a citizen of Sara's universe. It was too far from his own. No map had been drawn that would ever give him a sense of belonging there. And glancing about her at the neat, sterile office, at the two computer terminals, their screens flashing with green messages and symbols, Sara was forced to acknowledge that Randy would probably never want to be more than a visitor to her world. He would never apply for a permanent visa. He would never leave his own world.

"How are you?" Charlotte called out to her.

She peered up from her magazine, hoping her depressing thoughts weren't visible in the pallor of her cheeks, in the heavy slope of her eyelids. "What?"

"Randy wants to know how you are."

"I..." Sara's eyes searched the room, though she knew full well that Randy hadn't returned. "I don't understand," she managed.

Charlotte tapped her fingers impatiently on the keys of her word processor. "He just punched in a message from the conference room through the computer there. He wants to know how you're doing."

"Oh." Sara strained to read the brief message lit up on the word processor's screen, but was unsuccessful. "I'm fine."

"Thank you," Charlotte grumbled, clearly not thrilled about being cast in the role of messenger. Her fingers flew across the keyboard in quick communication to Randy. Then she read the screen and announced, "I'm supposed to ask you if you want a lift home."

Sara almost declined but then gave the idea serious consideration. She felt uncomfortable in Randy's building, surrounded by territory as unfamiliar to her as her mind must have been to him. She tried to ignore the look of mild disgust on Charlotte's face and said, "If it wouldn't be too much trouble..."

Charlotte harrumphed. "As a matter of fact, I've got plenty enough to keep me busy this morning. I don't have time to be doing chauffeuring chores."

"Oh," Sara acceded. "Well, then, don't bother."

Charlotte glared at her, then at the screen before her. "I'll find someone else to take you home," she offered, tapping a message into the computer.

Sara expected Charlotte to leave the office, or to try to reach a colleague on the telephone, but she continued to work at the computer. Evidently that was the way the employees of Zaleco communicated. Sara found it horridly impersonal, but she remained silent as

Randy's assistant hammered the keys with her long angular fingers.

After a few mintues, the outer door to the office opened and a tall, thin man with a slender, pleasant face, olive-toned skin and a mop of thick brunette hair peered in. His gaze immediately fell on Sara. "You're Sara?" he asked.

She flinched. "Who are you?" she asked.

"I'm Larry Canning. I guess I've been volunteered to drive you home."

Larry. Randy's friend Larry. Petey's father. Sara stared at him with unabashed curiosity. She immediately perceived the resemblance between Petey and his father. "If it's a problem," she demurred, "I can wait for Randy."

"Randy's meeting is going to take up most of the morning," Charlotte declared with such certainty that Sara suspected the grim woman would lock the men into the conference room rather than let them adjourn early.

"It's no problem," Larry insisted. "Come on."

Feeling like an unwelcome burden to be disposed of, Sara reluctantly stood up, smoothed out her skirt, and nodded her farewell to Charlotte. She followed Larry down the long hall, through the lobby and outside.

Larry's flashy red Firebird was parked next to Randy's Alfa-Romeo, giving the impression that Randy's good friend was the second in command at Zaleco. Yet clearly he did his boss's bidding, even when it came to driving home the previous night's date.

Sara took her seat beside him in the car, and Larry backed out of his spot. "Directions?" he cued her.

She provided him with the easiest route, using the Long Island Expressway. Once he was on the broad highway he hazarded several measuring glances at her "Randy's told me a bit about you," he revealed.

"Oh?" Sara was too tactful to mention that Randy had also told her a bit about Larry.

"He told me you were beautiful. I must say, he wasn't lying," Larry flattered her. When Sara said nothing, he continued, "He says you work at some restoration village, is that right?"

"Old Harkum Village," she told him.

"That must be weird," he pondered aloud. "Randy says you get paid to dress up in a floor-length uniform and knead bread." He shook his head. "Must make you feel like you're living in another world."

"It does," she admitted, not bothering to add that that was the job's major appeal, as far as she was concerned.

She pointed out her exit, and Larry turned off the highway. His car's engine was loud, its rumble echoing inside Sara's head. A vague discomfort enveloped her; she wanted to leave his car, to leave his company. She didn't want to be seated next to the man who was enmeshed in some ridiculously contrived difficulty with his wife. She didn't want to be seated next to the man who worked with Randy in some futuristic computer universe. She wanted to bolt from his car, to breathe some clean, clear air, to recover from her overdose of modernity.

She woodenly directed him to her block, to the drab, modest house she rented, so like the tract houses surrounding it, a remnant of an earlier philosophy of innovation. Yet that morning, her house looked more welcoming than it ever had before. Inside the house were her plants, her seedlings, the natural things she had nurtured. Behind the house was her garden. She would work the soil that day and thc next, and on

Wednesday she would be back at Old Harkum Village, back in period dress, back in the safe yesteryear world where she belonged.

With a hasty thank-you, Sara dashed from the shocking-red car up her walk to the front door and shut herself inside.

Chapter Eight

"I'm really sorry about this morning."

Randy's voice purred through the telephone wire to Sara. She had been outdoors mulching the soil of her garden when she heard the phone ring through her open kitchen window. She had rinsed the dirt from her hands but had not dried them before answering the phone, and now she blotted the excess water from her fingers on the legs of her overalls.

"Don't worry about it," she assured him softly.

"The meeting went on forever," he continued. "If I didn't need those folks to keep my company solvent, I would have walked out on them. I'm sorry Larry had to drive you home."

"It's all right," Sara insisted.

"So. Free at last." Randy sighed happily. "Can I see you tonight?"

Sara bit her lip and gazed out the window. She spotted the red-white-and-blue mail truck turning the corner onto her block. The letter carrier parked the truck and then emerged, toting a leather sack over his shoulder. Her gaze followed him for a moment, then alit on the Sharkey house next door.

"I'm afraid not," she told Randy. "I've been invited to dinner by some friends." It was the truth; less than an hour ago, Jean had accosted Sara over the lilac hedge that separated their yards and demanded that she have supper with the Sharkeys that evening. "You haven't had dinner with us in ages," Jean had pointed out. "I want an update on Randy."

As she tended her garden plot, Sara had been thinking about what sort of update she would provide. She was disturbed by thoughts of the morning she had spent in Randy's world. Those thoughts superseded her happy thoughts of the evening Randy had spent in her world. She felt out of sorts, out of kilter, suffering from time warp.

"Are you free tomorrow night?" Randy broke into her troubling ruminations.

She exhaled. "Randy, I... I don't know," she admitted. "I... I've got to think some things over."

He hesitated before venturing "What things?"

His voice was soft, husky, enticing. Closing her eyes, Sara could picture him as he was last night, hovering above her in the inn's fantasylike room, his body stripped of everything but the primal essence of his masculinity. Last night they had soared beyond the edge of time. But this morning... this morning he had eaten plastic food and run a nasally buzzing electric razor over his cheeks and raced off to sell computer systems to airplane manufacturers. "I've got to think about what happened to us," she confessed quietly. "I wasn't... I wasn't at all prepared for last night, and—"

"Sara," he broke in firmly. "That's the fault of both of us; we're both responsible. I'm not going to run out on you if... if there are consequences we weren't counting on."

"That wasn't what I meant," she told him, though his willingness to accept responsibility pleased her.

He hesitated again. "What do you mean?" he asked.

How could she explain? How could she put into words the confusion she felt? She and Randy had made a commitment to each other last night, but it was a simple commitment to make when they were so far from reality. Randy had been a tourist passing through her universe. Thoughts of love blossomed easily in a foreign country, where the atmosphere was laden with romance and the real world was forgotten. "I mean I need some time to think," she told him, her voice small and tight.

"To think about what?"

"About us."

He remained silent for a moment. "Sara, I thought last night was something special."

"It was," she readily agreed. *Too* special, she added mentally. It was the very specialness of it that allowed them to forget about their vast differences in outlook, in manner, in values. "Randy, I don't know what's bothering me. We're so...different. In spite of last night, we just seem awfully different to me." She waited for him to comment, but he said nothing, and she felt obliged to add, "Maybe...maybe I'm just not as ready as I thought I was last night." She knew that wasn't the truth; she was completely ready to love Randy, only not the Randy he actually was. She was ready to love the Randy she wanted him to be.

"Oh, Sara." He sighed. "Sara, I can't really get into a big philosophical discussion with you right now. I'm in my office with a dozen projects demanding my attention. When can we talk?"

"I don't know," she answered candidly. "I've got to do some thinking first."

He sighed once more, a broken, hoarse sound. "Why don't you call me when you're ready, then?"

"Fine," she promised. "I'll do that."

He gave her his home telephone number and then reluctantly bade her good-bye. Sara hung up the phone and realized that her shoulders were shaking. Her eyes were damp.

This was why she had shut herself off from men—because no man could ever totally fit her ideal. No man could ever truly understand her scheme of things, her wishes and desires and yearnings. Randy had come close, much closer than she had ever imagined a man capable of coming. But then he had left. He had returned to Zaleco. In spite of his efforts, he was a modern man.

It oughtn't to hurt so much, she thought as she abandoned her kitchen for the front door to fetch her mail. *It oughtn't to hurt so much to do the sensible thing.* She could never be comfortable with Randy and his toys. To break things off with him was only reasonable. She didn't need Randy Zale.

Her mailbox contained two bills—calculated and printed by computer, she noted—and a personal letter bearing the return address of the high school where she used to teach. She carried her mail back to her kitchen and slit the envelope open with a knife. Out fell a letter and three copies of a form. Sara read:

Dear Ms. Morrow:

Enclosed you will find, in triplicate, the change-of-grade forms needed to enable your former student, Vincent Chesler, to graduate from our school with his class this year. We have discussed his case on the telephone, and you have made your opinions known. However, I ask you to reconsider and to sign the enclosed forms and return them to my office.

We have debated many times your archaic theories regarding the evaluation of students, as well as our school's policy in this matter. I agree with you that Vincent Chesler is something of a troublemaker, but for the personal safety and satisfaction of the school staff and students, it would be most advisable for him to be graduated from this school.

I have spoken a number of times with Mr. Chesler, and he has expressed his deep concern about graduation. He holds you directly responsible for the one failing grade that currently stands as an obstacle to his graduation. It is clear to me that, at this point, whether or not Mr. Chesler learns the Articles of the Constitution or the particulars of the War of 1812 is irrelevant. He is a powder keg, and my concern is with the continued safe functioning of the school.

Therefore I strongly urge you to act on behalf of expediency in this matter. We cannot save every soul that passes through our lives. Sometimes we must take a more modern, pragmatic approach to such issues. All I am asking for is one letter upgrade for one student. Surely you can do this without betraying your admirable but rather outdated principles.

Sincerely,
Donald Corcoran

Sara grimaced. She reread the letter, her disdain evident in the curl of her delicate lips, in the deep crease denting the narrow bridge of her nose. Good Lord, the man was begging her to sell out just because he was afraid of one snotty student! He was asking her to be "modern" and "pragmatic" in order to solve his own problems.

No way. Not a chance. One hundred fifty years ago, a

petty thug like Turk Chesler would have been caned by the schoolmaster and, if corporal punishment were not effective, thrown out of the school to fend for himself Sara didn't exactly approve of thrashing misbehaving students, but she believed that strict discipline was more effective in shaping character than easing the path for troublemakers. Donald Corcoran wanted to get Turk out of his own hair by dumping the surly, nasty, ill-prepared youth on society.

The Articles of the Constitution were relevant, Sara fumed. So was the history of the War of 1812, the Monroe Doctrine and Manifest Destiny. The things that had shaped the nation in its adolescence were the same things shaping its current movement toward maturity. History was the greatest teacher. Turk deserved to learn these things—he deserved to be taught them Just because he had successfully resisted Sara's attempts to teach him didn't mean that he should be congratulated and granted a diploma for his complete lack of effort.

She didn't want to think about it. She didn't want to think at all. Striding to her back door, she stormed outside to her garden and immersed herself in the loamy black soil, relishing its damp, lumpy texture, its pungent smell, the wholesome essence of it, unencumbered by convenience or modernity.

At five, she returned to her house, showered, dressed in fresh jeans and a plaid blouse, and headed next door to the Sharkey house. Pipsqueak answered her knock on the back door with the shrill announcement, "Watch your step!"

When she entered, she saw the reason for his warning. At least a hundred baseball cards were scattered across the floor, and he was trying to gather them up in order. Jimmy was standing on a chair in the center of the room, changing a light bulb in the overhead fixture. Mick lounged by the refrigerator, still in his work clothes but with his tie loosened, slugging a beer directly from the can. Donna was polishing her fingernails at the table. And amid the bedlam, Jean placidly cut vegetables into a salad bowl. "Come on in, Sara," she called over her shoulder. "Join the fray."

Eventually Jimmy descended, the last baseball card was retrieved, Donna's nails were dry, and dinner—a tuna casserole—was served. Pipsqueak described to Sara his and his father's attempts to loft the kite she had helped him to build. "We went to Bethpage State Park. Sara, it was the plainest kite there," he complained. "There were these kids with aluminum foil kites, and then these kites that looked like snakes in the air, and box kites and stuff. These stingray kites, with wings. Mine didn't fly right. It was too plain."

"That's not why it didn't fly," Mick argued, reassuring Sara. "It's a fine kite. Like the ones I used to make as a kid. Those fancy ones gave me the creeps."

"The fancy ones are neat," Pipsqueak insisted. "I want an aluminum foil one."

"Enough," Jean silenced him before turning to Sara. "Now, tell us, how have you been?"

"Busy," Sara answered evasively. "I'm getting married."

"Married!" The entire Sharkey family erupted in squeals and gasps.

"At the Village," Sara explained with a smile. She told the Sharkeys about the lovely dress being sewn for her, about the apple and currant pies she was planning to bake for Ira Lipton, and the leather shoes he was making for her, about the Village's interpreters who had been selected to portray her parents, her maid of honor, the best man and minister. "You can all come, of course," she invited them. "It should be a lot of fun."

"Do we have to get all dressed up?" Pipsqueak worried aloud.

"What do you know?" Donna asked contemptuously, her fingernails glinting a garish pink in the light. "It's a wedding, stupid."

"You can wear whatever you want," Sara consoled Pipsqueak. "Jeans, shorts, whatever suits you. Only the members of the wedding have to dress appropriately."

"We'll mark it down on the calendar," Jean promised. "Of course we'd love to see you married."

Sara knew that her friend wanted to hear more about her relationship with Randy, but Jean politely refrained from asking questions about him over dinner. Once the casserole had been consumed and the children wandered off to do their homework in front of the television set, which Mick had turned on to an Islanders play-off game, Sara helped Jean to clean up the kitchen.

"A little peace and quiet," Jean said, sighing contentedly after pouring two cups of coffee and settling with Sara at the table. "Now, tell me, what's going on with you? How are things progressing with Randy?"

Sara exhaled. "I don't know, Jean," she replied. "He's so different from me."

"Oh?" Jean patiently awaited more.

"He's a computer whiz." When Jean remained silent, Sara went on. "Jean, he's so...so twentieth-century. When we're enjoying each other's company, it's only because one of us has bought a ticket on H. G. Wells's time machine. But it's always a round-trip ticket. Randy goes back to the twentieth century, and I go back to wherever it is I belong."

Jean appeared bemused, but she nodded sympathetically. "Do you like him?"

Sara studied her coffee. It looked so much more appealing in a ceramic mug than in a plastic cup. It tasted more flavorful, too, she decided as she sipped. "Yes," she admitted. "I like him. But that's not enough."

"What would be enough?"

"If... if he changed. But he won't. I couldn't possibly ask him to. I'm not dumb enough to try to change him." Sara sighed glumly. "I must be abnormal, Jean. His world is completely alien to me, full of gadgets and video gizmos and computers. I just don't fit in there. It's probably my fault, but—"

"It isn't a fault," Jean argued gently. "It's just a matter of personality. And you aren't abnormal."

"Maybe I am." She told Jean about the letter she had received that afternoon from her former boss concerning Turk Chesler. "A normal person would just go ahead and sign the change-of-grade forms and forget about it," she muttered. "Why can't I?"

"Because you're true to your beliefs," Jean replied. "That's nothing to be ashamed of."

"Even though I'm inconveniencing a lot of people?"

"Their convenience isn't your problem," Jean pointed out. "You've got to be true to your beliefs. If Turk Chesler runs amok, it's the school's fault, the system's fault, not yours. If the system operated on your values instead of on its own, Turk Chesler probably would have turned out much better than he did."

"You're so damned sensible, Jean," Sara teased. "How do you do it?"

"It's either stay sensible or go nuts. I'd rather not go nuts, so..." Jean shrugged placidly. A burst of activity in the living room—Pipsqueak shrieking, Jimmy responding in kind, and then Mick interceding in an ominously booming voice—caused Jean to laugh. "I teeter toward nuts a million times a day, Sara. Sometimes it just helps to tune out everything that goes against your grain. Just tune them out, pretend they don't exist, march to your own drummer and all that. It's the only way."

"You're right," Sara concurred enthusiastically. "You're absolutely right."

WOMEN, RANDY GRUMBLED bitterly as he climbed out of his car and loosened his poorly matched tie. He strode briskly up the walk to his house, let himself inside, and slammed the door shut.

Women. Sara. Why was she backing off? He thought they had finally made contact, reached each other, gotten beyond all the superficial stuff about microwave ovens versus fireplaces. So what *was* her problem?

She wanted to think. Fine, he grunted as he prowled to the kitchen. Let her think. Maybe if she thought long and hard enough, she'd realize that something far more powerful than their differences drew her and Randy together. He had to have faith that if she thought about it, she'd admit the obvious.

He flicked his hand across the refrigerator's electric eye and the door swung open. He stared blankly at the contents and found nothing particularly appealing to eat. Even after that ghastly fast-food breakfast, and after skipping lunch, he had no appetite.

Crossing to his rotating bar, he punched the button that brought his liquor supply back to the kitchen from the den. He poured himself a Campari, took a long sip, and lowered the glass. His eyes circled his kitchen, acutely aware of the whimsical paraphernalia that cluttered it. Was this really enough, he wondered. Was a rotating bar and an electric-eye refrigerator really enough to turn Sara away from him?

He liked his toys. He shouldn't have to defend them to her. He took pride in his inventiveness. The day he'd rigged the bar, he had invited Larry and Renee over for a celebratory drink, and they'd spent the better part of an hour making the damned bar spin around and giggling at its delightful novelty. It didn't make or break Randy's life, but it was fun. Couldn't Sara take it for what it was?

It wasn't his toys that bothered her, he knew. It was Randy himself. She was still afraid of men, and he supposed he couldn't blame her, given the life she'd lived. She was afraid of "normal, typical" men, the sort of men who were looking only for fun, for a moment's entertainment, for no-strings-attached physical compatibility. The way Larry was these days with Renee. The way Randy used to be before he met Sara.

He left the kitchen and wandered downstairs to his basement workshop. A wry laugh escaped him as he considered what Sara would think of the lablike room. Two computers—one personal, one for business—stood on a counter along one wall, and a workbench cluttered with various gadgets in need of repair or improvement ran along another wall. Randy dropped onto his swivel stool and studied the tangle of wires feeding out of a stereo speaker he'd been rigging from scrap pieces. He didn't feel like working, but his workshop was the place to which he usually retreated when he needed to think.

He ought to just write Sara off, he considered as he sipped his drink. He ought to just chalk her up as a weirdo, eye-catching and incredible in bed but with no future for them. He'd never thought of a woman in terms of a future anyway. Why not simply accept Sara as his latest conquest and move on?

Because he wasn't interested in conquests. He never had been. He had always viewed women as his equals, and making love with them was a mutual conquest, not a one-sided ego trip.

And besides, if anyone had been conquered, it had been Randy. Sara had captivated him; he was the one aching for her. She offered so much more than any other woman had ever offered him—commitment, principles. Values that, while painfully old-fashioned in their way, were refreshing, noble. He wanted what she had to offer. And now she was pulling back, refusing him.

Maybe if she didn't call, he'd get himself back on track, back into the groove he'd been gliding along for years. His life would run smoothly again, like a beautifully programmed computer system. He'd forget about the petite, dark-haired woman, the strongest, and ironically the most vulnerable, woman he'd ever met.

No, he wouldn't forget about her. He had to believe she'd figure out whatever was bothering her and call him. He had to. He didn't want to give her up.

ON WEDNESDAY at the Village, preparations for Sara's and Ira's wedding shifted into high gear. They and the other participants in the ceremony were issued a complicated schedule of activities to mark the celebration, and a rehearsal was planned. Sara and Ira were invited to participate in the design of their "wedding announcement" and "invitations"—Old Harkum Village's special publicity arrangements for the event.

Sara was excited about the wedding, but the exuberant planning didn't rouse her from the vague lethargy gripping her. She felt logy and tired, a bit queasy. Her head ached, and she found herself longing for five o'clock to arrive so she could go home.

When she finally arrived at her modest Levittown house, she discovered the reason for her ill temper and discomfort. She had gotten her period.

She showered, pulled on a bathrobe, and wandered to the kitchen to prepare herself a cup of tea. As she sipped it, she thought about Randy. She ought to tell him. Surely he was concerned about their carelessness last Sunday night, and she owed it to him to inform him that he need not worry.

Yet she wasn't sure what to say to him beyond that. Should she tell him she missed his magically sparkling eyes, his infectious smile, his warm humor, his hair tinged with fire and light? Should she tell him she missed his potent touch, his sweet kisses, the effort he made for her? That would all be true.

But it was also true that she knew his effort wasn't enough and never would be, and that she had no right to expect more from him. It was true that he was under no obligation to change himself for her—as if he even could. She wanted him to be as true to himself as she was to herself; she couldn't bear the thought of his changing just to satisfy her.

She drained her cup and stood, resolved. She did have to call him. Given his sense of responsibility, he might have been kept awake at night. She had to put his mind to rest.

On the counter beside her telephone she found the sheet of paper where she had jotted down his telephone number. Shoring up her nerve, she dialed.

"Hello." He sounded tense and breathless to her. What had she interrupted?

"Randy?" she asked hesitantly.

"Sara!" He was silent for a moment, then, "Sara, thank goodness you called. Something terrible has happened."

"What?"

"Petey's run away."

This time Sara was struck mute. Eventually her lips began to function again. "Oh, Randy! Tell me what happened."

"I had invited him to have dinner with me tonight. Renee thought Larry was going to pick him up and drive him to my place. Larry thought Renee was going to bring him over." He sighed wearily. "Somewhere in the crossed wires, he disappeared."

"Have you called the police?"

"Renee did, about a half hour ago. I just got off the phone with her again. She's beside herself. Larry's driving through the neighborhood. The police told me to stay here in case he shows up." He paused. "Sara, help me out. You understand him. What do you think he's up to?"

"Obviously he wants attention," she stated with certainty. How many times had she, as a child, contemplated equally foolish measures to capture her parents' attention when they seemed to be ignoring her and her needs? "He feels neglected. Maybe he thinks this will bring his parents back together again."

"Maybe," Randy mused. "Sara, look, I can't tie up the phone. Would you come over? Perhaps you could give the police some ideas. I bet Petey would love to see you. He knows you've been through it all. He relates well to you. Will you come over?"

"Of course." She didn't have to think. She understood Petey very well and she wanted to help him.

"Good. Just come. I'll see you soon." Sara heard a click on the line, and then dead air.

She hung up, jogged to her bedroom, and slipped on her jeans and a loosely knit rose-colored sweater. After a cursory brushing of her hair, she raced from the house to her car and headed for Randy's home.

She parked beside his Alfa-Romeo at the end of the long driveway. Ignoring the appalling avant-garde architecture of his house, she hurried up the lantern-lined walk to his front door and pressed the chime. Randy answered almost immediately.

Sara stood motionless on the doorstep, transfixed by his appearance. He looked so handsome, she thought, her gray eyes delighting in the clean angles of his face, in the plush thickness of his hair, in the tall, lean lines of his body, clothed in dark green corduroy slacks and a green-and-white striped rugby shirt. For a moment she was willing to suspend her memory of their differences All she wanted was to feel his arms around her, his lips taking possession of hers.

"Come on in," he said, ushering her through the door.

His slightly frantic tone quelled her erotic longings, and the loud rumbling noise emerging from his kitchen caused her to flinch. "What's that?" she asked, unable to identify the strident mechanical sound.

"An ice-crushing machine," he answered. "Larry's here. He's fixing himself a drink."

Sara followed Randy into his grotesque living room Within a minute Larry joined them, a tumbler filled with Scotch and crushed ice clutched in his hand. His face was ashen, his business suit rumpled. "Sara," he greeted her with a nod.

"Do you want a drink?" Randy offered. She shook her head.

Larry bore down on her immediately. "Sara, Randy says you've been through what Petey's going through.

Please tell me, why would he do something like this? Why would he do this to us?"

Sara bit back the harsh reply that instinctively rose to her lips—that Petey did this because he felt ignored, because he felt unloved and unwanted, because he needed his self-centered parents to prove that they still cared for him. "I suppose he wants attention," she said quietly.

"Attention!" Larry paced the length of the room, from the bas-relief to the abstract painting and back again. "Well, he's getting plenty, I'll tell you that. Two police cruisers, his mother calling everyone in the county... If that's what he wants, that's what he's getting." He subdued himself with a belt of Scotch. "Any ideas where he might have run off to? Do kids join the circus these days?"

Not kids who play Zinger, Sara thought. "I don't know much about Cold Spring Harbor," she answered, "so I don't know where he might have gone. But I'd wager that he hasn't gone far. He's probably just hiding."

"You think so?" Larry and Randy eyed each other. "Where would he hide?"

"The park by the shore?" Randy suggested.

"Nah. The police would have looked there by now."

The telephone rang, and Randy excused himself to answer it. Larry and Sara stood silently in the living room, Larry engrossed in his drink and Sara staring out the window to avoid having to look at the lumpy, shapeless leather furniture. "Renee?" Randy's voice drifted out to them. "No, no word yet.... Hang on." He returned to the living room and informed Larry, "She wants to talk to you."

Larry strode out of the room. Randy moved to Sara, his eyes caressing her face with their brilliant green light. "Thank you for coming," he whispered.

She studied his face. He looked tired, his eyelids ringed above and below with shadow, the corners of his mouth punctuated by downward-sloping creases. Worry about Petey darkened his brow. "He'll turn up," she declared, though she was in no position to make such a promise.

"I love that kid," Randy muttered, raking his hands restlessly through his hair and gazing out the window as if hoping to see the little boy magically materialize on the other side of the clear pane. "If anything happened to him, I don't know what I'd do."

"He's fine," Sara said, her only thought to reassure Randy, to assuage his fear, to calm and console him.

He gave her a wistful smile, obviously grateful for her presence. Larry rejoined them, the glass in his hand nearly empty. "I told Renee what you said," he addressed Sara. "She said to thank you for helping out."

"I haven't done anything," Sara protested.

"You're here," Randy murmured, something private underlining his voice. She *had* consoled him, she thought.

The door chime sounded, and he hastened to the foyer to answer it. When he returned, he was followed by a rotund, uniformed policeman whose hand grasped Petey's. The little boy looked incredibly tiny beside the huge officer, his face downcast and his expression forlorn. "Look who I've got," the policeman bellowed.

"Petey!" Larry ran to his child, his arms outstretched, and gathered the boy into a strong, staggering hug. Without releasing Petey, he peered past him at the policeman. "Where'd you find him?"

"In his school's playground," the officer reported. "He was hiding under the slide."

Larry turned back to his son and squatted down to view him at eye level. "Petey, why did you do this?

Why did you run away? Do you know how frightened we were?"

"Were you?" Petey asked, interested.

"I'll call Renee," Randy said, strolling from the room.

Larry thanked the policeman, who jotted down several notes for his records and then departed. Larry turned back to his son. "You must never, never do that again," he sternly lectured the boy.

Sara didn't think this was the appropriate time to scold Petey, but she held her thoughts in check. At least Petey appeared pleased by his father's overwhelming concern for his safety.

Randy entered the room with the announcement that Renee was on her way over. "Mommy?" Petey asked, turning his drawn face up to Randy.

"Yes. She's coming to see you because she was very worried, too."

"Oh." He shrugged and eased himself out of his father's embrace. "Were we supposed to have dinner, Randy? 'Cause I ate a bag of potato chips already."

"That's all right," Randy assured him.

Petey turned to Sara. "Hi," he said. "I ran away, huh?"

"So it seems," she concurred.

"Are you mad at me?"

"No."

The boy beamed a big smile at her. The dark space where one of his front teeth had fallen out made him even more endearing to her.

Renee soon arrived at Randy's house. She was an attractive woman in her early thirties, with dark, curly hair and the same soulful eyes as her son. "Petey!" she exclaimed as she darted to her son's side and gave him a hug. "You're all right! What a scare you gave us all!"

She loosened her hold but refused to release Petey as she glowered at Larry. "Remind me never to trust you to pick him up when you said you would," she snapped.

"Me? You told me you were going to drop him off!"

Before their argument could reach full steam, Sara reached for Petey's hand and whispered, "How about you and me playing some Zinger?" Anything, she thought, to get him out of earshot of his parents' silly spat. Petey eagerly clutched her hand and dragged her to the den.

Sara took a seat on the couch while Petey set up the machine, turned on the television and the large screen projector, and carried the two joysticks to the coffee table before them. In the distance she heard the muffled voices of Petey's parents arguing. She knew Petey heard them, too, but he kept his attention resolutely fixed on their game.

Sara's total lack of skill enabled Petey to score heavily against her. Again and again he annihilated her little yellow creature as it wandered clumsily through the maze. Sara felt absurdly inept as she maneuvered the joystick. She couldn't fight her memories of Randy's lewd teasing the first time she had been exposed to the video game. Still, she was glad for the distraction the game offered. Maybe if she'd had Zinger when she was growing up, she might have found playing the game a way of escaping from her sorrow about her parents, a safer way than planning to run away from home.

As Petey was racking up his fifth consecutive win, his parents entered the den, Randy behind them. "Petey," his mother said, "will you come home now?"

Petey stood up and turned to face them. He eyed his mother distrustfully, and then his father. "I was supposed to have dinner with Randy," he pointed out.

"You can have dinner with Randy some other time. Daddy and I would like you to have dinner with us tonight."

"With both of you?" he asked.

"That's right," Larry interjected. "If you'd like, we can even go to a restaurant."

Petey's suspicious gaze passed from one parent to the other. "We promise we won't fight," Renee maintained.

Petey glanced beyond her to Randy. "What do you think?"

"I think maybe you should have dinner tonight with your folks," Randy replied. "I'll take a rain check."

"What's a rain check?"

"That means we can have dinner together another time, soon," Randy explained. "How about it, tiger?"

Petey eyed Sara, then shrugged. "A restaurant? Really? Which one?"

"Your choice," Larry told him.

"Okay." Petey happily joined his parents.

Randy and Sara accompanied the reconciled family to the front door and waved them off. Then they ambled back to the den, where Randy shut off the video game. "They didn't really make up, did they?" Sara asked skeptically.

"A temporary cease-fire," Randy related. "I guess they've got enough sense left to realize they've got to focus on Petey for a while." He turned fully to Sara and examined her face, his own expression inscrutable. "You want to join me in a pizza?"

She sighed. Randy had clearly been upset by the evening's excitement, and she didn't think he was ready to be left alone yet, so she accepted his invitation. "All right."

She followed him to the kitchen, where, with a casual

swipe of his hand across the electric eye, he opened the refrigerator. He pulled a frozen pizza from the freezer compartment, then pushed several buttons on his microwave oven, removed the pizza from its box, and slid it onto the oven shelf. He crossed to a cabinet, pressed a button, and a panel slid open to reveal a small collection of wine bottles. He removed a bottle of Chianti, pressed the button to close the panel, and opened the bottle with a strange device that injected air through the cork into the bottle, causing the cork to pop out.

Sara cringed and drew in her breath. Here was Randy in his element, she thought, surrounded once again by his beloved junk. No corkscrew for him, no pizza with fresh dough and stewed sauce, but frozen this and gadgety that. She tried to concentrate her gaze only on him, but she couldn't block out his environment, the panoply of electronic stuff cluttering his home.

The oven timer buzzed to announce that the pizza was ready. Randy took it out and carried it to the dining-room table. He filled two goblets with wine, set two plates and napkins on the table, and lifted a gooey wedge of pizza onto Sara's plate before helping himself to a slice. Sara bit into the pizza. She chewed and swallowed, aware that it tasted exactly like what it was: a thawed precooked pizza that had spent the major portion of its existence sealed in cellophane and kept in a waxed cardboard carton.

She forced down several bites, then put down the slice. When she lifted her eyes she discovered Randy watching her, his pizza untouched. "I'm not very hungry," she mumbled contritely.

"Neither am I." He clasped the bowl of his goblet and studied the ruby wine, then drank some. Lowering the glass, he fastened his gaze on her. "Do you want to talk?"

"I'm not sure," she honestly replied.

"*You* called *me*," he reminded her. "You must have wanted to talk."

"I..." She sipped some wine for courage, then said, "I called to tell you I wasn't pregnant. I thought you'd want to know."

He stared at her, his expression again unreadable, and nodded slowly.

"I—I guess we were pretty reckless the other night," Sara stammered.

"I have no regrets," Randy observed softly. Detecting the silvery flash in Sara's eyes, he added, "I was even prepared to marry you if it came to that. I was... I was thinking it wouldn't be such a terrible thing."

His words shocked her, and she laughed nervously.

"You think it *would* be a terrible thing?" he asked.

"I think my having to participate in two weddings in one month would be a bit much," she remarked.

"What would you have done if you *were* pregnant?" Randy asked, leaning back in his chair and studying her curiously. "They didn't have abortions back in 1791, did they?"

"Not legal ones," Sara confirmed.

"Then what did the women do?"

"They had a lot of children," she told him. "Many of the babies died quite young."

"So did many of the women," Randy pointed out. "Sara, why do you think that was such a terrific time? Life was very hard then."

"It had meaning—"

"Life today has meaning, too," Randy countered.

"Different meaning."

"The same," he insisted. "It still means surviving, looking for love, making babies, sharing ideas... and dying. Preferably not at a young age. What's so different about it?"

"The style, maybe?"

Randy weighed her words. He fingered his glass, gazing at the wine, gazing through its deep red translucence. "So that's the problem? A matter of style?"

Sara let her eyes drop to his hands. Their strength seemed even greater when contrasted with the fragile glass they held. She watched his long fingers fan around the sides of the bowl of the glass almost like ribs, as if preserving and protecting the breakable crystal within. It reminded her of how he had cupped his hands around her slender waist. She had felt so delicate in his arms, so precious.

Her cheeks flooded with color at the memory; she could feel the heat rise along the gracefully defined bones of her face. "Randy," she murmured, concentrating on her own glass. "When you put it that way it sounds trivial, but it's not. I do like you, and you're more than I ever expected a man to be. But it's not enough."

"I've tried," he defended himself. "This past weekend I really tried—"

"That's just it. You tried," she stressed. "It isn't what you would have done naturally. You were *trying* for me. I appreciate it, Randy. It meant so much to me—" Her voice broke off, and she realized that she had been on the verge of telling him that what she had felt for him last Sunday was love, a stronger love than she had ever felt for any man before. "A modern woman would be so much easier for you," she admitted in a hoarse whisper.

Randy gave her words careful consideration. "Do you think I'm the sort of person who chooses the easy way?" he asked.

"Obviously not," Sara granted with a wry smile. "But...but I want you to be happy. I want what's best for you."

"You sound like my mother," he complained. He reached across the table and slipped his hand around hers. "I'm a big boy, Sara. I'll decide what's best for me."

"And I'll decide what's best for me," Sara rejoined, growing impatient. "I don't feel comfortable in your house. Doesn't that tell you anything? I don't feel comfortable at your office. I don't feel comfortable with what you do."

"Do you feel comfortable when I hold your hand?" he asked, lifting her hand to his mouth, brushing his lips with whisperlike softness over the tips of her fingers. "That's something I do, too, Sara."

She felt a dizzying rush of the heat again, that heat only Randy could kindle in her. She closed her eyes and fought against it. "Randy, don't," she moaned, wriggling free of his grip. "I want you." The honest words blurted out, and she couldn't bring herself to deny them, even after she hid her hands safely in her lap. "You know I want you, Randy. But that's not enough."

"What would be enough?" he asked, his patience now wearing thin. "If I wore a tricorn hat and knee breeches? If I ground my own wheat into flour? If Zaleco were a blacksmith's shop? What do you want from me?"

Nothing, Sara answered silently. She wanted nothing from him. She had discouraged his attentions from the start, but for some reason he had chosen her as his challenge. He had eroded her resistance until she finally agreed to attend the hockey game with him. And then he had insisted that he would prove that she couldn't do without men. But she could. She had been doing fine without men until Randy Zale had come along and forced himself into her life. She hadn't asked him to. She hadn't wanted him to. Her life as a reclusive celibate was less exciting than the hours she had spent in Randy's arms last Sunday night, but who needed excitement? Wasn't excitement exactly the thing she shunned?

"I'm leaving," she announced, rising from the table.

Randy scrambled to his feet, chasing after her as she stalked across the living room to the foyer. He gripped her arm tightly and held her in place. "Sara," he murmured, his expression a blend of confusion and anguish. "Sara, I don't know what you want, and I don't know why I want to give it to you, but I do. I love you, Sara. I'm not going to turn my world upside down for you, but you've gotten to me, and I love you. So tell me what you want."

She stood very still. His words reverberated inside her, and the shimmering light of his eyes penetrated her upturned face as she watched him. He loved her. But he wasn't going to turn his world upside down. And there was the paradox, there was the obstacle. Her world was the inverse of his; if neither he nor she could turn their world upside down, there was no hope for their relationship. "You can't give me what I want," she whispered, tears rimming her eyes, catching like bits of glass in her long lashes. "I want peace and simplicity. I don't want complications."

"You're scared," he guessed, letting his hand rise to her shoulder, urging her against himself.

She nodded, her face pressed to the cotton jersey covering his chest. "Yes, Randy. My life was a whole lot easier before I met you."

She felt his hands roam placatingly across her back, allowing her the expanse of his torso to cry upon. She shed only a few tears, managing to swallow back most of them, and when she stopped leaning against him, he let his arms fall to his sides. She dared to look up at him and found his face reflecting dissatisfaction and resignation, his eyes cloudy and his dimpled smile nowhere in evidence. "Go home, Sara," he ordered her, his voice touched by poignant gruffness. "Go home. I'll take a few aspirin, polish off the Chianti, maybe go out to a bar and play some video games and pick up a modern woman who wants to be ravished mercilessly, no questions asked, no commitments demanded. I'm a smart guy. I'll figure out a way to get over you."

"I'm sure you will," Sara sadly agreed. She lifted herself on tiptoe and kissed his cheek. "Good-bye, Randy," she breathed, then turned and hastened out of his house.

Chapter Nine

"The Willoughby boys slept upstairs in the loft," Sara told the group of twenty schoolchildren gathered before her in the Willoughby House. They were on a class trip, a crowd of well-scrubbed, well-behaved youngsters with their youthful teacher, and a class mother to keep them in line.

"All four boys in one room?" one of the children called out.

"All four boys in one bed," Sara replied, which elicited a loud chorus of grunts and disgusted noises. "Of course, only two of the boys survived past childhood, so by the time they were big, there were only two sharing the bed."

"How did the others die?" another child asked.

Sara tucked a stray hair beneath her bonnet and glanced at the fireplace. Despite the warmth of the afternoon, she had to keep the fire blazing in order for her pies to bake evenly. She added a log to the hearth before answering the child's question. "According to Julia Willoughby's diary, the first son, also named Josiah, survived to adulthood. The second child died of a fever before his twelfth birthday. The fourth son died at the age of seven, also of a fever. The third son grew up to become an itinerant lay preacher." Assessing the blank stares that greeted her, she elaborated: "That's a minister who travels from town to town, or from farm to farm, and gives sermons. You have to remember that the people lived all spread out, and they didn't have cars. So they couldn't always get to houses of worship. Sometimes the lay preachers had to travel to people's homes so they could observe their religion."

"How can you die of a fever?" a high-pitched voice sang out. "How come they didn't take aspirin or go to the doctor or something?"

"People didn't have aspirin in those days," Sara explained. "And the doctors didn't know everything they know now. They couldn't control a fever with medication, because most of the medicines we have today hadn't been invented yet."

The children grew solemn. "Life must have been hard in those days," one little girl observed.

"Yes," Sara agreed soberly, "life was hard."

"I'm glad I live now," another child contributed. "I wouldn't want to die of a fever."

Sara gazed down at the bright, attentive faces of the children. As much as she loved the nineteenth century, she was glad that these adorable girls and boys lived now. She wouldn't want them to have to die of fevers. As much as she hated to admit it, there were definitely certain benefits in living in the modern world.

It was a thought that had been haunting her a great deal lately. For the first time since she had begun her job at the Village, she was discovering that sweeping the hearth with a handmade broom was tedious, that lugging split logs indoors from the yard could strain her arms, that the long-sleeved, high-necked frocks she had to wear were occasionally uncomfortably warm. But that was how prim, proper ladies dressed a century and a half ago, and those were the chores that had kept them busy. The life of a farm wife in 1800 was... well, hard. For long stretches of time, Sara found herself struggling to remember the compensations of that hard life.

She ought to be happy. She was to be "married" the following day at two o'clock, and activities relating to the annual wedding at the Village were in full swing. Her gown was ready, flowers were being gathered, Annie had baked the wedding cake. The newspapers had printed announcements—a full-page feature article in *Newsday*, Long Island's daily newspaper, and smaller articles in the New York City, New Jersey and Connecticut papers. The air hummed with festivity.

But Sara felt detached from it all. She had felt detached since the day she had broken things off with Randy. Ever since that day over two weeks ago, when a sour mood had settled like a soggy veil over her, she had been unable to shake her dissatisfaction with her life, her work, her existence. Something was terribly wrong.

She tried to analyze it. She knew that her decision to end her relationship with Randy was a wise one, for him at least. He deserved a woman better suited to his own tastes, his own style. And Sara loved him enough to want that for him.

Loved him? No, she didn't love him. How could she? And how could she believe that he really loved her? She believed he was fascinated by her, intrigued, challenged. But that wasn't love. He would get over her, and she would eventually reclaim the simple life she had enjoyed before she had met him.

Sometimes, late at night, she found herself lying restlessly in bed and wondering whether it was something else that caused her to suffer from this depression. The strange mood that gripped her had begun before her final meeting with Randy. It had begun during the day, and she had suspected at the time that it was just a result of raging hormones, the typical gloominess that afflicted so many women at a certain time of the month. But Sara had never suffered from that syndrome before. And in brief flashes of what sometimes resembled honesty and other times resembled insanity, Sara pondered the possibility that she had been disappointed by her failure to become pregnant.

It didn't make sense. She was in no position to plunge into motherhood. That Randy would have offered to marry her was magnanimous, but it wouldn't have been a sound solution to an unplanned pregnancy. Sara was sure she wanted solitude, not matrimony and motherhood. She ought to be relieved instead of despondent.

"Did the mommies do all the baking?" a child asked, shattering Sara's reverie. "In my house, my daddy does the baking."

Sara's lips shaped an amused smile. "Families were less liberated in those days," she responded to the ingenuous question. "Daddies usually worked outside the home—in Josiah Willoughby's case, he ran their farm. His wife, Julia, was in charge of all the domestic chores—baking, cleaning, sewing. Sex roles were more restricted then." This news was greeted with another chorus of grunts and hoots, mostly from the girls in the class.

A motion to her left distracted Sara, and she turned to see Ira Lipton peering through the open upper half of the Dutch door. She grinned and gestured him inside. "This is Ira Lipton, Old Harkum Village's shoemaker," she introduced him as he pushed open the bottom half of the door and stepped into the kitchen.

Ira waved at the children. "They've already been to

the shoemaker's shop," he revealed. "How are you doing, gang? What do you think of my fiancée?"

"Your fiancée?" The children erupted into a shower of oohs and ahhs and a few obnoxious kissing noises.

"That's right," Sara said, nodding. "Ira and I are going to be married tomorrow right here in the Village. Holding a nineteenth-century wedding is an annual ritual at Old Harkum Village."

The children decided they wanted photographs of the bride and groom. Sara and Ira obediently posed, and then the children handed their Instamatics to the teacher and the class mother, who organized the children around Sara and Ira for a bubbly group photograph. Once all the children's cameras had captured the scene on film, Ira announced, "I'm not allowed to see my bride tomorrow before her wedding, so I brought a wedding present for her today. Would you like to see it?" At the children's encouraging cheers, he returned to the door, leaned out, and lifted a handcrafted pair of black leather shoes from the porch.

He presented the shoes to Sara, who took them and sighed, admiring their fine craftsmanship. They resembled ballet slippers in style, with layered leather heels and soles. The right and left shoes were identical, as was the mode of shoemaking in those days. Only by wearing them consistently on one's right or left foot did the shoe become broken in to the particular contours of each foot.

"Put them on!" one of the children demanded.

Sara dutifully removed her cloth shoes and stepped into the lovely leather slippers. They were the right size, though her outer toes pinched slightly from the symmetrical curves of the shoes.

The children applauded as she modeled the shoes for them. "What are you going to give him?" one asked.

"As a matter of fact—" Sara eyed the fireplace, then crossed to the oven and swung its iron door open "—his present is ready right now." Grabbing a thick cloth to protect her hands, she carefully removed three lattice-crusted apple and currant pies. She had baked three in the hope that at least one would come out satisfactorily, but they were all beautiful, their egg glaze giving the golden crusts a savory shimmer, their juicy fruit-and-honey filling oozing syrup between the neatly woven lattices.

More oohs and ahhs filled the small room as Sara set the pies on the table. "Three?" Ira gasped, clearly thrilled.

"I figured I had about a thirty-three percent chance of success," she explained with a modest grin.

"Well, I can't eat all three," Ira complained amiably. "I guess I can eat only one. Maybe we ought to cut the other two up and let these hungry tykes have a taste."

The children clapped their hands and ebulliently jumped up and down. Sara raised her eyes to the teacher, who nodded her permission. Then she handed Ira a knife, and he cut and distributed tiny tastes of the pie to each of the children. In no time, two pie plates were empty, not a crumb left in evidence of their former contents.

"We've still got a lot of buildings to visit," the teacher announced to her gaggle of charges. "It's time to say thank-you and move on."

"Thank you," the children recited in unison before filing through the door and out.

Sara fondly waved at the departing children. A vague sadness filled her as they vanished from view. Once again she found herself wondering what would have happened if she and Randy hadn't been so lucky several weeks ago.

She shut her mind to the troubling thought by turning back to Ira. "Thanks so much for the shoes," she said. "They'll look perfect with my wedding gown."

"I thought you might want to break them in a bit before tomorrow," he told her. "Otherwise your feet'll be killing you."

"Isn't that one of the bride's duties?" she chuckled. "I thought all brides were supposed to have aching feet."

Ira shared her laughter, then gathered up the remaining pie, which had cooled enough for him to be able to handle it without a towel. "And thanks for this," he said. "I'm going to devour it with my girl friend tonight. Maybe that'll shut her up. She's not too pleased by my impending marriage."

"Will she be coming tomorrow?"

Ira nodded. "She'll be the one with daggers in her eyes," he noted with a sly grin. "Have you invited any special guests?"

"My next-door neighbors," Sara informed him. "They're coming en masse. The youngest boy was reluctant, but when I told him he could wear jeans, he conceded."

"Well, I'll see you at the altar," Ira promised as he headed for the door. "Enjoy your last night of freedom." With a wink he was gone.

Abandoned, Sara cleaned off the table, dunked the two empty pie tins in a basin of water, and scoured them. Once again she found herself growing weary of the rugged task of scrubbing. Never before in her life had she fantasized about owning a dishwasher.

It must be insanity, she decided as she drove home. There was no other explanation for her state of mind. She didn't want a child. It took a man to make a child, and she didn't want a man. Not even Randy. He was better off without an insane woman like her. He was well adjusted, with his dishwasher, his toys, his modern life. Why couldn't she just count her blessings and forget him? By now he must have forgotten her. He was a smart guy. He knew how to get over a crazy lady like Sara.

THE BAR WAS DARK AND SMOKY. As soon as Randy entered, he was seized by the urge to turn and flee. He'd visited this particular gathering spot for singles countless times before, but tonight he felt as if he'd invaded an alien planet.

Sara would be getting married at the Village tomorrow, he remembered. Then he angrily shook his head. He didn't want to think about her and her beloved Village. He was here to forget about that. The world was returning to normal. Larry had moved back in with Renee, declaring a temporary cease-fire. Petey was ecstatic. Now that Randy's good friends had resumed their familiar life, he, too, wanted only to do the same.

Raucous rock music filled the air, amplified by enormous speakers suspended from the ceiling. He scouted the bar with a practiced eye, then meandered over to a row of coin-operated video games set up along one wall. He apathetically inserted a quarter into the nearest one and began to play.

The screen filled with enemy starships. He moved the control lever with precision and fired off a shot. His clean hit of one of the starships caused the screen to burst into a flamboyant display of multicolored light. Fireworks, he thought morosely, recalling the night Sara had sat beside him in his den playing Zinger. He didn't want video fireworks. He wanted the fireworks that only Sara could ignite within him.

Brusquely he turned from the machine, unconcerned about the fact that he hadn't played out his twenty-five cents. He drifted to the bar, ordered a Campari and paid for it, then surveyed the crowd.

An attractive woman with long dark hair caught his eye, but he purposefully turned away. He didn't want to meet anyone who even remotely reminded him of Sara.

He noticed a striking blond woman seated by herself at a corner table and sauntered over to her. "Are you alone?" he asked.

She smiled and nodded toward the empty seat opposite hers. "Not anymore," she said by way of invitation.

Randy took the seat and introduced himself. She told him her name was Trish. She was an insurance agent. She loved playing tennis. She was a Sagittarius, divorced.

Randy nodded, his gaze taking the woman in. Actually her hair was ash-blond, thick and wavy falling to her shoulders. She had dark eyes, which were enhanced by artfully applied makeup, and full attractive lips. Her tunic blouse hinted at a lush figure. "Would you like to come back to my place?" he suggested.

"I thought you'd never ask," she said with a warm smile.

She followed him in her car, a gleaming Corvette. Randy tried to assure himself that he was doing the right thing. He'd traveled this route dozens of times before, and he'd always enjoyed himself. A willing, mature woman, a satisfying evening, nothing serious. Trish, Randy knew, would be on the pill.

"I love your house!" she chirped as he led her into the spacious living room. Before he could offer her a drink, she had her arms curled around his shoulders.

"Show me how these couches work," she purred. "I've never seen furniture like this before."

I'm doing the right thing, he told himself. Forgetting about Sara had to be the right thing. Let her get married tomorrow—that was what she wanted. Her silly, artificial wedding. Playacting. Pretending to exist in another century, another civilization. That was what she wanted.

Trish's beautifully manicured hands slid down the front of his shirt, unbuttoning it. Then she gaily hoisted her tunic over her head. She flopped onto one of the couches and beckoned to him.

He stared down at her. She had golden skin, marked by the pale outline of a bikini. She must sunbathe under a sun lamp, he mused, since the beach season was still a month away. Her breasts were large and round. He tried to convince himself that he wanted her.

Hesitantly he dropped down beside her onto the leather cushion. She cupped her hands about his head and drew his lips to hers.

No. He couldn't will himself into wanting her. She was a lovely modern woman, but he couldn't do this. It wasn't right. He didn't want it.

"I'm sorry," he murmured, pulling away.

She stared at him. "Sorry about what?"

It was all too casual, too cool. He didn't love her—he didn't even know her. Maybe he had outgrown his desire for the sort of superficial sexual pleasure he could find with a woman like Trish. All he knew was that when he closed his eyes he saw Sara, Sara talking about love, honor, cherishing; Sara talking about the olden days, when men and women made commitments and abided by them. "I'm sorry," he repeated himself. "I really can't go through with this."

Trish sat up, uninhibited about her state of semiundress. She appeared curious. "Do you want to talk about it?"

"I'm in love with someone else," he announced. The words came out so easily, he knew they had to be true.

"Oh, it sounds messy," Trish giggled. "Not like something I want to be a part of."

"You aren't angry?"

"Disappointed." She shrugged nonchalantly and reached for her tunic. "You look like one hell of a stud."

Randy grinned wryly. He certainly didn't feel like one hell of a stud. In fact, he didn't *want* to feel like one. Trish had obviously intended her statement as a compliment, and he accepted it as such, but it was not the way he wanted to think of himself.

He wanted to think of himself the way he thought of Sara. Perhaps it was old-fashioned, but her values meant much more to him than a satisfying romp with Trish could ever mean. He wanted a woman he could cherish. He wanted Sara.

"No hard feelings," Trish assured him as she stood up and straightened out her blouse. "Work it out with that lucky lady if you can. And if you can't, come back to the bar. You'll find me there."

"I'll...keep that in mind," he mumbled as he escorted her to the door. She gave him a light kiss on the cheek and vanished.

He returned alone to the living room, buttoning his shirt. His eyes lingered for a moment on the hip-shaped indentations in the leather cushions, a souvenir of Trish's brief visit. He would have to go after Sara some way, he decided. He would have to convince her that things could work between them. Because if he didn't... if he didn't convince her of that, he'd be lost, truly lost.

SARA WAS UNABLE TO MUSTER much enthusiasm for her wedding. She arose to a clear, balmy Saturday morning. Her yard sparkled with dew in the sun, and the sky was graced by a few white tufts. A perfect wedding day, she tried to convince herself. A perfect day to immerse herself in an old-fashioned ritual, in the world she adored at the Village.

She arrived at the Village early, but already the visitors' parking lot was filling with cars. Old-timers at the Village had warned her that the wedding always drew an enormous crowd.

After changing into a frock in the dressing room, she walked directly to the Boodner House. Annie had been cast as her mother, and Edith, the Village's seamstress, and Kitty, who had been assigned the role of maid of honor, were on hand to pamper the bride-to-be. A professional photographer hired by Gil, the Village's curator, showed up to take pictures of them eating a typical breakfast of bread, boiled eggs and coffee. He took more pictures of them arranging fresh-cut flowers about the house and then left to photograph Ira and his best man enjoying Ira's final moments of bachelorhood.

"Nervous?" Annie asked.

"Not really," Sara confessed. In fact, she felt drained and disconnected. She hadn't slept well the previous night. Her eyes burned, her chest was heavy, and her fingers were awkward as they fidgeted with the daisies in a pewter vase on the dining table.

"You're supposed to be," Annie chided her playfully. "It's your wedding day."

Sara nodded absently. If she were pregnant, this wedding might have taken place with Randy at her side, she mused. She thrust the thought from her mind with a brisk shake of her head. "When should I start getting dressed?" she asked.

"May as well start now," Kitty urged her.

Sara removed her frock and brassiere. Kitty and Edith produced a pink satin corset and pulled it over her head. The corset was trimmed with white lace and lacked shoulder straps. Sara's colleagues tied its ribbons snugly around her waist. It offered a modicum of support for her breasts. "You can't wear a bra," Edith told her. "Not with the décolletage of the wedding dress."

After the corset, a wide petticoat was tied on her at the hips. Then Edith disappeared to her shop and returned a few minutes later carrying the bridal dress. Sara had already seen it during numerous fittings, but she was once again forced to admire its glorious appearance. It had delicate short sleeves that rode low off Sara's shoulders, a clinging bodice trimmed with sumptuous lace and a full, flowing skirt. The three women helped Sara put it on, then buttoned it and arranged the bustlelike bow to conceal the fastening at the waist. It was the most flattering, feminine gown Sara had ever seen.

Once Edith had made a few final adjustments on the dress, smoothing out the lace, plumping the bow, placing the sleeves precisely over Sara's graceful shoulders, she and Kitty tackled Sara's long, silky hair. They brushed it with brushes dipped in toilet water, separated two thick strands on either side of her face, and braided the strands. They drew the braided locks back from her face and clasped them behind her head.

Annie sighed deeply. "You look stunning," she crooned. "My real daughter should only look this good.

Come see yourself in the mirror." She led Sara to the slightly warped antique mirror over the bureau in the parlor.

Sara's large gray eyes took in her reflection. Objectively, she admitted, she looked lovely. Her jet-black hair set off the pale dress and her equally pale skin, and her features were set in a pure, virtuous pose.

But when her objectivity momentarily flagged, she saw something else: fear. She was scared.

She was visited by an unbidden memory of her last moments with Randy, when he had gently accused her of being scared. She had agreed with him then and had known that he meant she was scared of him, of his modern world, of the commitment he was asking of her. But now she knew her fear transcended that commitment. She was afraid to let a man destroy her complacent world. She was afraid of the horrors that developed between modern men and modern women. She had seen those horrors in her parents' lives and she shied from them.

She was scared by the temptation to take a chance with Randy. She was scared to step into the future with him. If she did, she might never find her way back to the peace and serenity she so desperately wanted, the peace and serenity she found only in solitude, in a reconstructed world of the past. She treasured the stability she had finally developed in her life. She was scared by the thought of losing it.

It was similar to the fear any bride must undergo, she meditated as she turned from the mirror. A wedding was a step into tomorrow, a commitment to the future. A successful marriage depended on compromise, on submerging one's own needs in those of one's spouse. It depended on buying a one-way ticket into one's partner's world. Those who entered into marriage with a round-trip ticket inevitably found themselves divorced.

"Ben's here," Kitty announced, ushering Sara to the front door of the Boodner House. On the porch stood Ben Stanley, the Village blacksmith. Behind him in the road, Sara spotted the chaise, a huge roan harnessed to it. Tomtom, she recognized. Ira would panic; Ginger was the less temperamental of the draw horses. Tomtom was more spirited, more stubborn.

The women left the house and Ben helped them into the chaise. It was only after she was seated between Annie and Kitty that Sara became aware of the multitude of people lining the road. Hundreds of visitors, dressed in civilian clothes and brandishing maps, souvenir wedding announcements and cameras, waved and pointed and snapped photographs as Ben lifted the reins and guided Tomtom away from the Boodner House toward the Village's church.

Kitty and Annie gaily waved at the crowds, but Sara kept her eyes fixed on her lap. It was the proper demeanor for a bride, she thought, to be bashful and reserved. But her demureness wasn't an act. It was real. She felt herself shrinking inside, thinking about what a terrible bride she would have made for Randy, thinking that she was too close-minded, too frightened ever to take a husband. She would never find a man better than Randy. And she would have made him miserable had she accepted the love he offered.

The crowd of onlookers grew denser as the carriage neared the church. Kitty pointed out the professional photographer, and Sara gave him a perfunctory smile as the carriage drew to a halt by the front steps of the church. Then she averted her eyes, once again overcome by a vaguely defined misery.

Richard Gladstone, another Village interpreter, who had been cast as Sara's father, took her arm at the church door. Sara was astonished by the teeming congregation, every inch of pew space occupied by period-costumed Village employees and visitors. The tall windows lining the church walls were jammed with onlookers, and as soon as Sara, Kitty and Annie entered the church the crowd gathered close behind them, peering eagerly through the open double doors.

Someone began to play a hymn on the reedy pipe organ. Sara, her Village "parents" and Kitty walked together toward the front pew, which had been reserved for them. Sara kept her eyes fixed on the floor. If Richard and Annie hadn't been holding her arms, she would have completely forgotten to move.

"Hey, Sara!" a distinctive cracking squawk rang out. Sara glanced in its direction and spotted Pipsqueak standing and waving beside a pew, surrounded by the rest of the Sharkeys. Mick snapped a photograph as she sent a smile in their direction. As soon as she passed the pew, her smile faded.

Ira dressed in a black morning coat, satin vest, white shirt, long pants and polished boots, waited for her at the front pew. She took her place beside him, and he grinned sheepishly at her. "Hey, good-looking," he whispered, evidently hoping to still the jittery glimmer in her eyes.

She politely returned his grin, but a ghastly thought cut through her, a wish that not Ira but Randy had been waiting for her. If only Randy could have dressed himself up in such clothes, come to this perfect representation of an early-nineteenth-century house of worship, and shared in this sort of marriage—not a marriage of necessity, to legitimize an accidental pregnancy; not a marriage of fascination that would wear thin in time;

not a marriage based on temporary visas, round-trip tickets, *trying* but never quite succeeding.

Sara struggled to concentrate on Gil's rambling sermon, but her mind wandered again and again to thoughts of Randy. How she wished he were different! How she wished *she* were different!

When Ira abruptly reached for her hand, she flinched. Gil pronounced them "man and wife," and then invited all the wedding guests to partake of cider and celebrate in the garden behind the Boodner House.

Clasping her hand in his, Ira led Sara up the aisle, his pace energetic and his smile radiant. Sara endeavored to match his buoyant spirit, but she was distracted by a glimpse of someone with richly hued hair that resembled Randy's. Her smile froze on her face, cramping her cheeks, and she swiftly looked away.

"Oh, God, it's Tomtom," Ira groaned as he led her to the carriage. "Why couldn't it have been Ginger? Tomtom and I don't get along."

"Maybe he'll behave today," Sara encouraged Ira.

He grunted doubtfully and helped her onto the cushioned front bench. Then he walked to the horse, whispered an admonishment into the beast's ear, and climbed onto the seat beside Sara. He flicked the reins. Tomtom turned and gave him a sullen look. He flicked the reins again, shouted a loud, "Gee!" and the horse reluctantly ambled down the road.

A long table had been set up behind the Boodner House. Pewter goblets and china plates stood at each place, and an exquisite white cake decorated with fresh lilies was on display at one end. On the back porch of the house were several huge kegs of cider to accommodate the visitors. The wedding participants and Village employees were all treated to wine.

Sara did her best to play the part of the happy bride,

accepting the guests' toasts and slicing the cake with Ira. The cake was delicious, but she had little appetite, and she was relieved when at last the rambunctious celebration began to wind down and she and Ira could make their ceremonial departure.

Enthusiastic crowds of visitors cheered and snapped more photographs as Sara and Ira emerged from behind the house to the waiting carriage. Once again Ira helped her onto the seat, and she dutifully smiled and waved at the throng of people surrounding the wide-wheeled chaise. Ira twitched the reins, hollered, "Gee!" and relaxed in his seat as Tomtom began an uneven lope down the dirt road.

The horse clomped as far as the Willoughby House, then halted. Ira flicked the reins again and again, and shouted urgent pleas and muttered mild oaths at the horse. Tomtom was adamant, however. He refused to budge.

"Do you suppose it could be a short in the electrical system?"

Sara heard the husky whisper at her elbow. She jumped, and turned to discover that Randy had emerged from the mob of people surrounding the chaise. He wore jeans and a beige shirt, and his beautiful hair was slightly wind-tossed. His eyes glittered with their usual green magic. Her jaw dropped; she was too astonished to speak.

"You know how it is with these newfangled contraptions," he teased in a soft voice. "They break down at the most inopportune times, and you're dependent on them, and then you're up a creek."

"Do you know this brash gentleman, dear?" Ira asked, reverting to his nineteenth-century personality.

"Yes," she mumbled, her hands clenched in her lap.

"Need I defend your honor?" Ira inquired, then turned to Randy. "This gentle lady is my bride, sir, and you had best address her with the respect accorded to the bride of Ira Lipton, shoemaker."

Randy laughed. "I'm handy with broken-down engines," he boasted. "Why don't I have a look under the hood?" Before Ira could respond, Randy jogged to Tomtom and scratched the proud animal on the white marking on his long nose.

Ira studied Sara. "It's all right," she tentatively assured him. "He's a friend of mine."

"If you say so."

Randy approached Ira's side of the carriage. "Let me give it a try," he advised. "Sara here can tell you, I know my way around transportation gizmos and gadgets."

Reluctantly Ira climbed down from the carriage, and Randy took his place. Casting Sara a hesitant smile, he lifted the reins, clicked his tongue against his teeth, and stirred the willful horse into action. Tomtom cheerfully lifted his head and began a leisurely trot toward the farm.

Sara twisted to look behind her. Ira was running after the carriage, but as Tomtom picked up speed her new husband dropped back, good-naturedly joining in the laughter of the swarms of visitors who had watched Randy abduct his bride. She turned back to Randy, who, rather than slowing down, continued to steer the moving chaise in the direction of the woods south of the farm. "Do you know what you're doing?" she asked.

"Kidnapping you," he replied.

"I mean with the horse!"

He scowled. "Are you kidding? I hope you know where the brakes are on this thing."

"Oh, my God!" Sara cringed, wondering if Randy was going to kill them both. She tried to calculate how fast Tomtom was moving, how many bones she might break if she tumbled over the side of the carriage. She hoped her falling body would clear the wheels.

But Tomtom was amazingly willing to behave for Randy. As soon as the forest swallowed up the dirt road in its dense, cool shadows, the horse slowed to a walk, then stopped. Randy kept one hand securely on the reins as he pivoted to face Sara. "Hello," he murmured.

"What are you doing here?" she breathed, no longer frightened about her fate in the carriage. Now her only concern was how to deal with Randy's unexpected reappearance in her life.

"I came to see you married," he explained. "You make a beautiful bride, Sara. You look spectacular."

"Thank you," she said, groping for courage. "Randy, you shouldn't have come."

"I came." It was a deceptively simple remark, and it caused a ripple of warmth down her spine.

"I thought you were going to get over me."

"I was," he admitted. "I tried."

"What did you try?"

"Exactly what I told you I'd try," he confessed. "I went to a bar and found myself the perfect modern woman."

Sara cringed inwardly. It was just what she had hoped would happen to Randy. She wondered why she didn't feel elated.

"We went back to my place," he continued. "She loved the house. She absolutely adored it." He lowered his eyes to the narrow leather reins in his grip. "Before I knew what hit me, we were on the living-room sofa, getting undressed."

"The sofa?" Sara choked. "Is that what that leather thing is?"

Randy laughed wryly. "Oh, Sara... I couldn't go

through with it. Before I met you, I might have had a swell time with her, a perfectly satisfying evening. But... I couldn't. I didn't love her. There was no... no commitment. It was all too... too 'exciting.' An 'interesting experience.' I couldn't do it." He exhaled. "So I told her to put on her blouse, and apologized and sent her on her way."

"Was she hurt?"

He shook his head. "She took it in stride. I guess I was an 'interesting experience' for her." He exhaled again, then reached for Sara's hand and wove it through the reins next to his. "So what am I going to do? Turn my life upside down?"

"I can't ask you to do that," Sara replied, sighing. "I—I don't even think I want you to do that."

"Then will you meet me halfway?" he asked hopefully. "Will you at least try?"

"Yes." The word emerged on its own, powered by her heart. She had wished for him to be waiting for her at the altar that afternoon. That told her more than all her mental debate about the wide differences between her and Randy. After all, the differences were only on the surface. Randy's confession about his meeting with a modern woman proved to Sara that in his soul he was no less committed than she to the archaic values she esteemed. Whether he kneaded bread dough by hand or by electric kneading hooks was irrelevant when his soul was willing to meet hers, willing to try. She, too, would try. For him she would try anything.

He slipped his hand to the back of her head and drew her into a long, languorous kiss. "Oh, Sara," he breathed against her cheek. "I've missed you. I've missed you so much." He kissed her again. "Is a nineteenth-century woman allowed to consummate her marriage with someone who isn't her husband?"

"Here?" Sara laughed. "On the chaise in the middle of the woods?"

His hand wandered to her shoulder, stroking the bare white skin above the lace of her gown. Her nerves responded ravenously to his touch. Her veins filled with fire, her heart throbbed against her ribs, her soul swelled with love and need. "Where does a nineteenth-century bride go?" he murmured hoarsely.

"Home, I suppose," Sara whispered. She touched his cheek and his lips, her fingertips reading the warm texture of his skin.

"To a bed in the kitchen?" he asked. "Like the Willoughby House? Where two people can figure out a way to stay warm on a cold winter night?"

Her eyes met his and widened. Was he seriously considering taking her to the Willoughby House to make love with her? The idea astonished her. "We couldn't," she protested giddily.

"Why not?"

"Because..." She was about to tell him that he wasn't showing due respect for the historic essence of the house, to say nothing of the Village rules—although she doubted anyone had ever bothered to write such a rule into the Village's charter. But there was another reason she didn't want to agree to Randy's suggestion. He had entered her world. Now it was time for her to enter his. "Because this is the twentieth century," she reminded him. "And a twentieth-century woman doesn't make love in a museum."

He perused her, easily discerning her earnestness. An amazed smile teased his lips. "Lead the way, then, twentieth-century woman," he urged her, handing her the reins.

Sara clucked Tomtom into action and steered them back out of the forest, past the farm to the stables. The crowds had dispersed as closing time approached at Old Harkum Village. Ben, the blacksmith, gave her a furious look as she guided the carriage into his looming barn. "Sorry about that," she apologized as she handed the reins over to him and Randy alit.

"You scared a lot of people," he scolded them both. "What the hell did you run off for?"

"We didn't scare anyone," Sara insisted, surprised by the evenness of her tone, which revealed none of the anxious yearning pulsing through her body. "They probably thought it was part of the show."

She left the stable, Randy at her heels, and they hurried toward the main building. A few of her associates gave them bemused looks as they entered the building, but Sara didn't bother to explain her abduction. She led Randy to the entry and said, "Wait here. I've got to change my clothes."

"No!" he protested, then lowered his voice. "Don't change. You look so lovely."

She gazed down at the flowing garment and laughed. "Randy, I can't go driving through the streets dressed like this."

"You won't drive," he told her. "I'll drive. You can come back for your street clothes later." He bowed and touched his lips to hers, his fingers trailing along her bare arms. "Please. Indulge a modern man's fetish."

"Well, if you're going to put it that way..." she conceded with a breathy laugh and followed him outside to the visitors' parking lot.

Randy helped her to gather the full skirt of the gown around her legs as she arranged herself on the Alfa-Romeo's bucket seat. Then he loped around the car and climbed in beside her. Sara didn't ask him where he planned to take her. She didn't care. All that mattered was that she would be with him in his world.

He cruised down a bustling thoroughfare and steered onto the driveway of a recently constructed motel. Its stark geometric lines and cold, crushed-stone facade ought to have bothered Sara, but it didn't. She refused to be repelled by the trappings of the modern world. She would enter it bravely; Randy would give her the courage she needed to do so.

Once he had parked the car, they strolled into the lobby, which featured a slate floor and green leather-and-chrome furniture. Randy marched directly to the desk, where a clerk stood gaping at the odd couple they made. "Have you got a honeymoon suite?" he asked. Sara tried unsuccessfully to stifle her laughter.

The clerk's eyes shifted from Randy to the strangely dressed young woman with him. "The honeymoon suite?" she echoed vaguely.

"Yes. I'd like to rent it."

Obviously flustered, the clerk thumbed through her reservation list. "I'm afraid that's already booked for tonight," she told him. "We've got a couple due in after their evening wedding reception—"

"How about for now?"

"I beg your pardon?"

Randy folded his hand around Sara's and drew her to the desk beside him. "Could we have it for, say, an hour? We'll be out by the time the people who reserved it show up."

The woman's eyes grew rounder. She glanced behind her at the digital clock fastened to the wall. It read five-eleven. "I don't think that would be possible," she managed. "The room would have to be cleaned and made up, and that does take time."

"How about a half hour?" Randy persisted. Another laugh slipped past Sara's lips.

The clerk turned back to him. "I really don't think..." she began.

Randy decided it was time to take a different approach. He reached into the hip pocket of his jeans and removed his wallet. Pulling a twenty-dollar bill from it, he poked it at the wavering clerk. "A half hour. How about it?"

The clerk stared at the proffered bill, then issued a tight smile. "Well, I suppose, for a half hour..." She snatched the bill from Randy's fingers and grumbled, "You'll have to pay for the room in advance."

"Whatever you say," Randy agreed. She quoted a price Sara considered outrageous, but Sara didn't intervene. Randy had played out her fantasy at the Colonial inn; now he would play out his own fantasy, as modern as hers had been historical.

After plucking the room key from a rack, the clerk muttered, "Follow me." She led them down an austere hallway to an unadorned elevator, and they rode to the top floor. She unlocked the door at the far end of the corridor and stressed, "One half hour."

"Fine. Thanks," Randy said, nodding her back toward the elevator. As soon as she was gone, he turned to Sara and scooped her into his arms. "Over the threshold," he whispered.

She cuddled to him, breathing his delicious aroma, savoring the strength of his embrace. She looked only at him, oblivious to the room until he gently set her down on her feet and returned to the door to lock it.

The room was large. The vertical blinds along the broad window were adjusted to admit the fading sunlight. The carpet was white, the ceiling mirrored. One wall contained a large-screen television set, beside it a page of instructions on how to dial up "adult movies."

The bureaus were white Formica. An enormous circular bed made up with royal-blue satin sheets consumed an entire third of the room.

Sara guffawed. "Randy, this is hilarious!"

He joined her laughter. "You think so?"

"Really... we could have just gone to your house."

"Uh-uh," he said, contradicting her and crossing to the bed. He bent down beside it and touched a switch. "I haven't got a vibrating bed."

"Does that thing vibrate?" she asked, approaching the bed.

He flicked the switch, and with a low, motorized roar, the mattress began to shimmy. He grinned and turned off the motor, then stooped lower to examine the bed's frame. "I bet I could rig one of these things up on my bed."

"Don't," Sara said hastily. "It would probably make me seasick."

He rose to his full height and peered down at her. "I take it you plan to spend some time in my bed?" he asked.

Sara colored slightly as she realized the implications of her remark. "Maybe." She shrugged shyly. "If you think an anachronistic woman like me could fit into such a modern house."

"I think... I think you'd fit in wherever I took you. Pick a century, any century..." He considered her for a long moment, his smile deepening, and then it faded as he covered her mouth with his. His tongue sought hers and greeted it with imperative thrusts. Once again Sara was inundated with heat, Randy's heat, the fire of her love for him.

His hands roamed her creamy shoulders before locating the buttons at the back of the gown. He deftly unfastened them, then tugged at the bow that covered the lower fastening. When the back of the dress was completely undone, he slid it from her shoulders.

Seeing her corset and petticoat, he caught his breath. "You never cease to amaze me," he whispered hoarsely, brushing his fingertips across the exposed upper halves of her breasts.

"Are old-fashioned underthings one of your fetishes?" Sara teased breathlessly.

"More so than back rubs, I'm afraid," he replied, bowing to kiss the swollen flesh above the corset.

Sara's thighs tensed, aroused by his tender assault on her breasts. His fingers worked on the corset lace, untying and loosening it, spreading the garment to free her slender midriff and waist. "Sara," he groaned. "Oh, Sara... there's a lot to be said for an old-fashioned woman."

"Yes," she agreed, her voice a musical purr. "An old-fashioned twentieth-century woman."

He nodded, sliding the corset over her head. Her fingers moved down the front of his shirt, opening it. He shrugged it off, and her cool, slender fingers seemed to float over the strong, male contours of his chest, feeling for his ribs through the firm planes of muscle, feeling for his heart through his ribs, for his soul through his heart. His erratic sighs, his hands eagerly clutching her waist, his lips showering her hair with kisses all informed her that she had found his soul, that it was hers to take.

He relished her gentle caresses until his hunger for her drove him to more insistent action. Drawing her hands to his mouth, he kissed each in turn, then removed her petticoat and panties. She stepped out of her shoes and melted into his outstretched arms.

"Sweet Sara," he murmured. "Beautiful bride. You don't know how honored I feel."

"Honored?" She laughed airily.

"Loved, honored, cherished." He unbuckled his belt, and she helped him shed his jeans. Then he lifted her into his arms and carried her to the circular bed.

Their bodies merged like old friends, like two halves longing for completion. Randy laced his fingers through hers, pinning her on her back as his tongue teased her flushed nipples, sucking them into his hot mouth. *This was how it should be,* Sara thought, *the timelessness of love, transcending boundaries, dissolving differences, meeting on the peak of eternity.*

He released her hands in order to slide lower, tasting her stomach, licking her navel. Her fingers clutched the soft thickness of his hair as he let his tongue rove lower.

She gasped as his kiss conquered her soft feminine flesh, sparking crazed impulses deep in her. She heard herself cry out from the exquisite sensation, her body arching of its own volition, seeking relief from his tortuous assault. "Randy," she sobbed, "Randy, please..."

He lifted his head. "Should I stop?"

"Yes. No," she moaned, her fingers convulsing into fists against his head.

He kissed her again, then lifted himself onto her and buried himself deep inside her, reaching beyond her body to ignite her spirit. Sara closed her eyes and then opened them again, seeing only Randy. No mirrored ceiling, no modern motel room, only him. He was her world, her anchorless, timeless world. No passport was needed, no ticket. They traveled together into an entirely new universe that belonged to both of them, only them.

She felt the inexorable building of passion, fueled by Randy as her own unfettered passion fueled him. And then the ultimate moment, the ultimate completeness that obliterated everything but him, her love for him. With a ragged groan she succumbed to it, letting him carry her away, letting him sweep her into a world of forever.

Chapter Ten

The Village appeared abandoned. Sara had to ring the bell at the front door of the main building several times before Sam, the night watchman, finally appeared.

A grizzled man in a khaki uniform, gnawing on the stem of an unlit corncob pipe, Sam stared at Sara, still resplendent in her wedding dress, and then at Randy. "So," he muttered, "this is the fellow you eloped with. I heard what happened at your wedding this afternoon, Sara. Running off with some wedding guest—I do say!" His tone wasn't quite disapproving, nor was it approving. But his eyes twinkled with amusement as he studied the couple standing at the entry to the deserted Village.

Sara turned to Randy and grinned. "That's the way it is in these old-time towns," she noted slyly. "Word travels fast. One rash move, and your reputation is completely destroyed." She turned back to Sam. "May I come in and change my clothes?"

He chewed thoughtfully on his pipe. "You know that's against the rules, Sara," he reminded her. "I'm not supposed to let anyone in after hours."

"Oh, come on, Sam," Sara wheedled. "I can't very well go home dressed like this. As a matter of fact, I can't go home at all. My purse is in the dressing room, with my keys in it. You've got to let me in."

Sam's eyes shifted from Sara to Randy, and then back to Sara. "All right," he relented. "But only you. The young man can't come in."

Sara glanced at Randy and considered. "Maybe the best thing would be for you to go back to your house," she advised him. "I might be a while here. I've got to get this dress back to the seamstress shop and packed up. And I'd like to shower when I get home. Why don't you go to your place, and I'll call you as soon as I'm ready?"

Randy mulled over her suggestion. "I don't mind waiting," he assured her.

She smiled. She didn't want to be separated from him, either. But it made more sense for him to return to his house to wait for her. She honestly didn't know how long it would take her to get changed, packed up and home. She told him so.

"Okay," he begrudgingly yielded. "I'll go home. But call me the minute you get to your house, would you?"

Sara was touched by his insistence, by the solemn glow of his eyes. She and Randy would be apart for less than an hour, and he was acting as if it were a lifetime separation. His attitude transcended flattery; she understood his reluctance to leave her because she was just as reluctant to leave him.

She rose on her toes and gave his lips a warm kiss. "Go home, Randy," she ordered him. "I'll call you soon." Then she turned and followed Sam though the door and out of sight.

Randy remained for a long moment gazing at the locked door, at the Village into which Sara had disappeared. He felt an odd pang, a twinge of anxiety at the thought that the make-believe Village world had taken her back, swallowed her up. What if she felt so at home there that she changed her mind and decided not to come back into Randy's world? It was a ridiculous thought, a groundless worry, he scolded himself as he turned resolutely and strode back to his car. Of course she would emerge to rejoin the modern world. After the bliss they'd just shared, the understanding they'd reached, he couldn't doubt that she'd return to him.

Sam waited for Sara to change her clothes, then accompanied her to Edith's seamstress shop, where Sara wanted to store her wedding clothes. She carefully hung up the beautiful dress and covered it with protective paper. Then she neatly folded the archaic undergarments she'd worn. Sam locked up the seamstress shop and escorted her back to the dressing room, where she retrieved her purse, the frock she'd worn that morning, and the lovely new shoes Ira had made for her. "All set," she said brightly as she rejoined Sam outside. "Thanks so much. I'll never breathe a word that you let me in after hours."

"When Edith comes in tomorrow and finds the dress there, she'll know I let you in," Sam pointed out. "But what the heck. I'm up for retirement in another year, anyway. Let 'em can me if they want."

"They wouldn't dare," Sara insisted, giving his arm an affectionate squeeze. "I'll stick up for you."

"The scandalous bride is going to stick up for me?" he teased. "Then they'll can me for sure."

Laughing, Sara bade him good-bye and left the building. She walked to her car, climbed in, and started the engine. Cars might be transportation, unwanted necessities on which modern people were dependent, but at that moment Sara believed she could have flown home on the wings of her own soaring spirit. She drove the roads leading to Levittown faster than usual, imagining her rickety automobile to be a high-powered sports car. There were advantages to vehicles like Randy's Alfa-Romeo, she acknowledged. They could carry one to where one was going faster than a horse and wagon could, which meant they could bring two lovers together again in less time.

By the time she arrived at her block, dusk had descended, casting the world in lavender shadows. Sara pulled to a halt in her driveway. She noticed that the Sharkeys' car was missing. Maybe they had gone out to dinner, still celebrating their neighbor's wedding. The thought made her smile, and her smile deepened as she contemplated the fact that not only had the Sharkeys' neighbor had a wedding today, but, more important than that, she was in love. Not just in love, but ready to admit it, ready to herald it. To Sara, that was far more significant than a wedding.

She hastened up the front walk and turned her key in the lock. The movement in the dense shrubbery beside her porch was so sudden she didn't have a chance to react before a large young man with straw-colored hair and an angry, surly face pressed up behind her. "Hello, Miss Morrow," he hissed.

Turk. Turk Chesler. Sara's brain was muddled, so crowded with her love for Randy that it took her a while to register that her creepy former student was at her house, his breath rasping against her neck, his hand clasping a strange, glittering object as his arm locked around her neck. A knife. He was holding a knife.

"Hello, Turk," she said, as calmly as if this were an everyday occurrence.

"Are you going to pass me?" he grunted.

"Are you going to stab me?" she countered. How could she be so calm, she wondered. Why wasn't she screaming? Why wasn't she fainting from sheer fright?

"Open the door," he ordered her.

She did. They entered her living room together, and he shut and locked the door behind them. She pocketed her keys, something she rarely did upon arriving at home. Somehow, her reflexes made her keep them in her possession. She might need them quickly, she realized.

"The forms," Turk growled. "Where are they?"

"What forms?" she asked stupidly.

"I know Corcoran sent you the change-of-grade forms," the sneering boy declared. "Sign 'em and I'll leave."

"Don't be an idiot," she reprimanded Turk.

Furious, he thrust the knife threateningly at her. "I ain't here to fool around, Miss Morrow. I want the change-of-grade forms signed."

"Too bad for you," she said, casually carrying her Village frock to her bedroom to hang up.

Turk seemed momentarily stunned by her apparent lack of concern, and then darted down the hall after her. Before she could reach her closet he had his hand wrapped bruisingly about her upper arm. The frock fell to the floor. "You don't seem to understand, Miss Morrow," he snarled. "I'm gonna graduate this June. You're gonna sign those forms."

"No, Turk," she explained. "*You* don't understand. I'm not going to sign them."

"Why? What's it to you?"

She gazed up at the hulking young boy. He hadn't changed much in the past year. His dark eyes still blazed with hatred and anger, his mouth still twisted in an automatic smirk, his hair was still matted and messy. He still wore a denim jacket with its sleeves cut off, a form-fitting black T-shirt and skintight jeans. He still was a bully. "What is it to me?" she reflected aloud.

"It's a belief that education is an important thing, and that students in my classes are going to learn or they're going to fail. You knew that from the start, Turk. I was an old-fashioned schoolmarm and I'm not going to change at this point. So put away your knife and get out of here."

His fingers squeezed unbearably tighter, but Sara resisted the urge to cry out in pain. "Lady, I'm not playing games. Where are the forms?"

"I threw them out," she lied. In fact, she had stored them in a carton in her kitchen with her other records from her teaching days.

He spewed a long string of invectives at her, then dragged her to her dresser. Refusing to release her, he clamped the handle of the knife in his mouth and yanked open her drawers, tossing out her underwear, her sweaters, her jeans, in search of the forms he was looking for.

"Stop this, Turk," she muttered sternly.

"So help me, I'll cut you," he warned.

"I've been cut before," she informed him. "I've already got a knife scar to show for my teaching career."

"When I cut you, Morrow, you'll be too dead to have a scar." Frustrated, he swept her toiletry items from the top of her dresser onto the floor and dragged her from her bedroom. "Corcoran said you were an old-fashioned lady. He was being nice, you know?" Turk growled. "There's worse words for you." He provided a few of them as he towed her back into the living room. "Are they here?"

"I told you, I threw them out," she maintained.

Enraged, he stormed to her window and spitefully knocked over her carefully tended seedlings. Each small planter fell to the floor, scattering dirt over the rug. He mashed several of the frail green sprouts with his heel. That made Sara wail—not his grip, not the menacing glint of his knife, but his heartless destruction of the plants she had nurtured.

"You want me to keep going?" he railed.

"I want you to walk through the door and then, yes, keep going," she spat out. "You have no right, Turk, no right—"

"This—" he brandished the knife "—this gives me certain rights." He heaved her against himself again, tickling her neck with the keen point of the blade. "Where are they?"

"In the town dump," she declared through gritted teeth.

He stroked the knife less lightly across her throat. "Where are they?" he whispered.

"Turk, killing me won't help your situation at all," she logically pointed out.

He swore some more, his voice grating her eardrums. Her head began to pound.

And then the telephone rang. Randy. Impatient, wondering why she hadn't yet called him. "I've got to answer," she murmured.

Turk refused to release her. The telephone rang five times, six, seven. Then deathly silence.

"Someone is expecting my call," she said. "If I don't call him, he'll come after me."

"And he'll find your corpse," Turk mumbled. "The kitchen? Where's your kitchen?" He half-dragged, half-carried Sara to the kitchen.

"How did you find me, anyway?" she asked, hoping to keep him from hurting her by engaging him in conversation. The longer she could stall, the more time she would have to plot her escape from him. She knew she wasn't listed in the telephone book; she had lived in the house less than a year.

"Today's your wedding day, ain't it?" he snickered. "I read about you in the papers. Marrying at some stupid museum village or somethin'. Yeah, I'm not an idiot, Miss Morrow, I read the papers. I read you worked at some museum village. And I called them up and they gave me your address."

Damn Gil's secretary, Sara thought vaguely. Giving out personal information on employees was terribly negligent. She would have to complain. If Turk didn't kill her first.

Was he really going to kill her, she wondered. Was she really going to die young? This wouldn't be an early death like the early deaths of nineteenth-century citizens. This would be a twentieth-century death, death by violence, the death of a woman of archaic values at the hands of a man with no values at all. Fear began to nibble at her innards. Her pulse accelerated, and her headache grew more intense.

Turk swung open several cabinet doors, knocking her cast-iron pots and pans onto the floor. "Come on, lady," he roared. "Where? Tell me!" He opened the cabinet door in which she had stored the carton, but apparently he didn't see it because he slammed the door shut and turned his attention to the seedlings on the kitchen windowsill. Again he vindictively knocked them down, their jars shattering on the counter, spattering clods of dirt across the floor.

"Why are you doing this?" Her temper flared, tears springing to her eyes as she viewed the destruction of the plants she had loved and tended. "Why are you killing my seedlings?"

"Just so you know what I'm capable of," he replied gruffly. "Now, where are the forms?"

The telephone began to ring again. "I've got to answer it," she said, risking a step toward the phone.

"If I don't, he'll know there's something wrong and he'll come here."

Turk stared at the shrilly ringing instrument. So did Sara. A modern contraption, she thought, an appliance, a gizmo. A lifeline, if she could reach it. She took another brave step toward it, and Turk once again gripped her arm. He dragged her back against himself, and they danced together toward the phone, his knife less than an inch from her breast. "Give me away, I'll kill you," he whispered.

She nodded and lifted the receiver. "Hello?" she said softly.

"Sara? Where the hell have you been?" Randy greeted her. "You said you were going to call as soon as you got home."

"I know," she managed, her eyes fixed on the shimmering blade creasing her blouse.

Randy waited for her to say more. "So? What happened?" he asked.

"Something's...come up," she faltered. Turk drew her more snugly to himself. She felt the raging heat of his chest against her back and shuddered.

"Care to elaborate?"

"I don't think I can," she told Randy.

Randy hesitated. "Sara, please don't tell me you're having second thoughts about us," he objected. "Or is it third thoughts by now? I thought...I thought after today—"

"No, Randy, it isn't that." She sighed, closing her eyes so she wouldn't have to see the knife anymore.

"Get off," Turk grunted into her ear. "Get rid of him."

"Randy, I can't talk now," she said hastily. Her headache mingled with a creeping sensation of nausea.

Randy fell silent.

"Please understand," she begged him, her voice wavering. "I'm not alone, and—"

Turk shoved her sharply against the counter and slammed his hand down on the telephone's cradle, disconnecting them. He screamed a curse at Sara and swung toward her, the knife outstretched.

She smashed the telephone receiver into his face. It was an instinctive thing to do. She couldn't reach any of her strewn pots, or even a shard of glass from one of the broken seedling jars in the sink. All she had was the receiver, and she bashed its rounded end into his nose.

He fell back, howling, clutching at his face. Sara saw a trickle of blood ooze from one of his nostrils. She wondered with detached curiosity whether she had broken his nose.

But she didn't have time to diagnose him. Her attack had only incensed him further, and he was coming at her again. She swung the mouthpiece at his jaw, and when it made contact its perforated plastic cover cracked and fell loose.

He staggered and shouted a curse. She ran. She raced for the door, dexterously worked the lock, and shot out into the yard. She didn't wait to see if Turk was chasing her. She dove for her car, scrambled inside, and revved the engine. She was three blocks away before she stopped to collect her wits.

Her hands were shaking, her eyes watering. The relief of knowing she was safe allowed her to surrender to several wrenching sobs. Then she composed herself and drove slowly to the police station.

A sympathetic desk sergeant listened to her story and brought her a glass of water. He sent two officers out to her house but insisted that she remain in the safety of the station. "I'm still not clear on this," he mumbled as he labored over the keys of his manual typewriter, trying to get her statement on paper. "This kid wanted you to sign some change-of-grade forms for him?"

She nodded dully.

"He was coming at you with a knife, Ms. Morrow. Why didn't you just sign the forms?"

"Because..." She exhaled. "Because he didn't deserve to pass my course. I know the current mode of school administration is to pass every student along, whether or not he deserves it—social promotions, they're called. It's still a popular theory in certain quarters these days, but I don't believe in it."

"Even when a kid is threatening to murder you?"

"I've got pretty strong convictions about it," she granted.

"You'd rather be dead?"

"I'd rather..." She sighed and sipped her water. "I don't know that I want to live in a society where principles are cheap and nobody is committed to his or her beliefs. Of course I wouldn't rather be dead," she swiftly added. "But I'm not about to go along with whatever happens to be faddish or convenient at any given moment. I do what I think is right. Changing this student's grade wouldn't have been right."

The police sergeant appeared bemused, but he didn't quarrel with her. She watched him wrestle with the sticky typewriter and thought about how much she preferred it to the slick, silent word processor Randy's assistant Charlotte had used. She liked the way the sergeant's fingers had a direct effect on the keys. A typewriter like the one he was using was something Sara could understand. If it broke down, she could probably fix it. It was her kind of machine.

On the other hand... She settled into her metal folding chair and meditated. On the other hand, she had been saved by the only modern implements in her life:

her telephone and her car. A telephone and a car, two twentieth-century gizmos, had emerged victorious against an antiquated weapon like a knife. This one time, she mused, when her survival was on the line, she was glad to have a car and a telephone.

A stir in the doorway caught her attention, and she glanced up to see Randy entering the room. He raced to her side and dropped to his knees before her. "Sara, are you all right?"

"Yes," she reassured him, running her hand consolingly through his hair. Randy's distress seemed much more acute than her own, and she wanted to placate him. "Yes, I'm fine."

"I drove to your house. Sara, I was so mad...I thought...I thought—"

"You thought I was going to leave you again?"

He nodded contritely. "I'm sorry."

She chuckled softly. "It was a logical assumption, given the nutty lady you're dealing with."

Randy refused to laugh. "Sara, I got there, and there was a police car in the driveway...." His trembling hands hugged her legs. "And there was blood on the wall of your kitchen."

"There was?" She frowned. "His blood. Not mine. I think I broke his nose."

"Are you sure you're all right?"

"Yes," she murmured, certain that as long as Randy was with her she would be fine.

The two officers who had been sent to her house arrived at the station. "He was gone," one of them reported to the sergeant. "We took some pictures. It didn't look like he stole anything, but the place is a mess."

The sergeant turned to Sara. "This should be an easy case to handle," he asserted. "Assault with a deadly weapon, vandalism, maybe kidnapping. We'll be able to track the kid down through the school, I imagine."

Sara nodded. Randy stood up and helped her out of her chair. "May I go now?" she asked.

"Sure. We'll be in touch," the sergeant promised. He glanced up at Randy. "You're a friend?"

"Yes. I'll take care of her," Randy swore as he gathered Sara's hand in his own. "As if she needs anyone to take care of her. You really broke his nose?"

"I hit him pretty hard."

"With your fist?"

"With the telephone mouthpiece. I think I broke it, too," she added.

"I'm a whiz when it comes to electrical gadgets," he impishly reminded her. "I'll fix it for you if I can."

They left the station. Randy escorted her to his car, and helped her onto the seat. She paused. "What about my car?"

"We'll come back for it later," he advised.

He *was* going to take care of her, she realized, and the thought sapped all the tension from her shoulders. She wilted into the bucket seat and felt her eyes grow moist. By the time Randy was seated beside her, she was freely giving vent to her tears.

He pulled her awkwardly across the pearl-trimmed gear stick, offering his shoulder to absorb her tears. She let them flow, releasing all the rage and frustration and fear that had clenched in a knot inside her since she had found Turk Chesler lurking in her shrubs an hour ago.

Randy combed his fingers gently through her hair, whispering sweet, soft words of comfort. "You're okay," he murmured. "That's all that matters. You're okay. He didn't hurt you."

"He killed all my plants," she sobbed.

"I noticed."

"Randy," she moaned softly, mopping at her damp cheeks with her palms. "I worked so hard on those seedlings. I started them from seeds. I wanted a garden so much!"

"You can buy seedlings at a nursery," he pointed out. "You can still have your garden."

"But I started them from scratch, Randy! They were real, original plants, *my* plants. The way gardens were started two centuries ago."

"I know." He sighed. "I know, Sara. Next year you can try again. There'll be other gardens in the future."

She nodded glumly and settled back into her seat. Randy switched on the engine, then turned to her. "Would you like to get a drink or something?"

She shook her head. "No, take me home, Randy. I've got to clean up the house."

"I'll help you," he offered as he eased out of the parking lot.

Sara nestled into her seat and closed her eyes. She thought of the dead seedlings on her rug, on her counters—crushed, thwarted, never having had a chance to become the fruitful plants they deserved to be. They were her plants, her babies, and she would never get to see them grow, flourish, mature.

Her babies. Like the baby she might have had with Randy. That baby wasn't to be. It had never happened. Randy's seed had never reached a fertile place inside Sara's body, had never had a chance to flourish, to grow.

But there would be other gardens, she knew. There would be other gardens in the future. If she was willing to step into the future... "Randy?" she said quietly.

He coasted to a halt before her house and shut off the engine. Then he turned fully to her. "Yes?"

"Will you...will you help me with a garden?" she asked.

"Of course."

"In the future?"

"Now and in the future," he swore.

She reached for his hand, held it in her lap, studied the long graceful shape of his fingers, the strength inherent in his palm. "Randy, I have to confess something."

"Uh-oh," he muttered ominously.

"Randy..." She sucked in her breath for fortitude, and addressed his hand. "Randy, I'm sorry I didn't become pregnant that night."

She could feel his surprise in the stiffening of his fingers. She could picture his eyes widening, their green brilliance glistening with bewilderment. "I thought you were relieved," he told her.

"I thought I was, too, at first," she conceded. "But Randy...you were right. The meaning of life is always the same. It's loving, making babies, raising a family, struggling for survival one way or another. And you—you would have made a good father. I could tell. The way you feel about Petey and all..." She glanced timorously up at him. "How is Petey?"

"Doing quite well, actually," Randy replied. "Larry's moved back in with Renee."

"He has?"

"They haven't exactly worked things out," he explained, "but they decided that Petey needed both of them around. And paying more attention to him helped them to regain their perspective about each other. The scare he gave them apparently did them all a bit of good." His hand moved against hers, rotating to capture her pale fingers. "They're seeing a counselor now. Trying to find some common ground."

"Petey is common ground."

"He certainly is." Randy lifted her hand to his lips and kissed it. "And you think that if we had a baby, maybe it would give us some common ground?"

"Yes," Sara acknowledged. "Even more common ground than we already have."

"Having a baby means taking a chance on the future," Randy reminded her.

"It also means creating new life from the past," she countered.

"Well," he said, sighing, "I'm willing to take a chance on the past if you're willing to take a chance on the future."

"I'm willing," Sara purred.

He smiled at her, a sparkling, radiant smile. He swooped across the gear stick to kiss her lips.

"One more thing," she whispered.

"Anything, Sara."

"I want...I want you to teach me how to play Zinger. To win, I mean. I want you to teach me the strategy."

He eyed her, amusement illuminating his face. "You do?"

"It was bad enough that Petey trounced me so thoroughly," she mumbled. "But I don't want to be humiliated when I play the game with our children."

A low chuckle slipped past his lips. "I'll do better than teach you the strategy," he promised. "I'll teach you how to program your own games."

"Hey, let's take this thing one step at a time, all right?" Sara protested.

"All right," Randy conceded. "One step at a time." He climbed out of the car and strolled around to her side to assist her out. "I suppose you're going to be wanting a big, old-fashioned wedding," he grumbled, feigning dissatisfaction.

"Complete with 'love, honor, and cherish,'" she confirmed.

They started up the walk. "If you really want to be old-fashioned about it, how about 'love, honor, and *obey*'?"

"This, from a supposedly modern man," she playfully chided him.

"Cherish it is," he conceded. He paused on the front porch as Sara manipulated her key into the lock. "Are you ready to face the mess?" he asked, turning his head toward the house.

"If I can face the future, I suppose I can face anything," she replied.

"We'll face it together," he vowed as he scooped her into his arms. He covered her mouth with an endless, timeless kiss as he carried her across the threshold and into the house.

Epilogue

Gil, the Village's curator, couldn't very well refuse Sara's request to use the Village church for her wedding. Old Harkum Village was a public place, after all—and besides, he himself had been married in the same church several years earlier. Sara and Randy offered a huge security deposit to insure the historic site against damages, and Gil agreed to let them use the building.

Edith, the Village's seamstress, also agreed to let Sara wear her Village wedding dress for the occasion. Randy adamantly refused to don a morning coat and top hat, but he looked devastatingly handsome in his classic black tuxedo and pleated white shirt.

After the ceremony, they and their guests departed to a neighboring motel for the reception. Jean Sharkey, Sara's matron of honor, expressed surprise that Sara would wish to host a wedding dinner in such a modern, impersonal building, with its stark architecture and characterless crushed-stone facade, but Sara had maintained with a laugh that the motel had a special significance to her and Randy. The banquet room wasn't too ugly, she decided. A bit contemporary for her taste, but as she readily admitted, her love for Randy had done amazing things to her taste.

In the past few months she'd grown to like his house—now *their* house, she reminded herself as she watched several dozen guests fill the banquet room's parquet floor and dance to the sprightly jazz tune the band was performing. She and Randy had scheduled their wedding for the beginning of August, when the lease on her house in Levittown expired. But she'd spent much of the summer at his modern home in Cold Spring Harbor, accustoming herself to its bizarre design and, with his assistance, clearing out a small, sun-drenched portion in the rear yard for a vegetable garden. She'd insisted on a few changes: the bas-relief and the abstract painting were moved to Randy's cluttered basement laboratory, and gentle impressionistic landscapes were hung in their places on the living-room walls. The leather furniture still looked strange to her, but she conceded to its undisputable comfort and let it stay. "I suppose I'll get used to the electric-eye refrigerator," she had allowed reluctantly, "but these mechanical dough hooks have got to go."

"Whatever you say," Randy had complied. "You're the official bread baker in this relationship. I can give the bread kneader to Charlotte," he suggested, referring to his assistant at Zaleco. "It's about time my favorite employee learned something practical—like how to bake bread."

Sara's drifting thoughts were interrupted by Randy's sister-in-law, who had sidled up to her with a cocktail in her hand. "Artie tells me you two are going to honeymoon in Montreal," she remarked.

Sara smiled and nodded. In addition to moving herself gradually into Randy's house before the wedding, she'd spent several delightful evenings with him at his brother's apartment, getting to know her future in-laws. "We decided Montreal is the perfect place for us to visit," she explained. "It's got a modern section and a historic section. And anyway, who wants to go to Aruba in August?"

Artie's wife laughed and turned with Sara to watch the dancers. Renee was attempting an awkward fox-trot with Petey but was rescued by Larry, who tactfully cut in and gathered his wife into a friendly, if not exactly intimate, embrace. By the bar, Sara's mother stood chatting with Randy's mother. Sara had to stifle a giggle as she compared the two women, Randy's mother attired in a formal satin gown and dyed-to-match pumps, and Sara's mother clad in a flowered peasant dress and leather sandals. At Sara's behest, her parents attended the wedding without escorts, and her smile expanded as she watched her father, dressed in a startling salmon-colored suit and open-necked lime-green shirt, cross the room, take her mother's hand, and lead her onto the dance floor.

She felt the warm, familiar strength of Randy's arm curling around her bare shoulders. "Aren't we supposed to be dancing or something?" he whispered, kissing the silky strands of hair that covered her ear.

"We've already had our official wedding dance," she replied playfully.

"In case you haven't heard, Sara," he returned her teasing, "it's the twentieth century. Anything goes. Even multiple wedding dances." He urged her to the center of the dance floor and closed his arms possessively around her. Bowing his face to hers, he kissed her lightly and murmured, "Have I told you how beautiful you look?"

"Several times," she answered, though the warm glow in her cheeks informed him that she didn't at all mind his repeating himself.

"May I ask what you've got on under that gown of yours?" he inquired with a lecherous grin.

"Randy Zale, you are the bluntest, freshest man I've ever met," she scolded him. At his expression of feigned hurt, she chuckled and nestled her head into his shoulder. "I really don't think our wedding dinner is the appropriate occasion to be discussing your fetishes."

"What would be the appropriate occasion?" he persisted.

"After we leave," she decided.

He glanced at his wristwatch—a new gold dial watch Sara had bought for him to replace his digital watch—and groaned. "How much longer do we have to hang around here? I understand they've got a hotsy-totsy honeymoon suite upstairs, complete with a mirrored ceiling and a vibrating circular bed."

"I'd rather we just go home," she admitted with a sigh.

His arms tightened around her. "I love you, Sara," he declared quietly, all traces of teasing gone.

Her cheeks grew pinker, her heartbeat faster, as she thought of the simple unvibrating brass bed that awaited them in Randy's bedroom—in *their* bedroom. "Just for that," she responded to his statement, "I'm going to give you a big hint about what I've got on under this dress."

"Oh?"

She pulled back to confront him, her lips curved in an impish smile. "It isn't a double-knotted camisole."

Randy's smile mirrored hers, and he drew her snugly against himself once more, tucking her head into the crook of his neck.

Together they danced the time away until they could leave for home.